Cranford Es

Wherever the siblings of Cranford Estate go, scandal is sure to follow!

As the future marquess, William must marry appropriately, yet he's tempted by his close friend's sister, Anna... A most inconvenient attraction indeed!

Tilly flees London with her reputation in tatters! And promptly meets Lucas, the Earl of Clifton, and his adorable baby nephew. But with scandal hot on her heels, will she make a suitable wife?

Eligible bachelor Charles is stunned when strikingly unconventional Lucy goes out of her way to avoid him. They have a connection, but Lucy is hiding a heartbreaking secret...

Read William's story in
Lord Lancaster Courts a Scandal
Available now

Tilly's story in
Too Scandalous for the Earl

And look out for Charles's story
Coming soon!

Author Note

Too Scandalous for the Earl is the second book in the Cranford Estate Siblings trilogy. The story is set in Devon, which is one of my favorite locations.

Having disgraced herself with a disreputable young man on the eve of her debut, Tilly's sent to Devon by her family until the scandal has blown over. Here she meets Lucas Kingsly, the Earl of Clifton. In the beginning there is conflict between the two, but gradually, against a backdrop of the sea and the beautiful Devon countryside, where smuggling is rife, their conflicts are resolved.

HELEN DICKSON

Too Scandalous for the Earl

ISBN-13: 978-1-335-59559-1

Too Scandalous for the Earl

Copyright © 2023 by Helen Dickson

Recycling programs for this product may not exist in your area.

For questions and comments about the quality of this book, please contact us at CustomerService@Harlequin.com.

Harlequin Enterprises ULC
22 Adelaide St. West, 41st Floor
Toronto, Ontario M5H 4E3, Canada
www.Harlequin.com

Printed in U.S.A.

Helen Dickson was born and still lives in South Yorkshire, UK, with her retired farm-manager husband. Having moved out of the busy farmhouse where she raised their two sons, she now has more time to indulge in her favorite pastimes. She enjoys being outdoors, traveling, reading and listening to music. An incurable romantic, she writes for pleasure. It was a love of history that drove her to writing historical fiction.

Books by Helen Dickson

Harlequin Historical

Caught in Scandal's Storm
Lucy Lane and the Lieutenant
Lord Lansbury's Christmas Wedding
Royalist on the Run
The Foundling Bride
Carrying the Gentleman's Secret
A Vow for an Heiress
The Governess's Scandalous Marriage
Reunited at the King's Court
Wedded for His Secret Child
Resisting Her Enemy Lord
A Viscount to Save Her Reputation
Enthralled by Her Enemy's Kiss
To Catch a Runaway Bride
Conveniently Wed to a Spy
The Earl's Wager for a Lady

Cranford Estate Siblings

Lord Lancaster Courts a Scandal
Too Scandalous for the Earl

Visit the Author Profile page
at Harlequin.com for more titles.

Chapter One

1812

Self-willed, energetic and passionate, with a fierce and undisciplined temper, Tilly had a charm and wit and beauty that more than made up for the deficiencies in her character. She hadn't a bad bone in her body and was just proud and spirited, so determined to have her own way that she had always been prepared to plough straight through any hurdle that stood in her path—but that was before she had made the dubious acquaintance of Richard Coulson.

Summoned to the drawing room by her brother Charles, who had been staying with friends in Sussex for the past month, an inexplicable premonition of dread mounted as she descended the stairs. When Tilly entered the drawing room, Charles was waiting for her.

He was still dressed in his travelling clothes, waiting impatiently by the fireplace, obviously in an angry mood. He had a handsome face—at least he would have been handsome had not a fierce scowl marred his features. The moment she closed the door behind her he embarked on a blistering tirade, denouncing her recent disgraceful behaviour.

'There you are. Aunt Charlotte has filled me in with what you have been getting up to in my absence. Really, Tilly, will you never grow up? You are clever, quick thinking and sharp witted. You are also problematical and a constant headache. You test my patience at every turn. You live for the moment and notice nothing that is not to do with outdoor pursuits and horses. In short, you are hell-bent on self-destruction.'

Tilly sighed. Her brother was adamant when administering discipline. 'I'm sorry, Charles, truly,' she said, only mildly repentant, 'for all the trouble I have caused. I never meant for this to happen. I didn't know.'

'There's a great deal you don't know.'

She nodded. 'It would appear so,' she replied, adopting a meek expression, although anyone who knew Tilly Anderson would know there was nothing meek about her.

'It would seem the task of learning to be the lady our mother intended you to become is seemingly impossible.'

'I am sure I must be a terrible disappointment to you, Charles, but I will try not to let you down in future. I will try harder, I promise.'

'It's too late for that. How could you let it happen? You haven't a grain of sense in you. How could you have been so blind to propriety? Coulson saw you as easy prey. You should have known better than to become entangled with him. You are too young and inexperienced to take on a man of his ilk. He eats young women like you for breakfast. He's played the field and gambled his way through his fortune. He'll beggar his father before he's done. Where did you meet him?'

'In the park when I was out riding.'

'Alone?'

'Well…yes. Aunt Charlotte wasn't very well…'

'And you didn't have the presence of mind to take a maid with you?'

'Aunt Charlotte's maids don't ride—and you know I don't like being confined in a carriage.'

Charles turned away in exasperation. Audacious and bold, Tilly could be a handful without any encouragement. 'Excuses—nothing but excuses, Tilly. Aunt Charlotte does employ two grooms to take care of the horses.'

'And one or the other has accompanied me on occasion.'

'Not often enough. Coulson has ruined your reputation.'

'No, he hasn't. He didn't dishonour me.'

'He might as well have done.'

'He—he did ask me to marry him.'

'And you refused him, thank God. At any other time and with anyone whose character was not mired in decadence I would have insisted you marry him—but Coulson is a rake of the first order. He would lead you a merry dance and you would be downright miserable.'

'I know. I didn't want to marry him. But it's very lonely for me sometimes with just Aunt Charlotte for company.'

'That's no excuse for what you've done. Friends have hastened to inform me of the scandal that is beginning to unfold concerning my own sister—a scandal that is entirely of your own making, if it is to be believed. It has already given you a certain notoriety—and I know perfectly well what happens to a young lady who falls short of society's expectations.

'I am incensed. Not in my wildest dreams did I imagine you would form a liaison with a man whose exploits are the talk of London. And where he is concerned, how dare he have the temerity, the effrontery to interfere with the half-sister of William, the Marquess of Elvington?'

William's father had died when William was just eight years old, and one year later his mother had remarried Sir Edward Anderson. Charles and Tilly were the result of that marriage, and William cared deeply for his half-siblings. Tilly had the grace to lower her eyes and fix them on her hands folded in her lap. No doubt when William heard of this latest escapade he would be as incensed as Charles.

Of course, Charles was quite right. On her rides in the park, she had garnered the favours of several young beaux and Richard Coulson, who stood out from the rest with his raffish good looks and sense of fun, was much sought after. He had approached her when she had managed to shake off her accompanying groom, who despaired of trying to keep up with her since she could ride like the wind with the devil on her tail.

Richard had become enamoured of her and he had soon turned to putty under the assault of her large violet eyes and sweet smiles. It was all a game to Tilly, who had done it out of boredom. His possessive attitude she soon found irritating. He had even had the audacity to kiss her when she had found herself alone with him, which she had thought presumptuous of him, and had shocked her and was not to her liking anyway.

Having captured him completely, the game had turned sour along with what she had seen of society. The idea of a Season and marriage in general—which, after all, was what having a Season was all about—she decided was not for her and had sent the young man packing, blissfully unaware of the consequences of their liaison. Her naivety and inexperience had not prepared her for a young man of Coulson's reputation.

'I could kill Coulson for this,' Charles said. 'The gossip will soon be all over town and you can expect no mercy.' Not to be made a fool of by an ignorant girl, Coulson had let his tongue loose to do its worse and turned the tables on Tilly, laughingly telling his friends that she was a game bird, an amusingly peculiar, pathetic little thing, and, if she was launched, he had no intention of plying his suit.

Charles looked to the door when a maid entered, carrying a letter on a salver.

'A letter has just arrived for you, Mr Anderson,' she said, bobbing a curtsy and leaving the room.

'Thank you, Betty.' Casting an eye over it, he shoved it inside his jacket unopened, turning his attention back to Tilly. Her head was bent, her shock of glossy black curls falling about her face. He sighed, shaking his head wearily.

'You have much to learn about life, Tilly,' he said on a softer note. 'I will take time off from the Company to take you to Cranford. Perhaps William—and Anna—can instil some sense into you, although with your difficult and unyielding nature they will have their work cut out.'

Tilly remembered when she had first seen Cranford Park. It was unlike anything she had imagined. She had been mesmerised by its splendour—imposing without being austere. This was her half-brother William's ancestral home. He had become the Marquess of Elvington on the demise of his grandfather six months earlier. When he had returned from India, he had insisted that his half-siblings made Cranford their home.

Employed by the East India Company in London, Charles resided at the Lancaster town house in Mayfair. Tilly flitted between the houses, recently spending a good deal of her time with Aunt Charlotte in Chelsea village as preparations were being made to launch her into society.

Adored by her family, Tilly had been petted and indulged outrageously by everyone all her life, but all the attention had left her unspoiled. Happy and always smiling, she had a warm and generous heart. Her greatest sorrow had been the loss of her father as a child and then later, on the death of her mother, something vital had gone from her life. She knew nothing of the harsh, cruel world that existed outside her own secure and comfortable existence.

Aunt Charlotte, her father's sister, with her gentle guidance and common sense, had become a kindly presence in her life. Having lost the love of her life in a riding accident, she had never married. She wanted Tilly to have a grand London Season, to associate with fashionable people of note, to attend balls and soirées.

Tilly was always very much aware that the moment she appeared in a room all eyes turned to her and she was soon surrounded by dozens of people, most of them young men, who obviously thought they might have a chance with the Marquess of Elvington's sister when she made her debut. She had a kind of aura about her that made her somehow unique, although she herself was quite unaware of this special quality.

Before her indiscretion with Richard Coulson she was given the distinction of being named as the most beautiful young woman who would grace the next London Season, that she would be the most desirable debutante to join the marriage mart, which was quite an achievement for any girl.

She wished she weren't so attractive because people, especially the young bucks, behaved like complete idiots around her. Aunt Charlotte said that when she was ready, she hoped the man she chose would be right for her—one who would appreciate her free spirit and love her for what she was, not for what he could make her.

But an interesting fact to some was, upon her marriage, the man who married her would become the recipient of a dowry generous enough to elevate his status considerably.

Tilly had met rich men, she had met handsome men, but she had not fallen in love. Disheartened and thoroughly disenchanted with the opposite sex, she scorned them all, much to her Aunt Charlotte's dismay, for she was eager for her to make a good marriage. She was certain that when the scandal had died a death and Tilly made her debut, there would be so many eager young males of good families posturing about that she would have the pick of the bunch.

The sun was sinking behind the gentle rise of the park when the coach carrying Charles and Tilly and Aunt

Charlotte travelled along the stately drive to the house. Despite being the sister-in-law to Charles and Tilly's mother, Aunt Charlotte had never visited Cranford Park. News of their unexpected arrival soon spread through the halls of the great house and it wasn't long before they were ensconced in the drawing room with the tea things arranged on a low table in from of them.

Tilly glanced at William, who stood with Charles across the room. He was as handsome as he had always been, although he possessed a haughty arrogance which some people took for coldness. He was a caring and compassionate man at heart and his love for Anna, his wife, was evident to all. Their first year of marriage had been blessed with a healthy son, Thomas James Lancaster, Lord Lancaster. After proudly presenting him to their visitors, Anna had taken him to the nursery to put him down for his nap.

Aunt Charlotte was an arresting woman. Her hair was no longer the dark brown of her youth and was liberally streaked with grey. She wore it on top her head, which made her appear taller. Besides being quite striking, if not intimidating, despite being short of stature, she conversed with such zest and charm that she could not be ignored. Ever since her sister-in-law's demise when Tilly was fifteen years old, she had stepped in to guide her beloved niece into adulthood.

Unfortunately, nothing had prepared her for the likes of Richard Coulson. With Tilly's reputation about to be shredded before she'd been launched into society, she had agreed with Charles that they should leave for Cranford until the gossip had died and some other unfortunate girl had transgressed for the *ton* to focus their attention on. It was this matter that was being discussed now.

'It was taken for granted that Tilly, a young woman with an impeccable reputation, would have a Season and make a brilliant marriage. It seems foolish to state the obvious,' she said, shaking her head as she spoke, her coiffure wobbling precariously, 'but she cannot do that now. It's out of the question. The *ton* would never stand for it. She would be humiliated and miserable. It cannot happen. At present no one will speak to her, let alone receive her or acknowledge her.'

'You're quite right, Aunt Charlotte,' Charles agreed. 'Of course it can't. Society will tolerate her because she is the half-sister of the Marquess of Elvington, but they will cut her dead whenever the opportunity arises. In short, she will be treated like a pariah.'

'I'm afraid you're right, Charles,' William said gravely. 'For my part I would like to tell the whole of society to go to hell, but that isn't going to do Tilly any good.'

Charles nodded. 'My feelings entirely. With any luck, next year this will all have blown over and she can be presented then.'

William, who had listened to what was being said with a deep regret, shook his head. 'I blame myself for this. Our mother trusted me to keep Tilly safe, not only from rakehells like Coulson, but from any other dangers that may come her way.' His voice was bitter as he added, 'I was so busy at Cranford, sorting out my grandfather's business affairs since my return from India, followed by his passing—and marrying Anna— that I failed to protect her.'

'It was my responsibility too, William,' Charles remarked. 'I have been so damned busy of late that I took my eyes off what matters. But it is important that she has a Season—which was what Mother would have wanted.'

Tilly sat there, listening as all this talk about her went on as if she was absent. 'What about me?' she protested. 'Does it not matter what I want? Who wants a Season anyway? From what I know of them they are a great bore—a gaggle of girls all doing the same thing, seeing all the same people at every event, all of them hoping to make the best catch.

'It doesn't appeal to me in the slightest—all that curtsying and bowing to goodness knows who and making empty conversation with beaus looking for a wife—the wealthier the better. All that time and effort for the sole purpose of procuring a husband. I hate all the restrictions of the social system that enslaves people like me. It all seems so silly,' she said, sitting up straight and raising her nose to a lofty angle.

'Be that as it may, Tilly,' Aunt Charlotte said as she sipped her tea, 'you will have a coming-out ball next Season. As the sister of the Marquess of Elvington you cannot hide yourself away indefinitely. With any luck this unpleasantness will have blown over by then.'

'And if it hasn't? What is to be done with me? I cannot impose myself on William and Anna indefinitely.'

'Do I have to remind you,' William said, 'that this is your home too, Tilly? I told you when I returned from India that Cranford Park is for my entire family.'

'I know—and I am indeed grateful—I do love being here, but I feel…' She faltered, not really knowing what she felt or what she wanted to do.

'You want more…excitement, perhaps?' William said with a twinkle in his eye.

'I suppose I do. But after what happened with Richard Coulson I'm confused as to what I do want to do now. I can't sit twiddling my thumbs until next year when the Season is upon us once more. And my transgressions may not have been forgotten.'

William looked at his sister. Despite this setback with Coulson, with her free and generous spirit and steadfast gaze, he had never been more proud of her, nor loved her more. She had grown more beautiful as she had reached maturity. She might be a handful at times, but with her willingness to please and her exuberance for life, her moods of warmth and generosity redeemed her.

'Perhaps I might make a suggestion,' Charles said. 'I've received a letter from our uncle's lawyer—Uncle Silas who lived in Devon.'

'Oh? What about? He's dead, isn't he?'

'Yes. He died three months ago. Being much older than our father and Aunt Charlotte just a child when he left home to indulge himself in his travels abroad, we didn't see much of him when we were growing up. He rarely got up to London. As you know, he died without issue and it would appear he's left his house—Drayton Manor, and the land that goes with it—to me as next in line. I don't know what to make of it—and I have neither the time nor the inclination to travel down to Devon to inspect it at this time.

'In fact, the Company is considering sending me to India some time next year, I think, which I would like to do. You could go to Devon for me if you like, Tilly. And you, Aunt Charlotte. A change of scene at this time would be good for you. I believe it is close to the sea. A touch of sea air will benefit you no end.'

Tilly stared at him. 'Devon?'

'Why not? I think Uncle Silas left his home in good order, but it will be comforting to know I'm not inheriting a ruin. Although what I will do with it—a house miles away from London—I haven't the faintest idea.'

All three looked at Tilly expectantly, waiting for her to make her decision. She didn't feel grief and shock at her half-uncle's passing. Silas Anderson was a man she had seldom met. She looked at Aunt Charlotte. 'Would you go, Aunt Charlotte? Uncle Silas was your brother, after all.'

Charlotte, who vaguely remembered her older brother and had last seen him on one of his infrequent visits to London, had listened with great interest as he'd talked at length about his extensive travels and his home in Devon. She could not wait to see what he had so avidly described. There was a broad smile of anticipation on her face for the coming trip. 'Yes—of course I would. Charles is right. The sea air might be good for both of us. Don't you agree, Tilly?'

'Oh, yes. It could be just what's needed at this time.'

'I doubt that,' Charles replied with misgivings, but continued in a more affectionate manner. 'When you look at me like that and smile that smile, I begin to understand why our parents and Aunt Charlotte—even you, William—spoiled and pampered you so outrageously. Hopefully there will be nothing in Devon to distract you.'

Tilly looked fondly at her brother and deeply regretted the disappointment he must feel. He was always the soul of discretion. Caught up in the grip of having betrayed her family, of having shamed the proud name she bore and that of William's own, she was aware of the carnage she had wrought by her careless, reckless behaviour with Richard Coulson.

'I meant what I said, Charles, I will do nothing to add to my disgrace.'

'Gossip is mischievous, often cruel and easy to begin, but ruinous and hard to get rid of. It never goes away entirely. People tuck it away, but they don't forget.'

'I know. So, yes, Charles, I rather fancy a visit to the coast.' Her eyes were alight with the spirit of adventure. 'As I recall Uncle Silas never married and when he stopped travelling he became something of recluse. It will be interesting to see where he lived.'

'Married or not, he did very well for himself, enjoying a long period of considerable prosperity with his many investments in Cornish mines and the like. The housekeeper and a caretaker have been kept on in anticipation of my journeying to Devon, so I expect the house will be in good order. I shall make all the arrangements. We can send a message ahead by one of the coaches going that way. Mrs Carstairs will have time to prepare for your arrival.'

The following days passed in a whirl of activity as they prepared for what could be a lengthy stay in Devon. William provided them with a splendid travelling coach drawn by six bay horses, a driver by the name of Dunstan and his son Graham, who acted as groom. Aunt Charlotte's maid, Daphne, was to accompany them. The coach was loaded with boxes above and behind. Goodbyes were said, Tilly promising to write as soon as may be. Anna, holding baby Thomas in her arms, waved, and the coach moved off. Tilly strained from her seat to get the last glimpse of her two brothers. For a moment panic about leaving them threatened to sweep over her, but when Aunt Charlotte squeezed her hand reassuringly, she knew everything would turn out all right.

They reached Devon after an exhausting journey. The early summer days allowed them to keep going. William had sent them off with six of his own carriage horses so the journey did take a little longer to allow the horses to rest, instead of changing horses at coaching inns along the way, but he thought they might be useful when they reached Drayton Manor. Coach travel was not exactly comfortable or relaxing. The roads were frequented by highwaymen and, to alleviate the dangers of being held up, they always stopped for the night at a coaching inn before the light faded.

Tilly had never seen the sea before and she gazed at the vast expanse of water with wonder. Seldom did the English Channel disappear from sight. A warm wind blew off the sea, pushing the clouds inland. Never before had she seen anything like it. She watched in fascination as the waves swelled and rolled in, breaking on the rocky headlands.

They drove through a village which she would later come to know as Biddycombe, where cobbled streets with a jumble of cottages and rooftops cascaded down the hillside to a harbour. Small boats bobbed on the water in the horseshoe-shaped harbour. Two tall-masted ships heading east could be seen on the horizon and triangular-sailed fishing sloops returning with their herring catch were heading for the harbour.

Tilly turned her eyes inland, her attention caught by a large house in the distance. Medieval in its architecture, it was beautiful in its desolation, its stones aged and grey, its mullioned windows facing south. Great chimneys rose proudly to the sky in competition to the backdrop of stately beech and elms.

'I wonder who lives there?' she wondered aloud.

Aunt Charlotte, eager for the coach to reach its destination and a comfortable bed, fought a sneeze and coughed. She had spent the last couple of days dozing in the coach, complaining of a headache. Now she had developed a chill. Tilly and Daphne were concerned about her. Unfortunately, she seemed to be getting worse. Her eyes were bright and feverish.

'I'm sorry you're not feeling well, Aunt Charlotte. As soon as we reach the house you must go straight to bed. I'll ask Mrs Carstairs to send for the doctor.'

Wiping her eyes, Aunt Charlotte looked too poorly to argue. 'I shall not be sorry to go to bed. I do hope the housekeeper has a room ready.'

Dusk had fallen when the heavy travelling coach eventually came to a halt outside the front door of Drayton Manor. The house was set slightly back from the majestic coastal cliffs in a sheltered valley, its origins dating back two centuries. It was certainly not Cranford Park, Tilly thought, with its stately, well-balanced design, but it was charming in its prospect and appearance, with ivy clinging to its grey stone walls.

Dunstan jumped down from the box and rapped on

the door. It was opened by a woman Tilly assumed to be Mrs Carstairs. She was wiping her hands on her apron and wisps of grey hair escaped her white mob cap.

'Welcome to Drayton Manor,' she said. 'We are expecting you.'

'Thank you,' Tilly replied. 'It's a relief to be here at last.'

'Come—come inside. Everything is in readiness for you.'

'This is Aunt Charlotte, Uncle Silas's sister. She isn't feeling well and really must go to bed.'

'Of course,' Mrs Carstairs said, casting a sympathetic eye over Aunt Charlotte as she tried to suppress another sneeze. 'There is a fire in the drawing room and the beds are aired.'

Mrs Carstairs ushered them inside. They were met by the welcoming scent of beeswax, and rosemary and lavender and other scented flower petals in a china bowl in the centre of a round table. With a brief glance, Tilly noted there were pictures of coastal areas and portraits of deceased strangers lining the wall of the curving staircase.

Mrs Carstairs bustled about, showing them into the drawing room and leaving to fetch refreshment. She was a friendly local woman who had been housekeeper at Drayton Manor for a good many years. Tilly sat in a high back chair before the fire while Daphne accompanied Aunt Charlotte to her room.

Gazing about the room with interest, Tilly thought that this would be where Uncle Silas had sat, drinking his brandy, all summer and winter long, listening to the wind sweeping in from the sea as he entertained company.

Mrs Carstairs showed Tilly the room she had selected for her, a pleasant room, aired and polished and the bed dressed with fresh linen. It offered a splendid view of the trimmed and scythed flower-filled garden. It also faced south and, Mrs Carstairs assured her, had an abundant supply of sunlight during the summer months.

'You don't have your own maid?' Mrs Carstairs asked.

'No. Aunt Charlotte and I will share Daphne, but it's not beyond me to take care of myself.'

'Very well, but should it prove too much for her we have maids who are familiar with the work. They come from Biddycombe daily to help with the chores.'

'Thank you, Mrs Carstairs. I'll bear that in mind.'

Later, when Tilly had changed in her room, she went to look in on Aunt Charlotte.

'How is she, Daphne?'

'Sleeping. I think a good night's sleep will put her on the mend.'

'I do hope so. If not, I'll ask Mrs Carstairs to send for a doctor to take a look at her in the morning.'

Downstairs, Tilly ate a solitary dinner. It was a lovely, simple meal and excellently cooked.

Afterwards, with a growing interest about her temporary home, she familiarised herself with the house, impressed by the quality of the furnishings and the library Uncle Silas had built up over the years. Drayton Manor was a house that gave one a feeling of permanence and importance, but Tilly could not see Charles living here, so far away from the bustle and excitement of London and his work at the East India Company.

As she looked out of the library window, in the far distance in the bright moonlight the tall chimneys of the house that had caught Tilly's attention earlier could be seen rising above the trees.

'Who lives in that large house, Mrs Carstairs?' she asked when the housekeeper appeared. 'It looks impressive and rather grand.'

'And so it is,' she said, coming to stand beside her. 'It belongs to the Kingsley family, the Earl of Clifton—Lucas Kingsley. He's the largest landowner in these parts, although he's been absent for the past twelve months. I believe he's kept on a skeleton staff and he employs a bailiff to administer the working of the estate, but apart from that no one knows where he's gone—although they have their suspicions.'

'But the bailiff must know where he is?'

Mr Carstairs shrugged. 'If he does, he isn't saying. I suppose the Earl will turn up one of these days.'

'So the house is empty—no other family living there.'

'Sadly, no.'

'You said everyone had their suspicions. What do they suspect?'

'The Earl has a sister—Cassandra. Everyone calls her Lady Cassie. She ran off—followed the man she was enamoured of to the Peninsula when he went off to fight Bonaparte.'

A romantic at heart, Tilly stared at her, her interest piqued. 'That was a brave thing for her to do, Mrs Carstairs.'

'Reckless, her brother will say. He has a temper. I've no doubt he was furious. Truth to tell, Miss Anderson, I think he's gone after her to bring her back.'

'Goodness me! Do you think he will? Bring her back, I mean.'

She shrugged. 'Only time will tell. If Lady Cassandra doesn't want to come back, she won't.'

'What is she like?'

'Very much like her brother—not just in looks, but in other ways, too. As wild as the countryside and the sea in the sense that is where she has been raised. She's like a bright light among the gentry—too spirited to be tied down. She's inclined towards downright rebellion, a wilful girl, determined to have her own way, becoming truculent when it's denied her.

'There are no conventions that restrict her mind and spirit as they do other young ladies up in London— hence her falling for someone whose spirit is as wild as her own. Lord Clifton often came over to spend time with Mr Anderson, who was a learned man. They would sit together long into the night, talking about things clever people talk about.'

Tilly could well imagine the scene. She looked around the room, at the cabinets full of fine china, beautiful surfaces polished to a shine over the years, the thickly textured carpets and even a harpsichord. Uncle Silas had made this room his own and on occasion invited the Earl of Clifton to share it with him. How she would have loved to have known Uncle Silas better.

The following morning, after looking in on Aunt Charlotte and relieved to hear she was feeling better and wouldn't hear of summoning a doctor, Tilly left the house, wearing a pale yellow dress and a wide-brimmed bonnet of the same colour atop her dark hair, to take a look at the gardens. They were well-kept with beautiful shrubs and flowers in full bloom.

Having looked at the gardens and unable to resist the pull of the sea, she followed a path that took her in the direction of the beach. Wild flowers sprang up everywhere and woodbine and sweet briar grew in tangles along the wayside, but dominating it all was the sea, glinting through the trees, forever beckoning. Breathing deeply of the air and with the taste of salt on her lips, she decided there and then she would be happy to spend the rest of her life within its sight.

She paused on the edge of a low cliff. Before her was a luminous expanse of jewel-bright sea, shading to darker green as it met the rocks jutting out to the water. Several fishing boats bobbed on the water and a sailing ship, its sails billowing as it caught the wind, could be seen further out.

Stepping on to the soft sand, shimmering from the heat, she walked towards the water lapping the shore, pausing to watch the activity on board the large vessel that was anchored some way out. A man climbed over the side into a rowing boat, where another man was manning the oars. A woman followed and when she was settled other items were lowered down to them.

The boat began to approach the shore. Lifting her hand to shield her eyes from the glare of the sun, Tilly watched the boat as it came closer to the shore. Who were these people? Curious, Tilly continued to watch, thinking it strange that the boat hadn't put in at the harbour she had seen the day before.

It took a while for the boat to reach the shore, time enough for a carriage to appear on the smooth wet sand, which told Tilly whoever was in the boat was expected. Ignoring the flutter in her chest, from a respectful distance she watched the tall, lean yet muscular gentleman climb over the side with an agility that bespoke his fitness, his boots landing in the shallow water. Wearing a dark green frock coat and a pair of black leather boots, his black breeches were snug, hugging his thighs.

He then lifted the woman out, placing her down out of reach of the lapping water. A well-rounded, buxom young woman, her skirts were full and a blue bonnet covered her brown hair. When she swayed suddenly, placing her hand over her mouth, Tilly assumed she might be ill. She thought the woman to be in her mid-twenties. She stood on the sand while the gentleman returned to the boat.

He moved with the assurance and lazy grace of a cat, lithe and arrogant. She sensed a tightly coiled strength in the lean body. His thick black hair was untied and waved freely about his dark face, giving him a feral, untamed air.

Extracting a couple of large leather bags and a wicker basket from the boat, he passed the bags to the driver of the carriage and the basket to the woman before turning to address the driver. The woman suddenly placed it on the sand and disappeared behind the carriage, where she noisily relieved her stomach of its contents.

The dark-haired gentleman took an impatient glance in the direction of the young woman, an expression of amused contempt on his face, then carried on talking to the driver, as if she was of no account.

Having seen the woman's distress, it would be unacceptable for Tilly to simply turn and leave without offering her assistance. Without considering her actions, out of concern she headed towards them, her attention focused on the young woman. The gentleman and the driver ceased talking as she approached. Going to the back of the carriage, she handed the young woman a handkerchief, placing her hand on her shoulder.

'Can I be of help?' she said softly.

'Florence is not a good sailor,' a voice said sharply. 'She has been indisposed since she boarded the boat at Le Havre. Get in the carriage, Florence. Now your feet are on *terra firma* you should soon start to feel better.'

Tilly stiffened and faced him squarely. His absolute disregard for the young woman's weakened state made her cheeks burn. 'And you, sir, might have the consideration to allow her a moment to compose herself before subjecting her to further discomfort.'

The stranger seemed momentarily stunned by her elegant speech and haughty manner. Then a sudden glow began to grow in his eyes as he stared at the proud young woman, whose disdain for him was only too obvious. She possessed a certain dignity that impressed him.

'I would thank you not to interfere in what is no concern to you, young lady. There is nothing wrong with Florence that dry land will not cure. Now, if you would be so kind as to step aside, we will be on our way. Well?' he said, when she failed to obey. 'Are you deaf as well as dumb?'

Tilly had to keep a close rein on her temper, for she had never before been spoken to so rudely. He had a hard mouth that curved grimly, if rather mockingly, up at one corner. His eyes darkened as she squinted up at him.

'I can speak and I can hear very well without you resorting to discourtesy. How can I help hearing when you don't have enough self-control to lower your voice?' She stood her ground and looked him contemptuously in the eye. 'You must forgive me if my concern to see someone in such distress seems out of place, but my concern is well meant. If you are an honourable man, you will see she is taken care of in a proper and considerate manner,' she said, appealing to his sensibility.

Any argument the stranger would have raised was silenced by her quiet rebuttal and her refusal to be cowed. He raised one dark brow, a gleam of humour in his eyes as he glanced at the driver.

'Devil take it, Brownlow. It would seem I am being accused of dishonourable conduct.' With his elbows akimbo, he looked down at Tilly from his superior height. 'I see you and I perceive Florence's situation differently. Just to set your mind at rest,' he said, his patience beginning to wear thin with this unexpected delay and wanting to be on his way, 'be assured that Florence will be given all due care and consideration at my disposal. Now,' he said, looking at Florence, 'please get into the carriage, Florence.'

'Yes, sir,' the woman whispered meekly, wiping her mouth with a handkerchief. 'I'm so sorry.'

Tilly turned her head to look at the gentleman. A frown of displeasure creased his brow. His voice was perfectly level, but it had a harsh, metallic quality that reminded her of steel. His face was expressionless, yet he nevertheless seemed far more formidable. He exuded an aura of hard ruthlessness that made her blood run cold. He was handsome, darkly so, and there was something undeniably fascinating about his piercing light blue eyes in a face burned brown by a hot sun. Black brows arched sharply above, brows that flared at the corners.

When Florence stumbled and reached for the carriage for support, on hearing an impatient tut from the stranger Tilly glared at him. 'Give her a moment—or perhaps a hand up would be appreciated.' Her voice was so authoritative that the arrogantly confident gentleman was momentarily stunned. Feeling a hand on her arm, she turned to find the young woman looking at her appealingly.

'It's all right—truly. I can manage quite well.'

'There you are, you see.' The stranger's soft tongue masked what was in danger of becoming outright anger. 'Now, for the last time, get into the carriage, Florence.'

The young woman obeyed him in silence, too much in awe of him and his authority to utter a word. She bowed her head, and Tilly was sure she glimpsed the sheen of tears in her large brown eyes. Picking up the basket, the driver handed it to her. She placed it carefully on the seat beside her. Only then did she look at Tilly.

'You are most kind,' she said softly, 'but please don't concern yourself. I do not travel on sea well. It's good to have my feet on dry land that is not moving up and down like a bucking horse. I shall soon feel better.'

'There, what did I tell you?' the man said, turning to Tilly. 'Florence is a robust young woman. Her discomfort will soon pass.'

Tilly glared at him defiantly, suspecting he was accustomed to total obedience, a tyrant who relished his power over others. She'd already decided that she disliked him immensely. 'Then I will detain you no longer.'

He looked at her, those piercing light blue eyes moving over her, taking in everything, betraying nothing. He raised one thick, well-defined eyebrow, watching her for every shade of thought and emotion in her. His lips lifted at one corner in a faint curl. Did those eyes linger on her face, her body? Was there a flicker of interest in their depths?

She stood back as he hoisted himself up into the carriage. He continued to stare at her boldly, a cool smile tugging at the corners of his mouth. Tilly found herself tensing and unconsciously took another step back, wishing she wasn't alone. Why she felt that way, she could not have said, but there was something in the expression in those piercing ice-blue eyes that warned her that he was no more impressed by her than she was with him.

After he instructed Brownlow to drive on, Tilly saw a feral gleam enter his eyes and realised she had made an enemy out of this ill-tempered man. Of course, that irritated her and she put an unusually haughty expression on her lovely face and her attractive nose firmly in the air. Not that she cared one way or the other for his opinion of her. Her sole concern was for Florence and how unfortunate it was for Florence to be ordered about by such a dreadful man.

Without more ado, she turned on her heel and began walking away in the opposite direction. Only then did she hear the whimpering and the cry of an infant. Spinning round, she watched the carriage make its way across the smooth wet sand, realising what had been in the basket.

A baby! It was the cry of a baby.

Tilly continued to walk along the shore, looking down at the waves lapping her boots while she thought of her encounter with the stranger. He was of good breeding, handsome, too. Handsome enough to tempt any woman. That thought confused her and angered her also because she wanted to feel nothing but the satisfaction of knowing Florence would be taken care of.

Chapter Two

Lucas felt as if he had been punched in the stomach, hardly able to believe that a girl who looked so feminine and lovely in her yellow dress and bonnet could be so single-minded and outspoken. He couldn't think of anyone, male or female, who would have stood up to him the way she had just done, verbally attack him and walk away as regal as any queen. The girl had spirit that challenged him. Her arrogance was tantamount to disrespect, yet in spite of himself he admired her style. Nor was she afraid of him. That was the intriguing part about her.

On hearing the infant cry, he recollected himself, pulling himself together, angered at the path down which he had allowed his thoughts to wander. For him to be so fixated on the first civilised woman he had seen with a pretty face in a long time, he must be losing his mind as well as his wits.

The carriage left the beach and joined the road to Clifton House. It was the crowning glory of the Devon countryside in these parts. His heart tightened with bittersweet pain as they traversed the fields and woods that lined the road. He was relieved when they passed through the ivy-covered towered gateway into a courtyard, the carriage halting before the entrance to the house.

Their arrival brought half a dozen footmen attired in black-and-gold-striped livery rushing out of the house and taking command of the baggage before the carriage was driven to the stables at the rear. Florence took charge of the basket with the now sleeping child.

As the Earl of Clifton, Lucas was used to the ceremony and scurrying of servants. Everything was quickly and efficiently taken care of, with Florence and the child ensconced in the nursery. With swift steps, he climbed the wide staircase, a magnificent work of carved oak that towered for three storeys.

The walls were lined with impressive family portraits and niches housed an extensive collection of porcelain vases and pieces of china. He moved along the wide, richly carpeted landing until he reached his rooms—large and comfortable and decorated and furnished in masculine tastes, with a view of the beautiful gardens.

Not until then did he pour himself a generous measure of brandy and feel himself start to relax, even though his return came with its share of troubles. His heart was not at rest. How could it be, after what he had seen, what he had experienced and endured in Spain? His beautiful sister was dead. No more would she grace these rooms. No more would her infectious laughter be heard. He found it difficult to think of what had happened, of the raw wound that festered deep in his heart.

In some strange way the woman he had met on the

beach reminded him of his sister. She had a healthy and unblemished beauty that radiated a striking personal confidence. She had an alluring face, captivating and expressive, he decided. Her chin was small and round, with an adorable, tiny little cleft in the centre. A rosy flush had stained her cheeks, her glorious wealth and vibrancy of glossy black hair streaming down her back from beneath the confines of her bonnet.

But it was her eyes he remembered most—enormous, liquid bright, the colour of damp violets, incisive and clear and tilted slightly at the corners—the kind of eyes a man wanted to see looking up at him when he was about to make love.

To Lucas, starved of a woman's beauty—of any kind of beauty—for so long, to behold so much loveliness, to find himself confronted by her, to be surrounded by the sweet scent of her, was torture indeed, yet that torture was sweet to endure. It made him feel that he wasn't entirely devoid of life.

After twelve months or thereabouts he had returned home, an event he viewed with little joy when he thought what he had left behind in Spain and an empty future that spread endlessly ahead. His home needed fresh life injected into it: a wife and children—an heir to inherit Clifton. Now he was home it was important that he made marriage a priority.

When Cassie had died in childbirth, a part of him had died, too. With her young husband killed in battle, with her dying breath she had made him promise that he would take care of her son, that he would raise him as his own, to keep him from the grip of his paternal family, his uncle Jack Price, and to ensure that, as heir to Trevean and the Price shipyard close to Plymouth, he would inherit what was rightfully his. Lucas had made that promise, a promise he intended to keep. But he did not look forward to coming up against Jack Price—a tyrant and a man who was not averse to obtaining money from any criminal means.

At this time news from the Peninsula was that Wellington and his troops were becoming victorious in Spain, giving his allies a tremendous victory. Other news was that the Grand Army, led by the French emperor Napoleon Bonaparte, was invading Russia. Across the Atlantic, America had declared war on the British.

All this was far from Tilly's mind the following morning. She left her room with the intention of taking a short walk. Mrs Carstairs had told her that Uncle Silas, who liked to walk on the shore, had had some steps hewn out of the rocks for easy access to the beach. They were only a short distance from the house and she couldn't miss them.

Climbing down them was easy enough. She gazed at the huge expanse of water with something like awe. The water flashed blue and was speckled with light. Standing on the sand in a horseshoe-shaped cove, unable to resist the pull of the sea, with not a soul in sight and in the shelter of the cliffs, Tilly removed her shoes and stockings along with her bonnet.

Leaving them in the shelter of the rocks, she padded the short distance to where the sea lapped the sand. The tide was on the ebb and the surf barely more than the lapping of wavelets against the beach. She watched as the water washed over her feet, the feeling exquisite.

Deciding to walk to the far end of the cove, curious to see what was beyond the headland, and holding her skirts in front of her, she made her way through the shallows. Driftwood and seaweed had been washed ashore and seashells were embedded in the wet sand. The sun was warm on her face and the breeze lifted her hair from her shoulders.

As she reached the far end of the cove, moving through deeper water now, and before she could round the tall granite cliffs to see what was beyond, a horse and rider came galloping through the surf. For a moment Tilly stood and gaped, then, with the force generated by the horse along with a forceful wave, she lost her balance and toppled into the water.

Suddenly the water was over her head as she was dragged under. The water roared in her ears and her clothes weighted her down as she tried to regain her balance. It felt like minutes before her head finally broke the surface, but it was only seconds. Gasping and spluttering, having swallowed a mouthful of seawater, she opened her eyes.

In the act of bringing his horse under control, the rider looked at the apparition that met his eyes. It was enough to stop all thought for the moment. When he saw the bedraggled head of a woman come spluttering to the surface, he flung himself off his horse and hauled her unceremoniously on to the sand. When she wiped the black hair from her face and he saw who it was, for a moment he couldn't believe his eyes.

'Devil take it! I might have known.' Her dishevelment and the fact that she was coughing and gasping for breath alarmed him. 'Here, take my hand.' Taking a handkerchief from his pocket, he proceeded to wipe her wet face.

Furiously, she shoved his hand away. Recognising the man she had met the day before and remembering their unpleasant altercation, she was tempted to crawl back into the sea he had just hauled her out of. 'Kindly leave me be. I may be half drowned, but I am not helpless.'

'I see you are upset—'

'I am not upset, I am furious.'

The stranger scowled down at her. 'Suit yourself. Not content with giving me a dressing down yesterday, now you almost unseat me from my horse. Do you have some kind of death wish or do you go out of your way to annoy me?'

She got to her feet, unaware as she did so that, from the soaking it had received, her gown clung far too revealingly to every curve of her supple young body. Tilly was so incensed she could hardly speak. Soaked through to the skin and her hair hanging heavy and wet about her face, filled with righteous indignation she looked down and surveyed her bedraggled appearance.

'You blundering idiot,' she fumed. 'You should look where you're going. You could have drowned me riding through the water at such speed. You have ruined my gown.'

'And you, Miss, have ruined my boots.' His voice cut through her accusation like a steel blade.

Almost bursting with rage and mortification, Tilly glared at him while taking the weight of her hair and wringing out as much water as she was able. 'I did nothing of the sort—and I don't care a fig for your boots.

The blame lies with you, not me. I feel sorry for your poor horse. What were you trying to do? Drown the poor beast?'

'That *poor beast* happens to like being ridden through water—he thrives on it, in fact, which is more than I can say for you looking as you do, like some bedraggled sea waif.' Throwing himself down, he proceeded to remove his boots, pouring the offending seawater out on to the sand.

Tilly jerked her head up, looking into his harsh-planed face and his mouth set in a hard line, a mouth she doubted ever smiled, but only curled in a mocking grin. Planting her hands in the small of her waist, she glowered down at him, tempted to snatch one of his boots out of his hand and beat him over the head with it. 'Not content with almost drowning me, now you insult me. This is all your fault, you…you loathsome, unfeeling scoundrel. You are certainly no gentleman… you… Oh!'

In frustration, she cut herself off, unable to find the proper words to insult him with, when he suddenly began to shake with helpless laughter, which only succeeded in incurring her wrath further. Staring at him in disbelief, she moved closer to him as he began to shove one of his stockinged feet back into his wet boot. 'I'm completely baffled at what you can find to laugh at.'

'Can you not? It's your use of the word *scoundrel* to describe me, I'm afraid. Given sober consideration, I suppose it might apply, even if it is rather mild compared to other more colourful terms I've heard to describe me before.'

'If I were acquainted with such terms you are accustomed to, which does not surprise me in the least, then be assured that I would use them.'

'You probably would—given the way you look and the sharpness of your tongue. If only you could see yourself as you are now, you would not dare give yourself airs and graces,' he said with unsympathetic amusement.

Quite suddenly, he no longer felt like laughing at her plight as his gaze took in every detail of her. Having donned one of his boots, he sat holding the other and, with one brow cocked, he studied her carefully, from her slender ankles to the top of her head, noting the way the material of her gown continued to cling to her slender body, emphasising the minuscule waist and the firm roundness of her breasts.

'I do believe,' he said, almost absently, 'that beneath all that wetness, there is a lovely young woman fighting to be released.'

His words hit Tilly like a slap in the face. Realising what was going through his mind and not liking one bit the way he was looking at her, fresh anger threatened to choke her. 'You hateful beast. How dare you be so...so forward?' Almost breathless with fury and mortification, something about the way in which he was looking at her, his eyes dwelling significantly on her breasts, made her suddenly aware of her appearance. 'Have you no shame?'

Lifting his shoulders in a shrug and shaking his head in that infuriating way of his, he said, 'None, I'm afraid. And now I think you have made your point. If indeed I was at fault in tossing you into the sea, then I apologise most humbly.' Ignoring her gasp of surprise, he continued ironically, 'So, you see, your eloquence has moved me enough to touch even my villainous heart.'

'Since my present predicament appears to give you cause for amusement, if you will excuse me, I will be on my way.'

Aware of her wet clothes clinging to her body and the gritty feel of sand against her face and in her hair, wanting to be as far away from this insufferable man as it was possible to be, with a toss of her head Tilly turned and marched across the sand to where she had left her belongings.

Lucas watched her go as if he had taken root. Troubled by his responsibilities since returning from Spain and with a nagging headache brought on by a sleepless night, he'd decided that a long ride would chase it away. After riding across fields and meadows, he'd come to the beach where he gave his horse his head.

He no longer felt his earlier urge to burst into laughter at the young woman's sorry plight. Shoving his foot into his remaining boot, forgetting for the time being that they were now ruined, then getting to his feet, he walked to where his horse stood patiently waiting. Unable to wipe the young woman from his thoughts, he thought of how she had looked—yes, she had been well and truly soaked through, but it did not detract from her temper or her loveliness. In fact, in some strange way, it had enhanced it.

Her breasts were high and firm, tapering to small peaks beneath the fabric of her dress, and her eyes, a wonderful shade of violet, had been huge in her pale face. Her haughty manner had marked her as a strong character whereas there was a certain softness about her, an elusive gentleness.

Clearly, she was a woman of ever-changing moods and subtle contradictions. While her physical beauty first arrested the attention, it was this spectrum, this bewildering, indefinable quality, that held him captive. A strange, sweet melting feeling softened his innermost core without warning, the place in him he usually kept as hard as steel.

Guilt engulfed him. He really should have been more sympathetic. The poor girl had been doused in seawater and no doubt had a long walk home. Feeling like a complete idiot and with the need to make amends, he mounted his horse and galloped across the sands in the direction she had taken, but she was nowhere to be seen.

He was curious as to her identity. He was acquainted with most of the people in and around Biddycombe, but she was a stranger. Although, he thought, having been absent for months on end, how would he know? On a sigh and feeling the discomfort of his wet boots, he headed for home.

As soon as Tilly arrived back at the house, aware of what a sight she must look and making the excuse that she had been knocked off her feet by a large wave, one of the maids who came to help Mrs Carstairs in the house brought hot water and a tub to her room so she could bathe. Nothing would induce her to tell the truth, that an insufferable man had almost drowned her and then insulted her most shockingly. If she was fortunate, she would not see him again.

When she was restored to looking decent, she went

to see Aunt Charlotte, who was seated in a chair by the window, a book on her lap. Glancing up when Tilly appeared in the doorway, she smiled.

'My dear Tilly, do come in and tell me what you have been doing. I hope you're not too bored. You're not used to so much solitude.'

'No, perhaps not, but I like being here very well. How are you feeling?'

'Oh, a little better. I'll soon be up and about. But this is such a restful house—so quiet.'

'So it is,' Tilly replied softly. 'It's certainly a change from the hustle and bustle of London. I'm tempted to asked Charles to keep the house so that I can live here for ever.'

Aunt Charlotte gave her an indulgent smile. 'You say that now, Tilly, but after a couple of months of complete solitude, you might change your mind. Have you been to the beach yet?'

'Yes—I—I was there earlier.'

'And?'

'I like it very well,' she said, having no intention of disclosing her encounter with the arrogant stranger who had knocked her into the sea. 'It's just like I expected. When you are better, we will go together. We can collect seashells.'

'I'm looking forward to seeing it with you. It will be a pleasant way to pass the summer until we have to return to London.'

Tilly laughed, perching on the window seat. 'It most certainly will. Why, you, too, might get to like it so well that you won't want to leave.'

'And miss your debut? Oh, I don't think so.'

'I know you won't miss the chance of playing match-maker, Aunt Charlotte.'

'Of course not, and you're hardly likely to find a title down here. Not only that, if Charles does go to India, then he will want to see you before he leaves.'

'Yes,' Tilly said absently, listening to a blackbird singing its heart out on the branch of a cherry tree close to the house and thinking how delightful it was. 'Although he doesn't expect to leave for months yet. I'm hoping we'll be here for Christmas. I will miss him dreadfully when he leaves. I would like to see India. Anna loved it, you know—although she was fortunate when her brother made her William's ward when she returned to England.'

'Yes, Tilly,' her aunt said. 'She certainly was. They are so happy together with young Thomas.'

They looked towards the door when Daphne entered, carrying a tray with tea and cakes.

'You will stay and take tea with me, Tilly? See, Daphne has brought two cups.'

'I'd love to,' Tilly said, looking out of the window while Daphne poured the tea, her thoughts turning to her unfortunate encounter with the stranger on the beach, as curious to his identity as he was to know hers.

Two days later, mid-afternoon, while her aunt was resting and Mrs Carstairs was visiting a neighbour, feeling hemmed in and restless at having to remain indoors on such a lovely day, Tilly left her room with the intention of taking a book to read out in the garden. On her way down the stairs she stopped, sensing there was someone in the house.

A man's heavy tread sounded purposefully through the hall, growing nearer from the direction of the kitchen. A tall man appeared, filling the hall with his presence, and then he spoke in the calm, assured voice of a gentleman.

'Ah—so the house is inhabited after all.'

Tilly stared at him. It was that insufferable man she had hoped never to see again.

'Oh—it's you,' she said, continuing down the stairs. 'Do you normally walk into other people's homes un-invited? Sneaking through the house like a thief. You certainly have strange ideas of the way to pay a call on your neighbours.'

One corner of his mouth lifted in a mocking smile. 'Not usually, but this is a house in which I was always welcome.'

There was no mistaking his air of familiarity. He stopped several yards from her, feet apart. She sus-pected he had no patience for the niceties of life. He had neatened himself up a little and pulled his windblown black hair back and fastened it with a ribbon at the nape, but he still wore the same threadbare coat he had worn on the two occasions they had met. All this was only surface deep and beneath it all the wildness was there.

Alone with him, alarmingly, nerve-rackingly alone, Tilly stood looking at him by the light slanting through the two windows. With his wide shoulders and lean waist, there was no concealing that here was a man alive and virile in every fibre of his being, arrogantly mocking and recklessly attractive. He had far and be-yond the most handsome face she had seen in her life.

Tilly found it was impossible to tear her eyes away.

He looked like an aristocratic pirate, arrogant, cold and remote, a man other men would be instinctively wary of and women fascinated by. His eyes in his perfectly chiselled face regarded her with calm intentness, unsmiling but not unfriendly. She looked him contemptuously in the eye before dropping her gaze to his boots.

'I see you have a new pair of boots.'

'I have several—but the boots you ruined were my favourites.'

'You ruined them all by yourself. I know you found the whole incident of almost drowning me highly entertaining, but I did not. Who are you? Why are you here? If it is to see my uncle Silas, then I'm afraid he is no longer with us.'

'So I've been told. So, you are Silas's niece. My commiserations. He was a fine man. A good neighbour. We dined together and visited each other on many occasions.' Despite their differences in age and neither admitting to a certain loneliness in their lives, they had been good friends.

Tilly had nothing to say to this, not having known her uncle well enough to make comment.

The stranger inclined his head slightly. 'I'm Lucas Kingsley, the Earl of Clifton, at your service.'

Tilly stared at him. So, she thought, this was the man who lived in the big house that had raised her curiosity. She was momentarily thrown on hearing this, but her resentment was not diminished. 'I see. And you only recently arrived home. Well, you may be Lord of the manor and own most of the land in these parts, but you do not own Drayton Manor. Do you hear me?'

'How am I to help hearing you when you have no

self-control to lower your voice? I don't know where you come from, but you'll make no friends in these parts if you go about with a face like a thundercloud and a tongue that can flay a man to within an inch of his life.'

'Friends? Ha! I am a stranger to these parts and if my neighbours are all like you, then I can do without them,' she retorted while asking herself what she was doing. She had forgotten her dignity and was shocked at herself and her lack of composure and self-control.

'And you, Miss Whoever-you-are, have a lot to learn. This is a man's world down here and, like it or not, get used to it.'

'I would not take you for a gentleman who indulged in afternoon calls, Lord Clifton.'

'There is always a first time. I apologise for my conduct yesterday. It was unfortunate, and I did try to find you afterwards—when I finally put my wet boots back on, I might add—but you had disappeared.'

'Why on earth would you do that? Come after me, I mean. I think we had said all we had to say to each other.'

'Nevertheless, I wanted to make sure you were all right—to offer you the loan of my horse to see you home—for you were in a sorry state as I recall.'

'Yes, I was. But as you see, Drayton Manor is close to the sea so I did not have very far to walk.'

'And you suffered no ill effects from your tumble into the sea?'

'No. None. Now, suppose you tell me what you are doing letting yourself in without a by your leave. Say what you have to say and leave the way that you entered.'

'Exactly,' he agreed lightly. 'My bailiff told me of Silas's demise. I came to call on Mrs Carstairs.'

'She's visiting a neighbour. She should be back shortly.'

'I brought Silas a keg of French brandy. He was rather partial to the fine stuff. He will have little use of it now. I have left it in the kitchen. Mrs Carstairs will know what to do with it.'

'Feel free to bring Mrs Carstairs a whole distillery, but do not enter this house again unless you are invited.' She thought she saw a look of surprise in his eyes, but it was soon gone.

'Worry not. I will not impose myself on you unless I am invited. We appear to have got off to a bad start,' he said coldly. 'The impression I have of you is that you would not spend your time in useless activities. I think you will get my meaning. With no husband—you do not wear a wedding ring, I see—and therefore no children, you think nothing of interfering wherever you think fit.'

'I believe you refer to my concern for the young lady when I saw her indisposed and rushed to her aid—which is what any decent human being would do. We have met on just two occasions, Lord Clifton, so I fail to see how you have had the time to form any opinion of me at all.'

She felt a moment of unease. It might have been the way his eyes were looking at her, touching her everywhere, an inexplicable, lazy smile sweeping over his lean face as he surveyed her from head to foot, that suddenly made her feel as if she had walked into a seduction scene, which momentarily threw her off balance.

'I recognise a lady who is charitable to others when I see one.'

'Really? I am surprised.'

'Oh, indeed I do. My mother was given to charitable works—quite the saint, in fact.'

'Oh, I am no saint, Lord Clifton. In fact, I am quite the opposite and certainly no lady—which is what my brothers are always telling me. I have an awkward habit of doing things I am not supposed to do and arguing when I should know better. There are times when I don't behave or express myself as a lady is supposed to and if my attitude causes offence, then that is for them to deal with, not me.

'I can be frightfully blunt,' she uttered, looking up into his dark face, which was relaxed into a noble, masculine beauty that drew her gaze like a magnet and brought self-reproach for her weakness.

'So can I,' he replied, his eyes the eyes of a hunter, instantly clear in the moonlight. 'You have inherited Drayton Manor?'

'No. My brother Charles.'

'He is here?'

'No. He remained in London. I am here with my aunt—Uncle Silas's younger sister, who is indisposed at present.'

'And your name?'

'Tilly, short for Matilda, but everyone calls me Tilly—Tilly Anderson.'

Lord Clifton's blue-eyed gaze, alert and watchful, was disconcerting.

'How is the young lady—Florence? Better, I hope?'

'Florence is recovered to perfect health, Miss Anderson. Thank you for asking. The way you leapt to her aid was, of course, laudable.'

'I was concerned.'

'That was obvious.'

'You were not sympathetic to her condition.'

'It is not in my nature. Many people suffer from sea sickness and recover quickly.'

'And you told me not to interfere when I tried to help her.'

'After an absence of many months I was impatient to get to my home.'

'And to be rid of my interference.'

'Yes, since you ask. Florence is a servant and knows her place.'

'She is still a human being and is entitled to be treated with consideration and respect.' Tilly was always one to speak her mind and was too angry to be intimidated by this illustrious neighbour. 'I should tell you that I have a streak to my nature that fiercely rebels against being ordered what to do. I think Florence should do the same.'

'Not if she values her position. I have a formidable temper myself,' he told her with icy calm. 'It may surprise you to learn that when we parted yesterday, I was prepared to give you the benefit of the doubt.'

'And now?'

'That still applies. You virtually accused me of being dishonourable, which was damning in itself. You summed up your opinion of me quickly,' he stated. 'No doubt you have listened to gossip from the locals, but whatever you have heard, forget it. You don't know me.'

Tilly could not look away from him—in fact, unconsciously her feet took her closer to where he stood, her eyes holding his. Angry colour suffused her cheeks. She stood close, her face tilted slightly to look up into his, her unbound black hair spilling down her back, her skirts brushing his black boots.

'You are wrong. I have not been here long enough to listen to gossip—and I wouldn't anyway. I prefer to make up my own mind. I may have met you only twice before, but I have made a very accurate assessment of your character.'

'Do you normally form an opinion of a person after so short an acquaintance?' he asked.

'In your case it was not difficult,' she replied. 'I found you overbearing and dictatorial and with little concern for the feelings of others.'

Lord Clifton arched his brows, mild cynicism and a stirring of respect in the icy depths of his eyes. 'That bad?'

'Worse. You are heartless and I cannot abide your superior male attitude—your insufferable arrogance and conceit.'

He looked at her with condescending amusement. 'And you, Miss Anderson, with a tongue on you that would put a viper to shame, can hardly be called a paragon of perfection.'

'My brothers would agree with you. Especially Charles. We are at war more often than not.'

'And are we at war?'

Tilly eyed him warily. 'I suppose it does seem like that.'

Lord Clifton's face was set in an almost smiling challenge. 'Don't be so certain.'

'Lord Clifton,' she retorted sharply, dark eyes locking with light blue ones, 'if you plan another battle, you can leave right this minute.'

'Nothing so dramatic—merely a mild skirmish. If nothing else, you are forward and recklessly bold.'

'I always believe in being direct and I enjoy walking on the wild side occasionally.'

'And I thought all young ladies sat at their needlepoint and painted pretty pictures.'

'I'm sure you may find it shocking and unfeminine that I do neither, but that's the way I am.'

'I do, but in your case, I will overlook your unfeminine interests. The informality of my call was not meant as an offence. Indeed, I had no idea who you were. I didn't even have the courtesy to ask your name or to thank you for your concern.'

'Because you are arrogant and conceited,' she reminded him.

'You do not take after your uncle.'

'And what is that supposed to mean?'

'You are nothing like him. He was the kind of man who saw the good in everyone and welcomed them into his home. No, you are nothing like him.'

He looked at her with as much dislike as she felt for him and this only increased her anger. 'Do you mean I don't show respect? Oh, dear. How annoying you must find that. I am no sycophant, Lord Clifton, who bows and scrapes to gentlemen and their titles. Those people have to earn my respect. I have met you on two occasions and I believe I have assessed your character correctly.'

When they had met on the beach, she had been angry with him, but that was yesterday. Today he had learned his good friend Silas Anderson was dead and he had come to Drayton Manor with condolences and to commiserate with Mrs Carstairs. Seeping into her consciousness, this thought was telling her that he could not be all bad and that he deserved the benefit of the doubt.

She had no idea how long she was to remain in Devon and, until the time came for her to leave, she could not go around making enemies of everyone, especially not the Earl of Clifton, her uncle's good friend and the most important land owner in these parts. Her manner had been anything but friendly. She must try to practise a little courtesy while he was in her brother's house. But that did not mean to say she had to like him.

'I would like to give you the keg of brandy as a peace offering.'

'I don't drink brandy—my brothers allow me just the one glass of wine, or champagne if I'm lucky.'

'I am not your brothers—and if you don't drink it then you can offer me a glass when I come to call.'

'And do you intend calling, Lord Clifton?'

'If you will allow it?'

'We are neighbours. I would hate to disappoint Mrs Carstairs. She…appears fond of you.'

'Then, in common agreement, we will portray ourselves as being both gracious and mannerly when we are in the presence of Mrs Carstairs.' Surprising her, he abruptly turned on his heel and walked in the direction of the kitchen. 'I will leave you now by the door I came in by. The next time we meet I can only hope you are in a better temper.'

Tilly followed him quickly. Pulling the door open that led into a backyard, he stopped and looked at her.

'You are here for how long?'

'I haven't decided—not that it's any of your business. All I ask is that I am left to live in peace for the duration of my stay.'

'Peace? In Biddycombe?' He laughed and there it was again—that mocking smile. 'You think it's as easy as that?'

She thought he must have read something in her face that made him change his mind about what he was going to say to her.

'When you are ready to listen, I will tell you—or someone else will,' he said flatly. 'A word of advice before I leave. See that your doors and windows are locked and bolted in future—especially at night. You might have the kind of visitors who would not be as amenable or as tolerant as I am.'

They were distracted when Mrs Carstairs entered the yard. When she saw Lord Clifton, her face broke into a welcoming smile. 'Why, Lord Clifton! Good gracious me! I heard you were back. The whole village is abuzz with the news. Welcome home. It's high time, too.'

'I was sorry to hear about Silas. He will be missed.'

'He will that. It's a blessing he didn't suffer. Caught a chill, he did, walking on the beach without his coat. He went out like a light. Can I get you some refreshment?'

'No, thank you. I'll be on my way. I just called to offer my commiserations and to leave a keg of brandy I intended giving Silas.' He looked at Tilly as Mrs Carstairs bustled into the kitchen. 'Good day, Miss Anderson. Thank you for your hospitality.'

Half turning, he hesitated. After some deliberation, when he next spoke his voice was low and serious. 'There is something I would like to ask of you. I'm sorry if it might put you on the spot, but my own need is urgent, which forces me to be blunt. The other day when we met on the beach, to avoid notice, it was my intention to get in the carriage and drive off, not to linger. Unfortunately, Florence put paid to that and I wasn't expecting to encounter a young lady intent on playing the Good Samaritan.'

Tilly looked at him in confusion. 'So, why did that matter?'

'As we were leaving you heard an infant crying.'

'Yes, I did. That was when I realised the contents of the basket was a baby.'

'It is important to me that on no account should anyone know there is a child living at Clifton House—at least, not for the present.'

'Oh, I see. Then…I will tell no one.'

'I would be grateful—not your aunt and certainly not Mrs Carstairs. She is a dear lady, but there are times when she lets her tongue run away with her.'

'I understand. Of course I will keep your confidence. I am not one to gossip. It is your affair, not mine. But you have servants at Clifton House. Can they be trusted to keep your confidence also?'

Frowning, he shook his head. 'As to that, I will have to depend on their loyalty to my family—although there are one or two who are inclined to gossip.'

Tilly followed him out of the yard to where he'd left his mount tethered to a gatepost. Swinging himself up into the saddle, he looked down at her.

'Good day, Miss Anderson. Enjoy your time at Drayton Manor.'

When he unexpectedly smiled broadly, Tilly noticed how white and strong his teeth were and how the tiny lines at the sides of his sharp eyes creased up attractively. He really was so handsome, so well made, so perfect to look at. She wondered at the effect he would have on the ladies who made up London's society.

For a moment she was confused and found herself striving for normality. It was difficult to organise her thoughts when those amazingly light blue eyes were focused on her so intently. Before the rogue thoughts could progress further, she lowered her eyes, quickly shaking off the strangeness of the moment that had caught her unawares. What was she thinking of? This man was practically unknown to her, yet just for a moment she had felt drawn to this handsome, desirable, insufferably arrogant stranger.

But she could not deny that he had a strange and strong effect on her—he invaded her consciousness and took over her mind. She found it hard to explain because it was something she had never experienced before. The way he had of looking at her was a new and very powerful and profound thing.

That something was happening against her will she knew. Men like Lord Clifton found it easy to manipulate a woman's heart and, after her debacle with Richard Coulson, who was a green youth compared to Lord Clifton, she could not allow him to do that.

Tilly stood and watched him ride away, noting his relaxed air and the splendid way he sat on his horse. He was hatless and his loosely tied black hair gave him a jaunty, nonchalant look. Whether or not he had been touched by the reeking decay and stench that hung over the battlefields in Spain, Lord Clifton had not been three days back in England and already he was firmly taking charge of his inheritance at Clifton House. Even with the journey from Spain still present in his mind, he was taking his affairs in hand and seeking her confidence to keep the presence of the child secret.

It was an attitude of which she approved, she thought, almost convincing herself that her admiration had nothing to do with his darkly handsome face, the midnight-blue depths of his eyes and the curl of his lips.

As she stood watching his retreating figure, she pondered the fascination she felt for Lord Clifton. She had met many handsome men in London, yet she'd felt no connection between them, no meeting of the eyes or quickening of her breath that she felt when her eyes were captured by the dark stare of the lord of Clifton House.

What was it about him that had the power to hold her so entranced, to arouse her rampant curiosity? It had to be something other than the classical perfection of his features, for Lord Clifton was an extraordinarily handsome man. She had never experienced with any gentleman that quickening of the blood she felt when his eyes captured hers. And who was the child whose presence at Clifton House he wanted kept secret? Was he the father and, if so, who was the mother and where was she?

Chapter Three

Lucas had been surprised to find the young woman he had encountered on the beach two days ago in residence at Drayton Manor. When his gaze had come to rest on her, on her violet eyes in which darker flecks blazed—a sure sign that their owner was under some urgent compulsion—he had looked at her with silent fascination.

He was easily moved by the beauty of a woman and the calm coldness with which Miss Anderson had looked at him intrigued him. He had tried to ignore her scent of jasmine and all her delectable attributes that stood just within his easy reach as she had lambasted his character. She was enchanting, part-spitfire, part-angel, and with an independent temperament.

Despite her acid tongue he was drawn to the freshness and vitality with which she carried herself. She was exceptionally beautiful, so beautiful that it was impossible not to stare at her. Her eyes were wide-set and accentuated by black brows. The patrician nose, the heart-shaped face, the fine texture of her skin, the haughty set of the queenly head crowned with a glorious shining black mane—all bespoke good breeding.

There was about her a warm sensuality, something instantly suggestive to him of pleasurable fulfilment. It was something she could not help, something that was an inherent part of her, but of which she was acutely aware. She was obviously intelligent with a poised manner that would charm all present at social events, but beneath her grace and poise she was also full of suppressed energy that lurked just below the surface.

Thoughts such as these brought to mind his need to find a wife, a woman who would be more amenable and biddable than Miss Anderson, who was far too headstrong and opinionated and reminded him far too much of his wild and tenacious sister. Miss Anderson was the type of woman most unsuitable to be his wife. But he was puzzled by her. A young woman with her debut to look forward to? It didn't make sense. What was the real reason her family had decided to bury her in the heart of Devon, in a house once inhabited by an old man?

As so often of late his thoughts turned to his infant nephew. He was a troubled man as he rode back to Clifton House. Jack Price posed a problem. While ever the boy was beneath his roof there was every chance that Price would find out and put two and two together and realise he was his brother's child.

Reaching the house, he made his way to the nursery, which was on the same landing as his own rooms. Pausing for an indecisive moment outside, he pushed open the door. Diaphanous white curtains were drawn across the windows to shut out most of the bright sunshine while the child slept. One of the windows had been opened and the curtain gently stirred in the slight breeze.

Pictures of animals and flowers hung on the walls, shelves crammed with books and baskets of toys were everywhere—toys that had once belonged to himself and Cassie—some more battered than others, but still able to give pleasure to a child. There was a clockwork dog and a doll's house in one corner and a child-size table and chairs. Set at right angles to the hearth were two comfortable easy chairs.

He could hear Florence moving about in the adjoining room. It was to the crib in which the child slept that Lucas directed his gaze. The child was lying on his back, his dark hair on either side of his face, his chubby palms open. He had kicked away the covers so his baby legs were bare. Not wishing to alert Florence to his presence and careful not to wake the child, he edged closer to the crib and looked down.

He was totally unprepared for the feelings and the emotions that almost overwhelmed him. As memories of the child's birth assailed him, remembering how he had taken him from Cassie's arms, promising he would take care of him and guard him from Jack Price with his life, he gulped in the air, trying to drag it into his tortured lungs as he remembered watching Cassie take her final breath.

He couldn't fail her. No matter what, he would honour his promise. She had told him that before he died, Edmund had expressed a wish that, if the child was a boy, he was to be named Tobias. Cassie had agreed, saying it was a lovely name. So Tobias it was.

The servants had been sworn to secrecy. Anyone

who uttered a word about the child's existence would be dismissed immediately. He gazed at Tobias. The fan of his dark lashes shadowed his plump, rosy cheeks. His lips were soft and pink and slightly parted. His head was covered with a mass of glossy brown curls. He accepted that he was his responsibility and his heart was stirred with a sense of pride in his infant beauty. His eyes were blue, the same blue as Cassie's.

Cassie. Remembrance of her twisted his heart. Cassie, glowing and strong, with the power to amuse and infuriate him and with a will of burnished steel as she had stood up to him when he had ordered her to stay away from Edmund Price. Defiant and brave and with blazing eyes, she had ignored him.

When he had caught up with her in Spain, finding her at her lover's bedside where he lay dying from wounds sustained in battle, and seeing she was big with child, he had arranged for them to be married immediately. When she had gone into labour, he could see that she was in pain and tortured with grief for Edmund's loss. Then she had subjected him to the most massive dose of guilt and emotional blackmail to ensure that he would take care of the child should she not make it.

Gently, he stroked Tobias's cheek with his finger. The infant stretched his tiny body and yawned. And then his eyelids fluttered and opened a little in sleep before closing once more, not yet ready to wake, but the man responsible for the disturbance in his nephew smiled to himself, a satisfying smile that warmed his heart.

Aunt Charlotte's recovery proved to be slow. She still refused to allow a doctor to visit, insisting her constitution was strong and she would soon be fully recovered. She was content to spend her time in her room with her embroidery or in the garden with a blanket over her knees, reading one of the many books that filled the shelves in the library.

With each new day that dawned, Tilly loved being at Drayton Manor more and more. During those first days as she was warmly greeted by neighbours as she wandered happily through the countryside and along the coast, she was unable to push the Earl of Clifton, whose house was never far from her sights, from her mind.

One day ran into the next so that she almost lost track of time. Never had she known such freedom, of being able to do as she wished, to live entirely for the present. How pleasant it was. Being out of doors so much, her face took on a golden shade and she had taken to braiding her hair so that it snaked down her back from beneath her bonnet. What did she care what she looked like? There was no one to see her.

Tilly couldn't have said what the sound was that woke her in the early hours. The wind had risen and was buffeting the house, but she thought it must be more than that. She closed her eyes once more as sleep threatened to engulf her, yet her ears continued to strain for the sound that had woken her. But there was nothing, nothing that could account for it.

However, she was restless and got up to look out of the diamond-paned windows. It was a dark, moonless night, but she could just make out the shape of the trees and the outbuildings housing the ivy-clad stables just beyond. Then she heard a sound that alerted all her senses. It was the sound of horse's hooves on the drive leading to the stables. That was the moment she thought she saw a light close to the stable doors. Surely it couldn't be Dunstan or Graham at this ungodly hour, unless there was something amiss with one of the horses.

Not wishing to disturb Mrs Carstairs, she decided to investigate herself. Shrugging herself into a dark blue robe over her nightdress, she left her bedroom and made her way through the dark house, letting herself out by a side door close to the kitchen. She started when a dog fox barked from somewhere beyond the house, shuddered, then pulled herself together, following a path lined on one side by the eerie trunks of ash and beech and guarding like sentries. She made her way silently to the stables.

She couldn't have said what alerted her to danger and caused her to shrink into the secluded, solid darkness of the trees. As her eyes became accustomed to the gloom, she saw the occasional flicker of light and weird shapes and shadows around the stables. There were sounds of movement, of horses shifting restlessly in their stalls. What on earth was going on? she wondered.

Although never of a nervous disposition, beneath the eerie canopy of the trees Tilly felt the chilling hand of fear clutch at her. Her heart began to race. Could someone be trying to steal the horses? About to step out and confront whoever it was, it was then that a powerful pair of hands grabbed her from behind. In an instant, she was pulled back against a hard chest and a hand was placed over her mouth, the fingers that gripped her lower face like a band of steel, stifling any sound she might have made. Then she was held quite still, held so firmly that she was unable to move.

'Hold still. There is danger.'

Hot breath touched her cheek as the warning was uttered softly in her ear. Her body was pressed hard to whoever it was that held her, their faces close together. She moved her head angrily to shake him off and heard a half-stifled noise that might have been a laugh. She could hear the sound of his breathing as the sounds she had heard coming from the stables earlier increased in intensity.

She heard the closing of doors and, in the limited light above her captor's fingers, her eyes grew wide as shapes began to materialise in front of her. She heard the hammering of her heartbeat in her ears as dark-clad figures, some ten or a dozen of them, passed by, some on horseback, each with their heads bent as they hurried on with a deadly-seeming purpose. Did she imagine it, or was that a flash of a scarlet coat she saw in the gloom?

'Be still,' the voice close to her ear repeated in a husky voice. 'Don't utter a sound.'

Unable to struggle, unable to move, Tilly did as he bade, too alarmed and afraid to do anything else. Holding her breath, she stood and watched the figures move quickly by and become swallowed up by the night. Only then did she feel the powerful grip release her and the fingers free her mouth. But he still held her close.

'You can breathe easy now. They have gone.'

Tilly was still tense, still anxious that those men would come back. Taking her shoulders, her assailant turned her to face him. She already knew his identity. Lord Clifton's unseen hands touched the nape of her neck and stroked the length of her hair. His close proximity was disconcerting. Her traitorous body tingled and grew warm. In the leather jerkin he wore, he smelled of the forest, of man and horse, but not unpleasantly so.

'Do you make a habit of prowling the countryside at night, Lord Clifton?'

'A man on foot who knows the land like I do and knows where he's going can hardly be seen—especially at night.'

Tilly looked at him haughtily, mostly to cover her self-consciousness at her state of dishabille. 'And tonight you were drawn to Drayton Manor. May I ask why?'

'For the same reason you were disturbed and came to investigate.'

Aware that his arm still encircled her and the hard set of his muscles flexed against her shoulder as they stood still in the dark shadows of the trees, she felt a shifting deep inside her. It was as if the very essence of him and herself, the very rhythm of his heart, was beating in unison with her own.

For all its intensity, the encounter lasted only a moment. His presence here at this time of night filled her with confusion, yet she was aware of an enormous relief, warmth and pleasure sweeping through her. Placing his finger beneath her chin, he tilted her pale face up to his.

'Are you all right?'

'Yes,' she replied quietly. 'Those men… Who were they? And I want the truth. Were they poachers? But… if so, what were they doing at the stables? Please don't tell me they intended to steal the horses. And why didn't Dunstan or Graham hear them and come to investigate?'

'They weren't poachers, Miss Anderson—nothing so tame.'

Tilly stared at him, trying to make out his features. 'I heard the horses and came to see what was happening.'

'You should have stayed in your room and kept the curtains closed. Those men were smugglers.'

Tilly gasped. 'Smugglers? But…what were they doing here?'

'You have horses?'

'Yes, six, the carriage horses.'

'Then I feel I must warn you that there may be nights when they are needed. I should have made you aware of the smugglers' activities when I called.'

'But…I don't understand. Why would they want our horses?'

'When a large cargo comes in, the smugglers may need extra horses to help carry it away before dawn.'

'You mean they may steal them?' Tilly was astounded by the audacity that such a thing could happen.

'Not steal—merely borrow them.'

Tilly looked at him coldly as the meaning of his words began to sink in. 'Are you telling me the smugglers take them and use them?'

'Exactly. They are always returned, to be used another night. It's a foolish person who tries to keep the smugglers out when their horses might be needed. See your curtains are drawn in future and your lips are sealed and you will find a gift on your doorstep the next morning.'

'And if I don't want a gift?'

'You'll get one anyway for the loan of your horses. The smugglers always pay for people's silence. It suits everyone very well.'

'I see. Well…thank you for telling me, although I'm beginning to wonder what I've let myself in for,' she said, concerned for William's fine carriage horses. 'But I don't understand why Dunstan wasn't wakened by all the activity. He loves those horses and would do anything to protect them if they were in danger. Unless…' She gasped. 'Oh, dear! I do so hope he hasn't come to any harm.'

'Don't worry. Your groom and his son are quite safe. I came to warn them. I was informed of the run—that the contraband would be bigger than usual. I thought your groom should be made aware of what might happen.'

'So that is what you are doing here. Thank you. I do appreciate your consideration.'

'Remember what I have told you. It would be prudent to keep out of the way of the stables at night. The smuggling fraternity is tightly knit and they keep to their own rules.'

'It's still a criminal offence. They make a living by not paying the King his revenue.'

'True. And there are many who say the King is rich enough.'

'Even you?'

He smiled slightly. 'I keep my thoughts to myself. It's easier that way. The smugglers are the law along the coast and they are well organised. Many of the Revenue men are terrified of them.'

'But how do so many horses pass along the road carrying contraband unnoticed?'

'They can and they do.'

'Have they taken the horses or made use of them and brought them back?'

'Relax. They've finished with them for tonight.'

'Thank goodness.'

The moon suddenly appeared from behind the clouds, spreading its light on them. Tilly was aware of him standing close, watching her so intently that he might have been trying to commit every detail of her features to memory.

Dropping his eyes to her waist and taking the ends of the belt which had come loose on her robe, exposing the stark whiteness of her nightdress beneath, he proceeded to tie it, drawing her robe together. Fires ignited inside Tilly at the intimacy of the act, fires that flared to a startling intensity when she found herself standing so close to him that she could almost hear the beating of his heart.

He gave her a long slow look, a twist of humour around his mouth. His direct masculine assurance disconcerted her. She was vividly conscious of his proximity to her. She felt a rush of blood sing through her veins. Instantly, she felt resentful towards him. He had made too much of an impact on her and she was afraid that if he looked at her much longer, he would read her thoughts.

'Come, I'll walk back with you to the house now the danger is past.'

He led the way on to the gravel path. His touch sent a flood of warmth through Tilly's body to settle in a hot flush on her cheeks. She was thankful it was dark and he couldn't see. With a great effort of will, neither of them speaking, she walked slightly ahead of him to the door through which she had exited the house earlier. Before she reached it, she stepped on some stony ground, twisting her ankle beneath her and stumbling in the process, falling painfully to the ground.

In alarm, Lord Clifton knelt beside her. Raising her head, her body feeling bruised and sore, she looked up at him looming over her.

'Here,' he said, reaching out a hand. 'Let me help you to your feet. Are you hurt?'

'I've twisted my ankle.'

'See if you can stand and I'll help you to the house.'

Placing his hands beneath her arms, he helped her to her feet. Putting a little weight on her injured foot, she cried out with the pain that shot through it. It was beginning to throb terribly.

'Here, lean on me.'

'No,' Tilly said quickly as he reached out his hand once more. 'It is only a sprain. I don't need help.'

Lord Clifton scowled at her, noticing the stubborn thrust to her chin which told him she would rather die than accept his help, but in the sudden light from the moon, he could see her eyes were swimming with the silently repressed tears that the pain from her injured ankle was causing her. It was evident that she would not make it to the house unaided. His eyes narrowed.

'I doubt that. Come—don't be difficult,' he said impatiently.

Before Tilly could stop him or protest, he had placed one arm firmly about her waist and the other beneath her knees, swinging her effortlessly up into his arms. Normally, she would have kicked and fought at being handled in such a way, but she was too stunned to say anything at finding herself pressed so close to him. She could feel his warmth and the strength in his hard lean body, which made her feel uncomfortable—and something else as well, something she did not care to analyse just then.

Pushing the door open with his foot, he carried her through the kitchen to the study that doubled up as the library, placing her in a chair by the hearth, where the dying embers of the fire still glowed. Lighting a lamp, he dropped on one knee and removed her slipper, flexing her ankle with the professional expertise of a doctor.

Tilly could feel the firmness of his fingers on her bare flesh as he twisted her foot to one side. She gripped the arms of the chair, almost crying out with the pain this caused her, but bit her lip in her determination not to let him know how much it hurt. At last, he put her foot gently on the carpet and looked up at her directly.

'There doesn't appear to be anything broken—just a slight sprain.'

'Why—*thank you*, Doctor,' she said with emphasis.

Ignoring her sarcastic tone, Lord Clifton curled his lips in a wry smile. 'I'm not a doctor, but I grew up on the hunting field where more people took a tumble than I care to mention. I soon learned how to deal with injured limbs and the like—although I have to say that none of the people I tried to help had such a charming ankle.' He looked to the door when Mrs Carstairs, wrapped in her dressing gown, appeared, carrying a candle.

'Goodness me!' she gasped on seeing Lord Clifton kneeling on the carpet in front of Miss Anderson dressed in her night attire. 'I thought I heard a noise. What on earth has happened—and how do you come to be here, Lord Clifton?' When he cocked an eyebrow at her, she sighed, shaking her head knowingly. 'Don't tell me. It's one of those nights, is it?'

'Yes, Mrs Carstairs. Unfortunately, Miss Anderson was unaware of the strange events that occur on certain nights and went to investigate.'

'Oh, dear. I should have told you,' she said, looking at Tilly with alarm. 'Did they see you? Did they hurt you?'

'They didn't see her—I got to her in time. Don't worry about it. She knows now and will keep to her room in future. On the way back to the house she stumbled in the dark and sprained her ankle. Some cold water and a bandage would not go amiss.'

'Of course. What am I thinking of? I'll get them at once.'

She was soon back. After soaking the bandage in the cold water, Lord Clifton proceeded to wrap Tilly's ankle. When he was done, he stood up and, with his hands on his hips, looked down at her.

'You'll have to rest it for a few days, but it should soon start to feel better.'

'Thank you. I'm sure it will,' Tilly replied, impatient for him to be gone so she could hobble up to bed—but Mrs Carstairs had other ideas.

'You will take a glass of brandy before you leave, Lord Clifton?' Mrs Carstairs asked, always kindly and seeming to have no notion of the impropriety of

Lord Clifton being with Tilly at that late hour, with her dressed only in her night attire.

To Tilly's annoyance, he readily accepted, seating himself in the chair across from her and stretching his long-booted legs out in front of him, looking very much at home. Mrs Carstairs went to the mahogany sideboard and poured a drink from one of several crystal decanters that sat there and handed it to him.

He sniffed and rolled it on his tongue appreciatively. He was silent for a time while he drank. Tilly couldn't believe it when Mrs Carstairs disappeared back to the kitchen, taking the bowl of water with her to be disposed of.

'Do you live in London, Miss Anderson?' Lord Clifton asked, swirling the amber liquid round the bowl of the glass.

'Yes, I do—at least, when I'm not staying with my eldest brother and his wife in Berkshire.'

'Tell me, what brings you to Devon?'

'My brother Charles is employed by the East India Company. He very much wants to work for the Company in India and he plans to leave shortly. He had no time to travel to Devon to see his inheritance.'

'So he sent you instead.'

'Yes, and my aunt.'

'He has no intention of coming to live in Drayton Manor?'

'Not for the foreseeable future, I'm afraid. It's too far away. He may even decide to sell it—which I think would be a shame. It's a lovely house.'

'Your older brother is the Marquess of Elvington, I

believe.' When she gave him a questioning glance he said, 'Silas told me something of your family.'

'I see. William is our half-brother. He spent several years in India with the East India Company until he decided to go it alone.'

Lord Clifton looked at her hard, then he nodded slowly, as if digesting this information. 'I am impressed. I had no idea when I pulled a lovely young lady out of the sea that she was the sister of the Marquess of Elvington.'

'Why? Does it matter? Does that mean you suddenly see me differently?'

'Yes,' he said quietly. 'I have to say it does.'

'Have you met my brother?'

'I know of him, but we have never met. And you are, what, Miss Anderson—eighteen, nineteen?'

'Since you ask, I am nineteen.'

'And ripe for the Season.'

'Next year,' she provided, conscious of his shadowed eyes upon her in quiet appraisal. 'At least, that is, if my aunt and brothers have their way.'

'And you? What do you want?'

'If you must know, the whole idea of the Season terrifies me,' she said, lowering her eyes. 'I have no interest in being paraded in front of society merely to acquire a suitable husband. Besides, I cannot see the point of going to all that bother and expense when I am in no hurry to marry. I'm quite happy as I am.'

Lord Clifton heard the intensity of her statement. It was said with deep conviction and more than a little pain, which stirred his curiosity. 'Perhaps when you return to London, you will have come to see everything in a different light.'

'No, I won't,' she told him with a quiet firmness. 'I meant what I said.'

He gave her a wry look. 'I know how society works, that there are standards to be upheld. As the sister of the Marquess of Elvington, when you fail to make an appearance when the Season starts people will want to know why. You will leave yourself wide open to a great deal of gossip and speculation.'

'I have little interest in what people think.' Tilly wondered how he would react if she were to disclose that she was already the object of gossip and speculation. If Charles allowed her to remain in Devon, then she would be too far away to worry about what people said about her.

As if reluctant to pursue the issue since it clearly troubled her, Lord Clifton stood and sauntered about the room. He looked at everything that had become familiar to him during his visits to his old friend Silas: ancient leather tomes filling the shelves, charts pertaining to the sea on tables and a jumble of magazines on a chair.

'I always thought this to be a pleasant room. I've spent many an hour discussing worldly matters with Silas.' He picked up a much-thumbed leather-bound volume from several on the desk. 'Armies of the world,' he uttered softly. 'The strategies of war always fascinated him. He should have been actively involved. He would have made an excellent leader of men with his common sense and no-nonsense attitude. His knowledge of matters military was as vast as Napoleon's and Wellington's combined.'

Placing it back on the table, he sat back down in the chair, making himself comfortable once more, seeming in no hurry to leave. He looked at the young woman seated opposite. With the orange glow from the lamp, she wasn't to know that her face was like a cameo, something so young and innocent that reminded Lord Clifton of a small bird.

Feeling compelled and at liberty to look his fill, crossing his long legs and resting his elbows on the arms of the chair, steepling his fingers in front of him, he found everything about her pleasing. She must have sensed his perusal because she suddenly raised her eyes, a flash of colour staining her cheeks as he met her gaze with a querying uplifted brow.

'I would be obliged if you would please stop looking at me in that way. Your critical eye pares and dissects me as if I was an insect on a slab.'

'Does it?' he murmured absently, continuing to look at her, at the soft fullness of her mouth and glorious violet eyes.

Her flush deepened. 'I have imperfections enough without you looking for more. Please stop it,' she demanded quietly, 'otherwise I will be forced to ask you to leave—which you should do anyway. The hour is late and your being here with me alone, attired as I am, is not proper.'

Her words brought a slow, teasing smile to his lips and his strongly marked brows were slightly raised, his eyes suddenly glowing with humour. 'And that bothers you, does it? It would be the height of rudeness if you were to do that. After all, am I not a guest? And I have tended your ankle…'

'Which was extremely kind of you, but it does not make me beholden to you,' Tilly retorted tightly.

'Nevertheless, I cannot help looking at you when you are sitting directly in my sights.'

Hot faced and perplexed, Tilly almost retorted that she was not a rabbit in the sights of his gun, but she halted herself in time. She had never known a man to be so provoking. She was suddenly shy of him. There was something in his eyes that made her feel it was impossible to look at him. There was also something in his voice that brought so many new and conflicting themes in her heart and mind that she did not know how to speak to him.

The effect was a combination of fright and excitement and she must put an end to it. She was in danger of becoming hypnotised by that silken voice and those mesmerising light blue eyes. The fact that he knew it, that he was deliberately using his charm to dismantle her determination not to weaken before him, she found annoying. She must learn to control her feelings and emotions where he was concerned. After her debacle with Richard Coulson, she was not looking for any sort of romantic entanglement.

'Will you not find Devon a trifle dull after the excitements of London?' he asked.

'I don't think so. I intend to adjust to the slow pace of country life. I intend to occupy my time getting to know the area—and I love being by the sea. It's the first time I've seen it.'

Lord Clifton smiled. 'Anyone who comes here to settle has much to learn about the place and its people.'

'Whether or not I settle here remains to be seen. It all

depends on what Charles decides to do with the house. I might try to persuade him not to sell it. I would like to know more about Biddycombe. What can you tell me?'

'Only that it's not perhaps what you expect. During the days the locals, the fishermen and country squires go about their mundane work, but when darkness falls it becomes another matter entirely.'

'Why? Is that when the ghosts come out to play?'

His lips curved in a smile. 'Nothing so exciting, Miss Anderson, although some might think so.'

'Well, if not ghosts, then what?'

'Smugglers, Miss Anderson. Smugglers. You have just seen them in action, have you not?'

'Yes, I have—and I have to say it does not sit easy with me. Tell me more about them.'

'Smuggling goes on the length of the entire south coast, from Kent in the east to Cornwall in the west. It's a way of life. For families with many mouths to feed times are hard and smuggling is a way of trying to make ends meet. It's criminal, yes, but it goes on. The coast round Biddycombe is favourable to the smuggling fraternity—reckless, desperate men. Brandy, tobacco, tea—exotic fabrics for the ladies—they break the law by not paying customs duty on them.'

'And do they get rich out of these activities?'

'They can do nicely out of one night's work. Some make fortunes, using any means—even murder. It's foolish to cross them. The smugglers are a law unto themselves along the coast—there's none that can stand against them. The life of anyone who informs on them isn't worth a penny piece. Those who are involved do so at a high cost, for the penalty will be found at the end of a rope.'

'Goodness, it sounds quite dreadful. It would appear I have a lot to learn about coastal affairs.'

'You can't be expected to know the ways of seafaring people. The entire county takes what can be got past the customs men. From the highest to the lowest most people have a hand in it. All it takes is a dark night and to know when the Revenue cutters are about—and even if they are, some go in fear and avoid the smugglers. Most of the community accept what goes on as a way of life and not as a crime.'

'And what of you, Lord Clifton? Do you take what can be got from the smugglers—or perhaps you have a hand in it yourself?'

'I'm not averse to taking the odd keg of brandy for turning a blind eye to their activities, but I am not involved. It would be more than my position is worth. As the Earl of Clifton, it is my duty to uphold the law, not break it.'

'I can understand that—although, where smugglers are concerned, I'm beginning to favour the ghosts.'

Lord Clifton fell silent, considering her carefully, twirling the glass in his fingers.

'How is Florence—and the child? Well, I hope.'

He nodded, suddenly serious. 'There is someone who would do the child harm. I cannot, will not, allow that. If he discovers the child's existence, he will stop at nothing to get his hands on it—one way or another.'

'The child is not yours?'

He shook his head. 'He is my sister's child. She died in Spain—giving it life.'

Tilly's heart contracted with sympathy. There was a deep sadness in his eyes. 'I am so sorry to hear that. You must miss her terribly.'

'Yes, yes, I do. We were close.'

'And how is he—the child?'

'Tobias. Despite the turbulence of his beginning he thrives, thank God. Finding Florence was fortunate for me—for her, less so. Her own child had died several days before, her husband before that. The war in the Peninsula has made many widows. Florence agreed to nurse my sister's child in return that I pay her passage back to England.'

'That must have been difficult for her.'

'It was—but she desperately needed the money. She has also agreed to remain with the child until he no longer needs her. By which time I may have a wife to concern herself with such things.'

Tilly stared at him, surprise registering in her eyes. 'A wife? You are to marry?'

'Eventually, yes—a woman who is eminently suitable to be mistress of Clifton.'

'And of excellent character, I expect—to preside over your house with grace and poise and has been trained to manage the demanding responsibilities of such a large house.' She laughed softly when he looked at her sharply. 'I know all about the way things are done. Aunt Charlotte is forever pointing them out to me for when I make my debut—should I decide to fall in with her wishes. A young lady has to acquire all manner of accomplishments before she makes her curtsy.'

'Of course. As the sister of a marquess, you will know how marriages work among the aristocracy.'

'You, too—and have decided it is time you married and produced an heir. You have a lady in mind?'

'Not yet.'

'It is evident to me that you are thinking with your head and not your heart, Lord Clifton. You are considering marriage to an as yet unknown woman with the same kind of dispassion and practised precision I imagine you employ when dealing with your business transactions.'

He shrugged. 'I am no more sentimental about marriage than anyone else. It's a contract like any other. Marriage to the woman I marry will be…favourable.'

'I think *excruciatingly boring* would be a more appropriate term to use. Do you not feel that where something as important as marriage is concerned, then it is essential that the two people concerned love each other?'

Shaking his head, he met her direct gaze. 'In my opinion that is sentimental nonsense. I cast a blight on love a long time ago, Miss Anderson. So, until the time when I take a wife, I have Tobias to take care of. He is my prime concern at this time.'

'Of course he is. May I ask who it is that is a danger to the child—a name, at least, so I will know who to be wary of?'

He thought for a moment, considering her request, then, deciding he could trust her, he said, 'Jack Price. He lives further along the coast. He's a man whose exploits are talked of all along the south coast. He's earned himself an admirable reputation in his field of free trading. He's a leader. He has agents in his pay— in Devon and beyond.'

'So, others take the risks and he reaps the rewards.'

He nodded. 'Price has the routes and markets for the smuggled goods all worked out. He is a man used to getting his own way and not averse to soiling his hands to get it. He is without common decency, without compassion, his emotions stirred solely by his greed for wealth. He also enjoys the earthly pleasures of life. He's good at impressing people who don't know that beneath his fancy clothes and affectations he is in possession of a ruthlessness and cruelty which will stop at nothing to possess or destroy what he cannot have. But there are those who are law-abiding and will not turn a blind eye to his activities for ever.'

'Then he would do well to remember that he is not beyond the reach of the law.'

'He is the younger brother of the man my sister was married to. Since his brother's death in Spain, he has inherited the property—which is considerable. By rights it is the infant's inheritance, but as yet Price is in ignorance of his existence. Until I can get legal advice on the matter it is imperative that it is kept secret. I have to keep him safe. There is bad blood between our families. That is all you need to know.'

'Then I shall know to avoid him.'

'You will respect my confidence?'

Tilly nodded. 'Yes, yes, I will.'

He fell silent. Tilly waited for him to go on.

'When I encountered you on the beach on my arrival back in England,' he said at length, 'you were the first civilised young woman I'd seen in a long time, Miss Anderson. It was a long way back to Devon.'

'Was it very bad in the Peninsula? We hear things—

about battles fought and won, or lost—but no one knows for certain what it is like.'

'It is bad. It was not what I hoped to find among the forces of the British and French armies and the utter carnage of the battle.' He got to his feet, looking down at her. 'Do you ride by any chance?'

'Yes—I love riding. Mrs Carstairs has told me I can hire a horse from the farrier in Biddycombe. I intend sending Dunstan to find something suitable for me to ride.'

'Thank you for the brandy. You are right. The hour is late. Will you manage to get to bed or would you like me to assist you?'

'Certainly not,' Tilly replied, prepared to climb the stairs on her hands and knees rather than ask his help. 'Mrs Carstairs will give me a hand and I am capable of hopping.'

'In which case I will leave you.'

'Thank you,' Tilly said stiffly. 'I'm glad you had the foresight to come and warn us about the smugglers coming to take the horses. I will speak to Dunstan in the morning and make sure they are unharmed.'

Lord Clifton nodded, crossing to the door. 'They won't be harmed. Now you are aware of what goes on after dark, you'll be prepared. Remember to turn a blind eye in the future.'

And then he was gone, melting into the shadows of the hall. Tilly waited and after a moment she heard a horse galloping away from the house.

With the help of Mrs Carstairs, Tilly returned to her bed.

'You know Lord Clifton quite well, don't you, Mrs Carstairs?' she asked, curious to know more about him.

'As well as most in these parts. Why do you ask?'

'His sister. Did you know that she died in Spain—along with her young man?'

She nodded. 'Lord Clifton told me himself. Terrible tragedy it was—such a lovely young lady—and coming so soon after the vessel carrying his parents went down in the Channel during a storm. They were going to Jersey to visit friends. What a dreadful time that was. It was a miracle their bodies were recovered and brought back to Clifton House. The whole of Biddy-combe and the surrounding towns and villages were in mourning. In the space of two years Lord Clifton lost his entire family.'

'That is tragic indeed, Mrs Carstairs. He has never married and he must be, what, twenty-eight or nine?'

'Twenty-nine, he is. Of course he should have married—when he was just a young man—but it all went wrong.'

'Oh? What happened?' Tilly asked, her curiosity piqued.

'Ran off with somebody else, she did—when her parents took her to London. Miranda, her name was. Some rich American gentleman, apparently. Broke Lord Clifton's heart, she did. Never looked at a woman in that way since. I doubt he'll ever get over it.' On a sigh, she turned to the door. 'He's had nothing but bad luck in the past. It's time something good happened to him.'

Left to her thoughts, Tilly was deeply saddened and ashamed of the way she had behaved towards Lord Clifton. His suffering must be great indeed. There was something about him that seemed to bring out the worst in her and made her act more outrageous than she thought was wise. Why couldn't she learn to control her tongue? Knowing what she now did, her conscience smote her. She had been quite horrid towards him. Should they meet again, she would try to be more amiable towards him.

And who was the woman he'd wanted to marry— the woman who had broken his heart? Having been let down so badly in the past, little wonder he spoke with such cold indifference about love.

Shrouded in darkness, as he rode, Lucas thought of what Miss Anderson had told him about having no wish to have a Season and her seeming reluctance to marry. He applauded her honesty, but suspected there was more than what she had divulged she was concerned about. There had been an unmistakable pain and desperation behind her words that had reached out and touched him in half-forgotten, obscure places. He had been made to feel uneasy by it, leaving him puzzled and with a curiosity to know more.

Chapter Four

Tilly slept badly that night. Her imagination was running rife. The night was dark and she tried to settle, but found her conversation with Lord Clifton played on her mind. She listened for sounds that would tell her the smugglers were active, but they were gone now. She was distressed at the thought of William's beautiful carriage horses being used to carry heavy contraband to goodness knew where for someone else's gain.

The following morning, the sun was already high when Tilly rose. Placing her injured foot gingerly on the floor, she was relieved to find it not as painful as she thought. Hobbling to the window, she looked out. Everything was still, with no sign of the disturbance in the early hours.

Later, managing to hobble to the stables, she found Dunstan putting fresh straw and hay into the stalls. He was a big man, a middle-aged widower, but tough and stubbornly dedicated to his work. He loved working with horses and had been more than happy to come down to Devon with his son Graham, who she could hear moving about up in the loft.

'I know what happened during the night, Dunstan. Lord Clifton told me. How are the horses this morning?'

'They seem to be all right. No harm done. I gave them a rub down earlier.'

'I have been told that this may happen on a regular basis.'

'So I understand. Bit queer if you ask me.'

'I agree, but we have no choice apparently. Make sure you look the other way in future and that you come to no harm. It is the way of things down here. Lock the stable doors to keep the smugglers out and they will think nothing to burning them down.'

Sitting astride his black gelding, its shining mane gently lifting as he rode, Lucas surveyed Clifton's precious acres for the first time since arriving home from Spain. The house was surrounded by woodlands of ancient oak, elms and beech, interspaced with sunny glades where streams meandered gently along on their journey to the sea. Berries and brambles clambered over the walls surrounding verdant fields and rabbits and deer darted for cover as he approached.

Riding out of the trees, he brought the horse to a halt atop a low hill and gazed at the gently rolling vista all around him. Each view kindled a memory—of his mother walking in the gardens at Clifton and the surrounding lanes, shielded from the sun by a gaily decorated parasol, of his father galloping hell-for-leather in the hunt, Cassie doing her ferocious utmost to keep up with him. He realised how empty the house was without Cassie and his heart wrenched when he remembered how she had filled the rooms with laughter. He couldn't bear the silence. And what was to become of Tobias? He couldn't keep him hidden for ever.

Clifton had always been the one place where he had felt in complete control of his life. It had always given him a feeling of fulfilment, of well-being, but no more. The house had never seemed so empty or so still. The servants had looked at him with anticipation on his return from Spain. On learning of that bright golden girl's death, they said little, but shared the silence on remembering. Never had he felt so alone, so bereft of family. It was as if all Clifton's life blood had been drained out of it with their loss.

And before that there had been Miranda, passionate and with a golden beauty, the daughter of Baron Enys and his wife who lived in a grand house in Truro. At twenty-one he had been unable to resist her. She had sent fire through his youthful veins, the woman whom he had so deeply loved, and at whose hands his pride had suffered so badly.

They met whenever he could travel into Cornwall and she would often come to Clifton House with her parents. Twining her slender arms about his neck and using all her wiles to captivate him, she'd made him her pliant, willing slave. She was a bright and beautiful beacon in his life. An honest man, who would later deplore the fact that he had such a large streak of naivety in his make-up, Lucas found it hard to grasp the guile behind the soft smiles or fond words, especially when they came from the mouth of this exotic creature.

He had believed Miranda loved him, but how purring

and persuasive and soothing the voice of hers could be. He could not have guessed for a moment what weight of treachery it concealed. On a visit to London with her parents she'd met a very wealthy American, who—her parents had told him when they had come to explain the conduct of their daughter—had swept her off her feet, married her and whisked her off to America. To his knowledge she never did return to Truro.

Lucas had been deeply hurt by what she had done. For the first time in his adult life his eyes had been blinded by a rush of scalding tears. When at last the tears had gone, what had come to take their place was rage at his own weakness. Never, he had vowed, would he allow a woman to do to him what Miranda had done.

As he lingered on that hill, still and silent with his thoughts, his eyes were shadowed by memories that haunted him, memories that banked the fires of his anger, anger at the unfairness of it all, of his life, of having his entire family taken from him in the space of two years. Both his parents had been lost to the sea during a storm, followed so soon by Cassie leaving for Spain and the tragedy of her death. Cassie's child brought so brutally into the world had awakened a response of warmth and love in him and he felt a need to protect the child.

The added worry at this time was that Tobias was his heir until he had offspring of his own. How Jack Price would react when he learned of the boy's existence, his own brother's child, remained to be seen. But it concerned him greatly. Should he himself meet with some unfortunate accident, he had no doubt that Jack

Price would lose no time in trying to control the actions and decisions on how the Clifton estate would be run.

Should he not provide Clifton with an heir of his own, he had to prepare for every eventuality. At some point he would travel to Oxford to see his lawyers. To prevent Jack Price taking charge of the estate, he intended setting up a board of trustees to run the things until Tobias was of age.

He still loved every blade of grass, every tree, every hollow and hill of Clifton, in all its seasons, but it was no longer the same. He was struggling with his feelings of fear that everything else he held dear would be wrenched from him. Now there was something missing, something vital, something of immense value he had always taken for granted. Would he ever know peace?

Seeing the tall chimneys of his home above the trees brought a lump of emotion to his throat. Clifton House, with its air of solidity and permanence, had been in the Kingsley family since the Commonwealth and he vowed on the memory of those he held most dear, though lost to him, that he would create for his descendants the greatness of its heritage. The Kingsley name was a loved and revered one, one he was proud to belong to.

He must marry and produce heirs in order to go forward. But first he must find himself a wife. Since his unfortunate experience with Miranda, he no longer believed in love matches. It would be a marriage of convenience. He sighed dejectedly. There wasn't enough fire in the world to thaw him out and make him feel the way he had for Miranda in those heady, golden days of his youth when he had fallen in love, and even if there

were, he could not let it happen again. Behaving like a
lovesick calf was not his style.

Unable to sleep and impatient to be out of doors,
Tilly left the house before anyone was awake and made
her way to the steps that would take her to the shore
below. Halfway down she found herself a perfect vantage spot between the rocks. Settling herself between
them, she took in her surroundings.

How beautiful it was, a magical, enchanted place,
especially as early as this, with the dawn breaking and
the sun just peeking over the horizon, a perfect example
of the beauty of nature itself. How gentle the sea was,
with hardly a wave to break its smooth surface. It was
a place where one could disappear into the realms of
fantasy and imagine herself to be a fairy princess, to
float on the surface of the water and close her eyes and
wait for her prince to come.

And then there he was, entering her fevered imagination. Sitting there languidly, she watched him ride
on to the beach and dismount, tethering his horse to a
rock. Sitting on the sand, the man removed his boots
and threw off his upper garments, before striding across
the sand towards the sea.

Losing all power of motion and scarcely capable of
thought, she could not take her eyes off his naked chest,
covered with a smattering of dark hair. He was like a
Greek Adonis. There were the muscles rippling beneath
the smooth, golden skin, the width of his shoulders narrowing down to the hips. For a moment she wondered
if she'd conjured up some spirit by accident.

From her vantage point she watched him walk into

the sea until it was up to his chest. He dived underwater like a fish and came up some moments later to shake back his black hair before beginning to cleave his way from the shore, as if some unnamed nightmare could be banished only with an early-morning dunking in the sea. Tilly tried not to dwell on what it was that he felt the need to wash away, what he needed to exorcise, but it did not seem to have worked because the dark, troubled shadow in his eyes when next they met would still be there.

She continued to watch him, her knees drawn up to her chin. She was mesmerised by him, in some kind of trance as a dreamlike feeling of unreality had taken hold of her. He swam out to sea so far that he almost disappeared from view. Afraid that he might be caught in a strong current or an undertow, anxiously, she waited for him to reappear.

And then there he was, his head bobbing just above the waves as his arms stretched out before him, strong and sure. Closer to the shore, he stopped swimming and turned on to his back, floating lazily, letting the swell of the water rock him while he stared up at the sky. When he reached a place where he could put his feet down, he stood, shaking wet hair from his face.

Completely unaware that he was being observed, he walked across the sand to his waiting horse. Dressing quickly, he leaped on to its back and rode away. Tilly remained where she was, unable to believe that what she had just witnessed had really happened and was not a figment of her imagination. She remained there another few minutes before she got to her feet and returned to the house.

* * *

Tilly was surprised when a groom from Clifton House appeared with a horse gifted to her by Lord Clifton for the time she was in Devon. She was deeply touched by his generosity. It was a lovely horse, a spirited grey mare called Gracie, which suited her well. With no visitors paying calls, or when not sitting with Aunt Charlotte, Tilly enjoyed riding Gracie, accompanied by Graham on one of the carriage horses following at a sedate pace in her wake.

It was a fine and sunny day when Tilly accompanied Mrs Carstairs into Biddycombe. She had asked Aunt Charlotte to accompany them, but she had declined, preferring to sit in the garden and read. It was market day and Mrs Carstairs wanted one or two things. Tilly had not been as far as the village. Dunstan hitched two of the horses to a carriage that had belonged to Uncle Silas and off they went. Tilly's ankle was feeling much better, so walking about the village shouldn't be too taxing for her.

Biddycombe was a picturesque coastal village, with a huddle of thatched and slate-roofed cottages and bay-windowed shops. Being market day, the traders had set up their brightly coloured stalls in the market square. People were milling about along with horses and wagons carrying all manner of goods. The pungent smell of fish came from the work sheds where, Mrs Carstairs explained, the wives and daughters of the fishermen gutted, salted and packed the fish.

The quayside was an animated scene, alive in a chaos of sight and smell and the laughter of children. Lobster pots were stacked high and sailors sat about mending nets and talking among themselves, seagulls circling overhead. It was a scene that would have changed little over the centuries.

Accompanying Mrs Carstairs round the market stalls, she became the focus of everyone's scrutiny because they had heard that a Miss Anderson had taken up residence at Drayton Manor. Had it been a larger seaport, with strangers coming and going all the time, her presence would not have been noted, but Biddy-combe was a small fishing village where strangers were conspicuous.

When Mrs Carstairs had acquired what she had come for, Tilly left her basket in the carriage watched over by Dunstan and decided to have lunch before returning to the manor. Mrs Carstairs assured Tilly that the local tavern was a respectable place to eat and the food was good. It was close to the market square and had a wooden sign above it bearing the name the Lobster Pot.

It did appear to be a pleasant enough place, catering to tradesmen, farmers, travellers and local people alike. Being market day, the inn was busy. Despite the warmth of the day, a fire burned brightly in the hearth, the flames reflected in the gleaming tankards on the wooden bar, where men quaffed tankards of ale and conversed and laughed in good-natured ribaldry, enjoying themselves immensely.

'It's always like this on market days,' Mrs Carstairs explained. 'We'll find a quiet corner to eat.'

Serving girls threaded their way through the crowded room. They were assailed with the fragrant odour of tobacco, along with the appetising smell of roasting meats and spices, increasing Tilly's pangs of hunger. They sat at one of the oak tables, where they were served with a good wholesome meal.

As they were ready to leave, someone entered and Tilly's eyes were drawn to the door. It was filled with the figure of a tall man. Sweeping off his hat to reveal sandy locks of hair secured at his nape, he had to duck his head as he came into the room. He was followed by several other men, but it was the man in front that riveted Tilly's attention.

She had risen from her seat and when his eyes picked her out for his attention he paused, oblivious to the awkward silence that had fallen on the usually noisy room. Tilly eyed the man who stood boldly before her, eyeing her with a look not to her liking. He was a large man, firm of muscle, a sensual attractiveness in his coarse features, which carried a countenance that was merciless. It instilled fear. He sauntered towards her as she was about to follow Mrs Carstairs out of the inn.

'Well, and who have we here? Never seen you before so you must be new to these parts.' Looking from Tilly to Mrs Carstairs, he put two and two together. 'So, staying at Drayton Manor, are you? Now old Silas has gone to keep his maker company. I heard someone had moved in. I should come round and welcome you proper like—if you'd care to extend an invitation.'

'I would not,' Tilly said coolly. 'I am not receiving visitors.'

'Excuse us, Mr Price. We are just leaving,' Mrs Carstairs said, edging further to the door.

Tilly eyed the man with distaste. So, this was Jack

Price, the man Lord Clifton had told her about—a
smuggler and disreputable sort. She recalled Lord Clifton telling her that he liked to cut a dash. As if to prove
it he was flamboyantly dressed in scarlet velvet braided
with gold and an embroidered waistcoat beneath, a froth
of lace at his throat and wrists—clothing more fitting
for a soirée in London than riding the waves in a smuggler's sloop in Devon. Two pistols were thrust into a
black sash about his waist and the hilt of a knife was
visible above his black riding boots. The man was obnoxious and there was an ugly glint in his eye. Little
wonder people feared him.

'Why the hurry?' He looked at Tilly. 'You'll stay and
have a dram with Jack Price?'

'I don't think so,' Tilly said in her clear-cut voice,
which told Jack Price and his loyal vassals standing
around—accomplished thieves every one—that she was
a lady. Lord Clifton had told her Jack Price was dangerous, a man to avoid. 'Mrs Carstairs is right. We are leaving.' She didn't bother to hide her distaste, much to Jack
Price's amusement. He liked a woman with fight in her.

Tilly turned to leave the inn, aware that all eyes were
on her. Turning her back on Jack Price, dismissing him
with no more attention than she would give an annoying fly, she was about to walk away when a heavy hand
landed on her shoulder, the bejewelled fingers digging
into her flesh.

'Not so fast,' Jack Price said, his voice close to her ear.
'Uppity, aren't you? There's no need to be unfriendly,
is there now?'

'Tell her where you live, Jack,' someone shouted.
'She might like to pay you a visit some time.'

He leaned closer to Tilly. 'If I thought she might find her way to my lair to help me wile away the daylight hours, I would tell her, but since she isn't too friendly and might take it into that pretty head to turn me in, she's better off not knowing.'

He spun her round and Tilly found herself looking up into his coarse features. 'Kindly let go of my shoulder.' She spoke in a commanding voice, trying not to show her fear or that she was in the least intimidated by him.

'I beg your pardon, my lady,' he said sarcastically, bowing his head in mock respect. 'I meant no offence. But when a man sees something as sweet as you, pretty and smelling of roses, how can he resist such a tempting morsel? This is an unexpected surprise to find someone as lovely as you in Biddycombe. You can't blame me for trying to be friendly now, can you?'

'Then find someone else to be friendly with, Mr Price.'

'You're a proud one,' he said with a quick, dangerous sneer, but he schooled it to a taut smile. 'Elude me if you will, but now we've met I intend to spend some of my time getting to know you. We might find we have things in common, things we can share. Biddycombe is a small place—with not many hiding places that Jack Price doesn't know about.'

'I have no intention of hiding from anyone, Mr Price. You may be accustomed to easy conquests, but I find the thought of sharing anything at all with you utterly distasteful.'

Jack Price's eyes narrowed. The mockery had gone and his voice was purposeful. 'Maybe so—but you won't always feel that way—and you have a stable of fine horses by the way,' he said quietly, close to her ear. 'I look forward to making use of them again—very soon as it happens.'

Tilly glared at him, unable to think of anything to say that would not jeopardise matters for her and Aunt Charlotte while at Drayton Manor.

'You will learn to be nice to me,' he went on, 'not now, not tomorrow, but you will, and you will no longer speak to me with such haughty disfavour.'

She stared at him, emotionless and defiant. 'Threaten me all you like—it means nothing to me. Just leave me be.' Hoping to make her escape, turning away, once again she felt the heavy hand fall on her shoulder.

'What's the hurry? Don't you like Jack Price?' His gaze lingered on her lips.

'Don't think you're going to have any luck there, Jack,' someone called, the words followed by the sound of raucous laughter.

Jack Price laughed, a horrible, brittle sound that bounced off the walls of the tavern. 'You think not? Me and this little lady are just getting to know each other.'

Tilly tried to step away from him, but he held her shoulder in an iron grip. Her flesh crawled at his nearness. His eyes slid over her, making her flinch. Instinct told her that he was a man who would find resistance and cold indifference far more intriguing than mere submission. She lifted her chin with a show of bravado. There was arrogance in the tilt of his head and a single-minded determination in the set of his firm jaw that was not to her liking. She had an uncomfortable feeling that her angry words, far from discouraging him, had acted as bait to this obnoxious man.

'Release me at once,' she demanded, enunciating each word clearly, her voice quivering with anger. In spite of herself, even surrounded by a room full of people, she flinched.

'Not yet.' He was enjoying her discomfort. 'Forgive me if am so enamoured of you that I want to keep you with me a while longer. I reckon I'll find my way to the Manor one of these days—to pay my respects.'

'Please get out of my way. We are in a hurry.'

'Please, is it? I like politeness in a woman.'

Tilly realised no one would come to her aid. The men whose services Price enlisted were afraid of him. According to Lord Clifton, smuggling was his forte and upon it he profited. His men feared him, some would die for him—any death was preferable to the fury that would rain down on them should they fail him.

Mrs Carstairs stood near the door, observing what was happening with fear in her eyes. Everyone else, cowed by this man, observed what was happening with fear. None had the nerve to speak up. Aware of his rampant maleness, Tilly felt an instinctive awareness of the danger she was in. This man was not the kind of London fop she was used to. What he wanted he took.

Encouraged when she didn't pull away and unaware of the moment when all eyes turned to the door, he pulled her close, his grin widening. Not until someone let out a curse did he look above the head of his captive towards the door. The smile of triumph on having this young woman almost at his mercy froze on his face.

Tilly's head spun round. Lord Clifton stood there. His tall, broad-shouldered figure blocked out the light and seemed to fill the whole room. With his hand resting on the pistol at his hip, he was looking directly at Jack Price.

Tilly's gaze never left Lord Clifton's eyes, which were narrowed and savagely furious as he looked at his adversary in murderous silence, his lips curling with disgust as he absorbed the scene. Such a transformation had come over his features that she recoiled before the change. All that had been controlled and good-humoured when he had visited Drayton Manor had given way to hot fury and positive revulsion.

'Release her, Price.' He spoke calmly, but with deadly intent.

The atmosphere inside the inn was heavy with tension. The arrogance had gone from Jack Price's eyes, replaced with a murderous glint. His expression tightened as he stared at the tall figure in the doorway watching him closely. Tall, handsome and carelessly dressed in a snug-fitting leather jerkin, his shirt neck loose, his hair untidy, his high leather boots accentuating the long lines of his body, she might have taken him for a local tradesman, if the voice and stance had not been so firm, so sure. It was impossible not to respond to this man as his masculine magnetism was dominant in the room.

'I said, release the lady, Price,' Lord Clifton demanded, walking further into the room.

When Jack Price's eyes rested on the cold, steely features, he released his iron grip on Tilly's shoulder and stared at him, momentarily stunned speechless, as if he were looking at the Devil himself. 'So, Kingsley, you're back in one piece. You survived your time in Spain.'

Lord Clifton's lips curled in derision. 'I am the sort who clings to life, Price.'

'So...you went after that whorin' sister of yours.'

Lord Clifton would not be drawn in by Price's vile slur.

'Find her, did you—and that renegade brother of mine? Bring her back, did you?'

'I buried her,' Lord Clifton provided, 'alongside her husband, your brother—in Spain.'

If Price was surprised, shocked or aggrieved by this in any way, he didn't show it. He merely stepped towards the bar, a sneer on his lips as he said callously, 'Then be thankful for small mercies. Edmund made his own bed when he took up with your sister and took himself off to Spain to fight the Frenchies. There's no remorse on my part.'

He glanced towards Tilly, who had made her way closer to Lord Clifton. 'I was just getting friendly with Drayton's newest resident—until you showed up.'

'You're a scurrilous villain, Price. I don't want to know what you intended—I can guess. I do not think it's an association she desires. If you make any forward move to touch her again, I'll blow your head off. And if you don't think I have it in me to kill you, you are mistaken.'

Price met his opponent's gaze and, reading the simmering anger in his eyes, knew he was dealing with a dangerous man. Price's eyes glittered with malice. A dangerous tension emanated between the two of them. 'I do, Kingsley. I have no illusions where you are concerned.'

Tilly watched and listened to the two men with bated breath. Jack Price's anger was barely held in check as he parried words with Lord Clifton—none too successfully, which riled the smuggler. There was an uneasy muttering among the men who stood around.

Lord Clifton continued to glare at him. Price was a criminal, a scoundrel, with blood on his hands. A powerful force within the smuggling fraternity, he intimidated, seduced, deceived others into obeying his will and thought nothing of resorting to violence. The idea of him touching the delicate flesh of Miss Anderson, having possession of all that beauty, woke the sleeping demon inside him. 'Move away from her,' he demanded.

Indecision written clearly across his features, Jack Price gazed at Tilly. Her hands were clenched by her sides, her head thrown back as she glared at him with defiance and pride, her hair in a plait as thick as a man's wrist snaking down her spine. She was lovely and Jack Price felt lust stirring within him, but then he looked at Lucas Kingsley, his greatest enemy.

As if deciding that nothing was to be gained from furthering hostilities just then, he backed away. He seemed to hesitate for a moment. Something in Lord Clifton's words and the way he was looking at him must have awakened a curiosity inside him to know more about his brother's death.

'They were married, you say—Edmund and your sister?'

'On your brother's deathbed. I found a priest. It was what they both wanted.'

Price looked at him sharply, eyes narrowed. 'Why the hell would Edmund do that if he was dying? And your sister—dead, you say. How did that come about?'

'Let's just say the toils of war and a broken heart.'

Price's lips curled and his nostrils flared. 'There's

more to this—things you aren't telling me, Kingsley. If I find you have been lying to me, keeping things back, you'll regret it.'

'You're nothing but a black-hearted villain, Price. Threaten me all you like—the law will catch up with you eventually.'

Neither man was aware of those who stood around. They only saw each other. The hatred they felt was a tangible thing as they looked at each other over the distance that separated them.

'If you do have the audacity to touch me again, Jack Price, I will kill you myself,' Tilly retorted scathingly.

In spite of herself, despite her brave words and even with Lord Clifton's intervention, Tilly flinched when Price's lascivious gaze slid over her slim form—the pressure he had applied to her shoulder she still felt. Her revulsion was plain to see, but not one bit of his cocksure attitude faded.

'Don't be too sure of that,' he said nastily. 'The next time we meet you won't have His Lordship on hand to give you protection.'

'If I were you,' Lord Clifton drawled dangerously, 'I would not make promises that you haven't a hope in hell of keeping.'

'Is that so?'

'At the end of the day you will have me to reckon with.' Lord Clifton looked at Tilly. 'You have finished your meal?'

'Yes. We were just leaving.'

'Then allow me to escort you to your carriage.'

Chapter Five

They drew notice as they emerged from the tavern. Lord Clifton was a well-known figure in the community and everyone was happy to see him back at Clifton House, although they felt a great sadness on hearing that Lady Cassandra wouldn't be coming back.

Lord Clifton took Tilly's arm. 'Come, let's get away from here—away from Price. Do you have to get back to Drayton Manor right away or will you walk with me, if your ankle will permit?'

'I'm with Mrs Carstairs—but I don't think you will mind if I have a word with Lord Clifton, will you, Mrs Carstairs?' Tilly said to the housekeeper standing beside her.

'No, in fact I've seen a friend of mine I would very much like to speak to.'

'Then I'll see you back at the carriage shortly.'

Tilly realised her mistake immediately. They would be seen walking off together and, in such a close-knit community as Biddycombe where nothing ever happened, she suspected they were in danger of becoming the subject of a good deal of senseless gossip and conjecture. But it was too late to do anything about it now.

'How is your ankle? Easier, I hope.'

'It is much improved,' Tilly said in answer to his enquiry. 'I am able to walk very well.'

'I'm glad to hear it.'

'I want to thank you for your generous loan of Gracie. I certainly wasn't expecting it. She's a lovely horse. We get on well.'

'I knew you would. Gracie belonged to my sister, Cassie.'

'Oh…then…then perhaps I shouldn't—'

'Of course you must. She has to be exercised. The grooms have enough to do as it is.'

'Well…thank you. I'll take good care of her.'

He looked down at her. 'I knew you would, otherwise I would not have trusted her to you. And you needn't worry about her being taken and used by the smugglers. Dunstan knows to move her elsewhere on the nights when the other horses might be needed.'

'That's a relief. She's not as sturdy as the carriage horses. I'd hate to think of her carrying a great weight.'

They began to walk away from the market and down to the quay. Taking a turn, they strolled along the beach, which was sheltered by a steep cliff. Few people were about so it offered them some privacy.

'So,' Tilly said when they found a quiet place to sit on some boulders on the edge of the beach, 'that was Jack Price.'

'That's right.' There was concern in his eyes when he looked at her. 'I'm sorry you were subjected to that.'

'Why? It wasn't your fault.'

'Did he hurt you?'

'No,' she replied, taking comfort from him, his presence and manner helping to dispel any lingering effects of her encounter with Jack Price.

'Please tell me you are glad I turned up to rescue you from our obnoxious neighbour.'

'Relieved, I think. Your arrival was timely. I was beginning to wonder how I was going to extricate myself from his unwelcome advances without resorting to violence,' she joked.

He cocked an eyebrow in mock horror. 'Violence? I would never believe it of you.'

'Nevertheless, I'm glad you arrived when you did.'

'I had people to see in Biddycombe. I've been shut away in my study for the past week with my bailiff, concentrating on estate matters—of which there are many that need taking care of. Most are routine, easily delegated to those who work on the estate.'

It was warm. They could hear the sounds from the market and the gentle sloughing of the sea as it caressed the shore. Tilly gazed at the channel, wrapping her arms round her drawn-up knees and breathing deeply of the salty air.

'It's so beautiful here.' She turned her head and looked at him. 'I imagine you have grown up with the sea, that it's as familiar to you as the woods and the fields that surround you.'

'It is. I have to confess that whenever I go away, further inland, I miss the sight and sound of it. I'm always glad to get back to it.'

'Do you travel much—to London or other faraway places?'

'I've done my share. London is not high on the list of places I like to visit. I have extended family, cousins, in London. Some of them often come down to Devon to take advantage of my hospitality—more often than not to escape some scandal or other or if they wish to escape the high life for a while. They enjoy nothing better than to come down here for the fishing and hunting and any other country pursuit they like to indulge in.'

'Have you always been at loggerheads with the Price family?'

He nodded. 'Always. It started when Elizabeth, my grandmother, rejected Jack Price's grandfather when he wanted to marry her. She was a widow by then—still a very beautiful woman. My grandfather died after ten years of marriage. They had three children—my father was the eldest. By all accounts, Jack Price's grandfather was a violent man—not unlike his grandson. When my grandmother became a widow, old man Price wanted her for himself. She did not reciprocate his feelings—quite the opposite.'

'I cannot blame her if the grandfather was anything like Jack Price. What did she do?'

'Unable to accept rejection, he abducted her and violated her. Unable to live with what had been done to her, she threw herself off a cliff. Her body was found on the rocks below. It was a great blow to my father—he was eight years old at the time—but he soon learned to hate the Prices. So you see, the vendetta that started with my grandmother is still there.

'There is a portrait of Elizabeth at Clifton House and, every time I gaze upon it, I thank the Lord she had the courage to escape him, that she preferred death to living with what he had done to her. The enmity is still there.'

'Yet your sister married one of them.' Tilly glanced at him. Although she could not blame him for his hatred of the Price family, she could not help but wonder what Jack Price would do when he discovered the existence of the child and that Lord Clifton had kept it from him.

He nodded. 'She did. Cassie didn't care about such things. She loved Edmund Price and that was that, even though I tried to dissuade her—even though he was nothing like his brother and grandfather. Because of who he was, I couldn't sanction the match.

'Edmund was the elder of the two brothers. He was not by nature or inclination a smuggler. The family own a boatyard further along the coast. Jack Price has never shown any interest in the business—unlike Edmund, whose whole life revolved around the yard. Edmund didn't see eye to eye with his brother. His nefarious activities were the cause of many a battle between them. He chose a military career to get away from him. But no good could come from him marrying Cassie.'

'Perhaps the child, a product of both families, will bring reconciliation.'

Lord Clifton threw her a dark look. 'That will never happen. Our families have been enemies for too long, the elders passing their loathing on to the next generation.'

'Is it not foolish to keep up these old feuds?'

'The Prices have kept up the feuds as firmly as any of us. If I were to let Tobias go to them, he would be raised to be like the rest of the Prices—of whom there are several scattered up and down the coast—who think they are some kind of divine beings put there to rule over everyone else.'

'I dare say that is what the Prices think about the Kingsleys.'

Lord Clifton frowned, looking at her. 'You've met Jack Price. Do you really think he would want to bury the hatchet?'

'No, perhaps not,' she agreed, 'unless it's in your head. I don't think he is a man to reason with.'

'Quite.'

'Tell me about your sister. What was she like?'

'Cassie was a wilful girl, determined to have her own way in all things. She would try my patience on a daily basis. Our parents coped with her as best they could, but in the end, they found it was easier to let her have her way, to do as she pleased, within reason, than face the awesome force of her hot temper.

'The death of our parents affected her very badly. She was inconsolable and when she met Edmund Price there was no reasoning with her. When I finally tracked her down in Spain, she was still in love with him, still defended him.'

'Then she must have loved him very deeply.' It was evident to Tilly that his sister had mattered to him, and to lose her so soon after their parents must have been devastating for him. Her gaze focused on his bent head. She felt the sudden urge to shove back the heavy lock of his hair that had fallen forward to better see his features.

With a strength of will, he lifted his head and stared unseeingly before him. She looked into his proud face. His eyes were dark with suffering. Did he ever give in to the struggle of emotions that must tear him apart?

'She did,' Lord Clifton said at length. 'To the very end.'

'And she was his wife.'

He nodded. 'Yes, she was.'

When he spoke of the loss of his sister, he looked up. Tilly was trapped by the intensity of those thickly lashed light blue eyes. There was such suffering in their depths, such anguish that she wanted to reach out to him, to offer him comfort. Yet, despite his evident pain, there was also something else warring with the anguish—the hatred he felt for Jack Price.

'Before I left for Spain, I encountered Jack Price. I damned his black soul to hell. It was because of him that his brother went to Spain to fight—that my sister followed him and is now dead. He stood arrogantly before me and laughed at my concern, showing no emotion.'

He got up and leaned against the rocks, looking down at her. He was smiling slightly. It was more reflective, even with a trace of wistfulness in it. Her questions had recalled memories to him.

'Is Jack Price's father still alive?'

'Ned Price. Yes, but he suffers ill health.'

'And Jack is his only remaining son?'

'Now Edmund has gone, yes—Jack revels in the power he has over others.'

'You say the family own a boatyard. Who works it?'

'Ned Price, when he's able, and they employ an overseer. When Jack deems to show up, he works the men for a pittance. My bailiff informs me his father is thinking of selling the yard. If so, then I intend to buy it.'

'Do you know anything about building boats? Is it a profitable business?'

He shook his head. 'I know nothing about the business. I know Edmund turned over enough work to secure its future. The craftsmen are still there. Edmund and his father shared a love of boat building. Ned taught Edmund all he knew. He was disappointed by Jack's lack of interest and turned a blind eye to his smuggling. If the yard does come up for sale, then I will buy it and not disclose ownership to Jack Price or his father until I decide how to handle it. They would never accept it, but I have to do this for Tobias's future.'

'And if he doesn't want to build boats?'

'Then he can do with it what he will. He can sell it or pass it on to any offspring he might have.'

'You have it all worked out, don't you?' Tilly said in a quiet voice.

'I have to do this for Cassie.'

'Why are you telling me this? I am a virtual stranger to you.'

'My instinct tells me you are trustworthy, Miss Anderson—and I always follow my instinct.'

'Thank you.'

He smiled at her. 'You're welcome.' Falling silent, he stared out to sea. 'So much has happened to me over the past two years that I have lost track of what is important,' he said quietly, as if speaking his thoughts aloud. 'Several months ago, I wouldn't have thought that I would be dashing across to Spain to find my sister—and yet here I am, Cassie dead and with the responsibility of a child whose life is dependent on me.'

'And you still insist his existence is kept from Jack Price.'

'To keep Tobias safe, it has to be.'

'What I don't understand is that if he is a free trader, why has he not been arrested before now?'

'To be suspected of smuggling is one thing, but to be caught doing it is another matter entirely. He also has some of the Revenue men in his pocket. They fear him, along with everyone else hereabouts. He doesn't always dirty his hands with the smuggling. He controls activities from Trevean—his home. He has his spies scattered about—knows where the patrols are going to be, both on land and at sea.

'Over the years he's forged his own kind of power. He thumbs his nose at the powers that be—the only way to settle disputes is with fists. Few men are foolish enough to cross him. When my parents were crossing to Guernsey to visit friends, their boat went down. It was reported that it was as a result of a storm and not at the hands of smugglers, which was what I suspected— the vessel my parents were on was perfectly sound and there was no storm that day.

'Afterwards I listened to words spoken furtively here and there and began to envision what had happened, unable to tear the ugly pictures from my mind. I knew Price was on a run at that time. Whether he was involved I never did find out—but I am almost certain he had something to do with it.'

'And if he was? What would you do?'

'He would not escape justice. I would see to that.'

'And you are such an important figure in the community you would be able to bring that about.'

'Yes, yes, I would.' He looked at her for a long moment and Tilly fancied there was a strange expression on his face she had not seen before. 'Because you have met Jack Price, because he knows you are alone at Drayton Manor, be wary.'

'Why? Do you think I may be in some kind of danger?'

'One never knows with Price what he will do. If, at any time, you should find yourself in danger, will you promise to come to me? I will help you. I promise you.'

Tilly paused to look at him. He was sincere, that she knew. She nodded. 'Thank you—although I imagine he has more to do than trouble me.'

He was smiling, a smile Tilly found almost endearing. He did seem to have a way about him and she could not fault any woman for falling under his spell, for she found to her amazement that her heart was not as distantly detached as she might have imagined it to be. Even his deep mellow voice seemed like a warm caress over her senses.

Shoving himself away from the rock, he held out his hand. She took it and he drew her to her feet. 'I would like to show you Clifton House.'

'You would? Mrs Carstairs tells me it is quite magnificent.'

'So it is—but then, I am biased.'

'I would love to see it.'

'And what about its owner? Are you not tempted to know me better?'

'It is true. I hardly know you.'

'We could soon remedy that. I think you would find it interesting to discover more.'

'I am sure you are right, Lord Clifton,' she replied, trying to still the rapid beating of her heart.

'I am having a few friends to dinner next week— the first time I've entertained anyone since returning home. So, will you honour me by joining us? You and your aunt, of course. She is recovered, I hope.'

'Yes, quite recovered—although she gets more tired than usual.' Tilly smiled. 'She puts it down to the sea air. I am sure I can speak for her when I accept your invitation.'

'It will give you the opportunity to meet the local parson, Reverend Leighton, and his wife, and Mr and Mrs Ainsley. Mr Ainsley is a magistrate.'

Tilly glanced up at him to find he was looking at her strangely, as if he was preoccupied. She was bewildered by his mood and, caught up in a rush of irrational confusion, she looked away from him—she felt mesmerised, uncertainty flooding over her.

He touched a lock of hair that had escaped the confines of her braid and rested on her neck and she felt the brush of his fingers on her flesh. When they lingered, her heart beat erratically, a thrill of anticipation spreading through her. Brief though the touch was, his fingers left their imprint upon her flesh.

Every nerve in her body piqued at the feel of his touch, which was like a brand of fire against her skin, and a searing excitement shot through her. She felt overpowered by his nearness. Her whole body throbbed with an awareness of him, but she would not give any hint of her weakness. She was conscious of the power of his masculinity, so great was the pull.

His face creased with concentration as he studied her upturned face. Slowly, his finger gently traced the line of her jaw. It was strong and soothing, his touch impersonal, as if he were examining an object, yet it was gentle and Tilly did not feel like an object—far from it. She felt cosseted. There was something agreeable in his touch, almost sensuous. Her whole body felt as if it were unwinding, growing weak with the pleasure of what the tip of his finger was doing to her.

Vividly conscious of the strange things happening to her, she abruptly turned her thoughts away from this new and dangerous direction and averted her head, before he could realise just how much he affected her.

'You are a lovely young woman, Miss Anderson. I don't imagine I am the first man to say that to you.'

'No, as a matter of fact, you aren't. My brothers can be complimentary when the mood takes them, which isn't very often. They only flatter me to improve my humour.'

'I am tempted to taste what your lips offer.'

'I am certain they offer nothing that is different to what you have experienced before, Lord Clifton,' she said, feeling the heat and vibrancy of him reaching out to her. For her own safety, and her own sanity, she knew she had to try to stay one step ahead of him. 'So, if it's seduction you have in mind, then please forget it.'

His lips curled in a crooked smile. 'Here on an empty beach, hidden from prying eyes, with the sun shining and the sea as blue as can be, with a beautiful woman— what man in his right mind would not have seduction on his mind?'

'Then please don't. If you tried, I'd resist you with all my strength—only I'm afraid I don't know how my strength would hold out with you.'

He tilted his head at her. 'Afraid?' he said. 'Are you afraid of me, Miss Anderson?'

'Yes,' she whispered. 'I'm afraid of both of us.'

With the sun warm on her face, a tautness began in her breast, a delicious ache that was like a languorous, honeyed warmth.

As he sensed the change in her, Lord Clifton drew her towards him. Curling his long masculine fingers round her chin, he tilted her face up to his. Her eyes were large, her lips soft and quivering. It seemed a lifetime passed as they gazed at each other. In that lifetime each lived through a range of deep, tender emotions new to them both, exquisite emotions that neither of them could put into words.

'Are you still afraid, Miss Anderson?'

'No,' she murmured. 'I'm not afraid.'

'And will you resist me if I kiss you?'

'No.' The word issued forth from her lips. It was uttered softly, barely audible, her breath warm on his flesh.

As though in slow motion, unable to resist the temptation her mouth offered, slowly Lord Clifton's own moved inexorably closer. His gaze was gentle and compelling, when, in a sweet, mesmeric sensation, his mouth found hers. Tilly melted into him. The kiss was lingeringly slow.

Raising his head, Lord Clifton gazed down at her in wonder. Her magnificent eyes were naked and defenceless. 'My God, Miss Anderson,' he whispered, his voice hoarse, 'what a delightful surprise you are turning out to be.'

The pressure of his body, those feral eyes glittering with power and primeval hunger, washed away any measure of comfort Tilly might have left. A strange, alien feeling fluttered within her breast and she was halted for a brief passage of time when she found her lips entrapped by his once more and, though they were soft and tender, they burned with a fire that scorched her.

Closing her eyes, she yielded to it, melting against him, finding herself at the mercy of her emotions as he savoured each intoxicating pleasure, glorying in her purity.

When they finally drew apart, Tilly could not believe how easily she had succumbed to his kiss. She turned her head away, wanting to conceal how deeply she was affected by what had just happened between them. 'I—I think we should be getting back.'

Raising her hand to his lips, he pressed them to the soft centre of her palm. 'Yes. We should stop now before things go too far. I'll escort you to your carriage before Mrs Carstairs comes looking for you—and since I am impatient to see you again, I will call the day after tomorrow. I would like to show you more of the area. Do you approve?'

Tilly was about to refuse, but the words died on her lips when she looked at the lazy, relaxed man with the slightly smiling mouth and eyes like soft blue velvet. Suddenly a ride in the countryside or wherever he chose to take her seemed immensely appealing. 'Why— I— yes, that would do very well. I shall look forward to it.'

'Excellent. We'll lunch at a tavern I know some miles from Biddycombe. It provides the best food in the area.'

Lucas took her hand to help her over the boulders that littered the beach. He was unable to believe this innocent temptress had surrendered in his arms and returned his passion with such intoxicating sweetness. The times they had been together, the tension and explosive emotions that her presence elicited had been disturbing. Like a siren in Greek mythology whose singing was believed to lure sailors to destruction on the rocks, her vulnerability had finally broken all bounds of his restraint.

He walked beside her to where Dunstan waited with the carriage. Mrs Carstairs was already seated inside. He stared at his companion's profile, tracing with his eyes the beautiful classical lines of her face, the softness of her shapely mouth and the brush of lustrous dark eyelashes shadowing her cheeks. A strand of her hair nestled in a dark spiral in the hollow of her neck. She really was quite extraordinarily lovely.

He sensed an untamed freedom of spirit hovering just below the surface, yet, haughty in bearing, she was undoubtedly a true lady and represented everything that appealed to him, everything that was most desirable in a woman.

He had seen the way Jack Price had looked at her and the remembrance of such familiarity sent a sudden surge of cold fury through him. Seeing Price with his hands on her when he had entered the inn had caused something to snap inside him, shattering his emotions almost beyond all rational control. The intoxicating beauty before Jack Price would arouse lust in any man and, dressed in a pale yellow day dress, she looked so damned lovely.

The smugglers came again. Tilly heard them in the early hours. She had promised Lord Clifton she would turn a blind eye and she had meant it, but her curiosity got the better of her. Going to the window, she half opened the curtains. The sky was moonless, but she was able to make out the eerie figures of men and horses. They were leaving the stables, which were in darkness. The front rider was a big man wearing a cocked hat, his frock coat spread over his horse's flanks. Instinct told her it was of a scarlet hue, that the rider was none other than Jack Price.

As if sensing her watching, he lifted his head and directed his gaze to her window. She didn't move or attempt to hide herself. She sensed he was laughing at her. When he removed his hat and waved it with a flourish in her direction, she knew he was.

It was a lovely morning for their ride, carrying the promise of a lovely summer's day in the faint sea breeze. Looking extremely fetching in a ruby-red riding dress, with a matching hat cocked at an impudent angle atop bunches of delectable ringlets that bounced delightfully when she moved her head, Tilly went to the stables. Lord Clifton rode into the yard. Bringing his horse to a halt, he dismounted, the heat of his gaze travelling the full length of her in a slow, appreciative perusal, before making a leisurely inspection of her upturned face.

'You're looking very fine this morning, Miss Anderson,' he said as Dunstan appeared leading Gracie.

'Why, thank you, sir. I'm looking forward to the ride.'

Placing his hands on her waist, he lifted her with gentle strength into the saddle. Wide-eyed, she met his gaze and saw his brows lift, a quizzical expression in his eyes. He watched as she hooked her knee around the pommel and placed her foot in the stirrup before settling her skirts, then he hoisted himself on to his mount.

'I've never seen you ride. Do you ride well?'

'As well as most,' she replied, taking the reins as Gracie moved restlessly. She controlled the horse effortlessly. 'You can judge for yourself.' She turned and looked behind her to where Graham was already mounted. 'Are you ready, Graham?'

'I am, Miss Anderson.'

Lord Clifton looked from Graham to Tilly, a scowl on his face. 'Graham is to come with us?'

'But of course. It wouldn't be proper for me to ride out with you alone now, would it? When I told Aunt Charlotte I was to go riding with you, she insisted Graham accompanied me.'

'Of course, and your aunt is quite right. Now, shall we get going?'

Tilly urged Gracie forward. Lord Clifton on his mount moved off from the stable yard and along one of the paths that led off into the woods. There was no room for them to ride abreast, so they didn't speak as they went through the deep shade, a kaleidoscope of shapes and colour. Sometimes they had to duck under low branches.

It was beautiful in this shadowed world, with the smell of damp earth and the coolness of the trees. Eventually they came out of the woods where the vegetation grew thick and rampant and they were able to ride side by side across the rolling countryside. Graham kept at a discreet distance. Fresh, cool breezes were fragranced with an invigorating scent of the sea.

Casting a sidelong glance at her companion, Tilly admired the way his body flowed easily with the big gelding's stride, both horse and master strong, a picture of combined, harnessed power. For a man of such imposing herculean stature, he had an elegant way of moving in his casual clothes.

He wore a tan coat, his long legs encased in biscuit-coloured trousers and highly polished dark brown riding boots. His hair was dishevelled from the ride, the black curls brushing the edge of his collar. The sun illuminated his bold, lean profile and that aquiline nose that gave him a look of such stark, brooding intensity.

Lord Clifton was no less admiring of her, gracefully perched side-saddle. When she soared over a wide ditch, he grinned approvingly. Tilly was light and lovely on horseback, managing her horse with expert skill. She urged it into a gallop, her skirts flying out behind her. She let the horse have its head as she charged full pelt laughingly along the rutted track. The speed and the air brought colour to her cheeks and made her feel more alive than she had in days.

After riding for several miles, Graham doing his level best to keep up with them on the heavier carriage horse, Lord Clifton drew up on the clifftop overlooking the sea and dismounted, then walked over to lift Tilly down from her horse. Graham pulled his horse to a halt some way away from them and sat on the soft grass with his knees drawn up, looking out at the sea.

'My compliments, Miss Anderson. I know few men who ride as well as you,' Lord Clifton told her. 'I am certain that the huntress Diana could not rival you.'

'That is a compliment indeed.' The genuine warmth and admiration in his voice and in his eyes flooded Tilly's heart with joy.

'Gracie is clearly to your liking.'

'She most certainly is.'

'The ride has done you good,' Lord Clifton said, noting the blooming colour in her cheeks and sparkling eyes.

'I always enjoy riding. I try to ride most days, but never venture very far from Biddycombe.'

'It's good for you to explore, to learn to see your surroundings through your own eyes. I am biased about the charms of Devon, but I've no doubt you shall fall in love with it, too, and want to come back.'

'That's up to Charles. I shall have to wait and see what he intends doing with the house,' she told him, perching on a large rock and smiling up at him. 'But I do like Devon—at least what I have seen of it—and the people seem to be friendly enough. You are fortunate having been raised by the sea. I can't imagine anyone would want to leave it for the city.'

'It does make one feel like that, although one gets used to it.'

'Do you swim in the sea?'

He nodded, walking towards the edge of the cliff and gazing over the water to where a large brigantine was heading east. 'Often.'

Tilly wondered what he would say if he knew she had watched him that day from the cliff as he cleaved his way through the water. She hugged the memory to her, considering it prudent not to reveal her voyeuristic moment.

'I don't sleep well and I come to the beach early in the morning,' he went on. 'It's the best time of day—the stillness, everything fresh and at peace. Sometimes

I come before daybreak when the sky is still dark and the stars so low you imagine you could reach out and touch them. There's something mystical about that time of day.

'I like to watch the dawn. It's as though, with the faint light on the horizon, the whole universe is holding its breath—waiting. I can sit among the rocks and listen to the scurrying of the land crabs and a multitude of other creatures that make up the sounds of the night. And then there's the sound of the surf.'

Tilly listened to his voice, which was soft and wistful. *Yes*, she thought, *he really does love this place.* 'I envy you your sense of belonging. I haven't lived anywhere long enough to feel that way—not even when my mother was alive—and then when I went to live with Aunt Charlotte. And as much as William wants me to make Cranford my home, as beautiful as it is, I have no sense of belonging. But you have Clifton House and a fine estate in this glorious part of the country. Knowing of the loss of your family, it must have been a difficult time for you of late.'

'Yes, it has, but I have no choice but to carry on.'

Tilly seemed to have touched on a tender spot of his vulnerability. 'You are strong. It is not impossible. I am sure you have the will to survive.'

They sat in silence for a while, content to sit and admire the view and watch the sweeping, squawking gulls circle the rocks. Tilly watched as her companion lifted his hand and, as he absently rubbed the muscles at the back of his neck, her treacherous mind suddenly imagined how skilfully those long fingers might caress her body and the exquisite pleasure he would make her feel.

Her heart suddenly swelled—with what? Admiration? Affection? Love? No, not that. She did not know him well enough to feel that. Recollecting herself, she shook away such thoughts angrily. She was being an utter fool romanticising Lord Clifton, simply because he was an attractive man, sleek and fierce as a bird of prey, with his raven-black hair. He had been incredibly skilled at raising her desire when the only time he had touched her was on the night when the smugglers had come and as they had shared the kiss on the beach, because she was helplessly attracted to him.

Standing up, she took a few steps to stand by his side. He was preoccupied with his thoughts, his gaze fixed on the distant horizon. Looking up at him, she wondered what he was thinking. Was it the loss of his family, or was it because he was pining for the woman who had stolen his heart?

'What are you thinking?' she asked softly.

As if he hadn't heard her, he continued to look straight ahead. When her voice finally penetrated his thoughts, he looked down at her and then fixed his gaze on the distant horizon once more.

Something hard flared in his eyes for a moment, but then he shrugged resignedly. 'I was thinking of nothing in particular—nothing that would interest you.'

'You could try me. I'm a good listener.'

'I was thinking of Spain—but you were not there. You would not understand.'

'That's nonsensical. Perhaps if you were to speak of it, the pain would ease. I am persuaded that you must talk about it. Why have you closed your mind to it?'

'Out of necessity.'

Something about the way he looked stirred Tilly's sympathy and she felt her heart wrench agonisingly. 'I would like to think you could talk to me,' she said quietly. He turned his head and looked at her. Her eyes were full of concern. 'How else can I understand? Is it your sister you are thinking about—or about the war?'

'Both. After all, I would not have been there had it not been for Cassie.' His eyes had grown as distant as the horizon, as if he had withdrawn into himself, into that painful time still so recent.

'Where did you find her?'

'I eventually tracked her down to a town called Ciudad Rodrigo, not far from the Portuguese border, where the French garrison was besieged by Wellington's Anglo-Portuguese army. It was January and it was very cold. Cassie was with more soldiers' wives and those who follow the army. She was heavily pregnant. I begged her to return with me to England, but she wouldn't hear of it. I was shocked by the conditions she was having to endure—it was not for the faint-hearted.'

'And you saw Edmund Price.'

'Yes. He was concerned about Cassie and he didn't want her there any more than I did, but there was nothing he could do. She was dead set on remaining. Aware of Cassie's condition, I made sure they were wed. When the town walls were breached by the British artillery, the British and Portuguese armies went on the rampage. There were hundreds of casualties—many killed. Edmund eventually died of the wounds he sustained in battle. Just hours after he was buried Cassie was delivered of her child and followed Edmund into the earth.'

'That must have been dreadful for you,' Tilly whispered.

'It was the worst. Before I left for Spain, I was sure that the men who'd gone to fight, so valiant in the field, with military discipline instilled into them, would deal with whatever was thrown at them. But what I witnessed at Ciudad Rodrigo—the mindless slaughter and deplorable lapse in human nature—shocked and horrified me to the core of my being. My saving grace was finding Florence to take care of Tobias. We travelled overland for many weeks, dodging French soldiers and desperate men. Eventually, we reached northern France and took ship for England.'

When he fell silent, Tilly moved closer to him, feeling his pain. 'I'm sorry, truly. There is nothing I can say to ease what you went through. But in time, in another life, that terrible time in Spain will ease.' *But it will not be forgotten*, she thought. What he had seen would continue to haunt him for evermore.

'What can I say except that I hope you are right.' He looked at her and held her eyes captive. 'You were right. You are a good listener and I apologise if what I have told you has caused you distress.' Suddenly, he smiled— it was as if the sun had suddenly broken through a dark cloud. 'Come, let's be on our way. I promised you lunch. The Bell Inn is not far from here. The ride has given me an appetite.'

Chapter Six

They spurred their horses on, riding some considerable distance following the coast before arriving at the Bell Inn on the edge of a large village. It was a respectable establishment, frequented by ship's masters, owners and brokers of merchant vessels based in nearby Plymouth. Carriages were drawn up outside. Inside, it was plain from the bustling clientele that business was good.

The landlord was a genial sort with a sunburnt face and a thick black beard and looked more like a sea captain than an innkeeper. On recognising Lord Clifton, honoured that one of the most important gentlemen in the district should visit his hostelry, he ushered them to a quiet alcove that offered a degree of privacy. Graham hung back, preferring to eat outside at one of the tables.

'Might I suggest that you aid the digestion of your food with fine wine and brandy brought in from France?'

'It surprises me that such luxuries are available, when Britain and France have been at war for so many years,' Tilly remarked, making herself comfortable across from Lord Clifton.

'A war fought by soldiers on behalf of politicians,' the landlord replied.

'And we in Devon—and Cornwall—have never allowed such considerations to stand in the way of trade, have we, Landlord?' Lord Clifton remarked with a knowing wink.

'By God, never! It benefits us all.'

The landlord left them alone to order one of the serving girls to take their order. Tilly glanced around the inn, observing the looks cast their way.

'You are a popular man, Lord Clifton. You are attracting attention.'

'Not just me. Who could not but notice you? And I must say that you look extremely fetching in your riding dress.'

She laughed. 'Why, thank you.' She took a sip of the lemonade a maid had set before her. 'Tell me, how is Tobias?'

'Thriving. He's a fine boy.'

'And Florence?'

'She is well—glad to be settled for the time being. She's had a difficult time.'

'Will she stay with Tobias permanently, or does she have family of her own?'

'She has a sister in Dawlish. She mourns her husband—and her child.'

'That's understandable. Her suffering must have been great indeed. It must have been a godsend to her when you befriended her.'

'I needed her very badly at the time. She's devoted to Tobias, but she's a sensible, educated young woman and realises the time will come when she will no longer be needed. But that will be discussed at a later date. For now, I'm glad to have her.'

'And Jack Price is still unaware of his existence?'

'As to that, I cannot be sure. People talk. Most of the servants at Clifton House have family connected to the smuggling fraternity one way or another. It's just a matter of time before Jack Price learns of his existence.'

Their meal came and they ate in companionable silence. Tilly enjoyed watching a variety of people come and go, greeting each other and going on their way or staying to enjoy a meal. And then it was over and they were heading home, riding through the woods once more.

'Who do the woods belong to?' Tilly asked casually when the track opened up and they were able to ride side by side.

'I own them.'

'I see. And do you mind people using them?'

He laughed. 'Not at all. I am not mean-spirited. The woods are too vast to patrol. Besides, people need to pass through them to go from here to there. All I ask is that they are sensible and do not damage the trees or light fires.'

She looked at him. His eyes were brilliant—full of laughter. 'And poaching?'

'Ah, now that is a different matter entirely. I employ gamekeepers to keep an eye out for poachers—although I'm not averse to anyone taking the odd rabbit or two. Those pesky animals do a lot of damage to crops when they come through.'

'And they provide a good meal for a family.'

'Exactly.'

Suddenly, they emerged into the open and ahead of

them was Clifton House. Seeing it from a different view-point, Tilly caught her breath.

'Oh, it's quite magnificent.'

'I totally agree. I shall enjoy entertaining you and your aunt when you come to dine. It is quite impressive—but then I am biased.'

'And so you should be. I look forward to seeing it.'

They rode on, eventually arriving at Drayton Manor.

'Won't you come in and meet my aunt?' Tilly offered.

'I will look forward to meeting her when you come to Clifton House. I have business in Biddycombe shortly. I must get back.'

'Of course.' Tilly was sorry the ride was over. 'Thank you for today. I've enjoyed it so much.'

'You're welcome. We must do it again soon.'

Tilly watched him ride away. Something was happening to her. She was too much aware of him—and he of her. Physically. He gave her a feeling of disquiet, yet at the same time he stimulated and excited her. Was their banter and meetings leading up to something, and, if so, what? Would he have kissed her if he hadn't intended to take their relationship forward?

He had been let down in the past—had he not told her that he did not believe in love and that when he married it would be one of convenience? It was early days and Tilly had no experience of men like Lucas Kingsley. Where was their relationship leading? Clearly his former lover had broken his heart. Could she, Tilly, be the one to put it back together again?'

They rode together again, but this time he took her up on to the high moor. It was a place where misleading mists often took travellers by surprise, mists in which one could get hopelessly lost, even those who believed they knew the moor. On the hem of the mist the moor was like some petrified and silent world. It was rich with legend, of highwaymen and smugglers and ghosts. The ground was strewn with rocks and for miles around it was littered with ruined druid temples and ancient stone circles. When darkness came it infused itself into the rock rising like sharp blades into the sky. Tilly felt drawn to the moor, finding beauty in its bleak and desolate landscape.

Having left Tilly after their ride, thinking how ravishing and invigorated she always looked, her cheeks adorably pink and her eyes sparkling, alone at Clifton House Lucas had much to think about. Finding a wife was very much on his mind. Perhaps he wouldn't have too far to look. Did he not have the ideal woman, with all the proper requisites to grace the halls of Clifton House?

Having overcome her initial hostility towards him, he felt that she enjoyed his company the more they were together—and he had the whole of the summer to win her over. Most of the women he was acquainted with were available to him at the crook of his finger, some of the most beautiful women in Devon and beyond, but none of them especially stood out and appealed to him—only one, who had particularly warm violet eyes and a wealth of gleaming black hair.

He had no doubt the chase could prove both difficult and exciting. He sensed her wariness. This young woman with her beauty and spirit affected him and she was not immune to him, as the kiss they had shared on the beach confirmed. Whenever they met, he felt a current of emotion between them, like the charged air on the sea before a storm strikes with all its devastating violence. He didn't have the slightest doubt of his own ability to lure her into his arms.

He was aware that she was young and that her brothers might insist that she make her debut, but he was prepared to wait. Before she had to return to London, he would court her with such ardour that she would return to Devon as soon as her brother left for India.

The next time Tilly rode out Lord Clifton was not with her. Having ridden through a shadowy world of muted sounds, where damp and decay rose from the undergrowth and assailed her nostrils, and squirrels skittered in the upper branches of the trees, without the sun a bitter chill had fallen on this twilight world.

Relieved when she came out into the open, Tilly looked about her, having ridden further than she'd intended. Accompanied by Graham, she had been tempted to ride once more to the high moor, with its craggy peaks and purple heather, but instead she had followed the coast to the west, seeing the occasional tall chimneys of the engine houses of tin and copper mines. Slowing her horse to a walk, she rode in the direction of the sea just ahead of her. She could make out the phosphorescence of the breaking waves below.

A large stone house was perched on a promontory high above the sea where it was under siege by the storms that blew in from the Channel, buffeting its walls during the winter months. Its surrounding battlemented wall gave it the look of a castle rather than a house. Never had Tilly seen a more desolate or gloomy place.

Hearing the sound of sawing and hammering, she looked down a steep hill to an inlet, seeing a large boat-yard. Labourers' cottages lined the hillside set further back from the inlet. The not-unpleasant smell of sawdust and tar assailed her nostrils. There was a good deal of activity as labouring men went about their work, car-penters sawing planks and caulking the hull of a large vessel. A dry dock held a large vessel having barnacles scraped from its hull, another was being painted and cradles held the keels of fishing smacks. A prepared launch way ran down to the sea.

Could this be the Prices' boatyard? she wondered. She turned to wait for Graham. Then she heard the bark-ing of dogs. They sounded fierce and angry. And then there they were, two great big black hounds, bound-ing towards her. Gracie half reared and shied away. The dogs stopped and looked straight at her. Then they began to bark again. It intensified.

Her heart almost ceased to beat when a tall figure suddenly stepped out of the trees in front of her horse. It was Jack Price. His eyes were gleaming coldly. There was a sneer on his mouth, and it was a cruel mouth, twisting in perpetual contempt for those who were be-neath him. He was looking at her with impudent admi-ration, letting his gaze travel from her eyes to her mouth and then, after lingering on its soft fullness, moving down to the gentle swell of her breasts beneath the bod-ice of her sapphire-blue riding habit.

'Well, well, if it isn't Miss Anderson! They do say as how, if one is patient enough, one will get what one wants in the end. I had no idea you would come calling to Trevean quite so soon. I am flattered.'

All the colour drained out of Tilly's face. At this point her pride played the better part of furthering her association with Jack Price. 'Don't be. I had no idea you lived this way. If I had, I would have taken a different route. Call off your dogs.'

Surprisingly, he did. They ceased their barking and retreated to sit beside their owner, but their eyes remained on Tilly. She glanced at a worried-looking Graham, who had halted his horse close by. 'It's all right, Graham. Mr Price and I are already acquainted.' She patted Gracie and murmured soothing words. She shivered, still disturbed by the dogs. 'She does not like your dogs,' she said to Jack Price.

'Not many people do. They do what I tell them.'

'I imagine they do. Kindly step out of my way,' she said coldly.

He smiled thinly, unconcerned by her hostile demeanour. 'What? You are wanting to leave so soon? You offend me, Miss Anderson. You don't know me well enough to show me such hostility.'

'I know *what* you are, Mr Price.' In the depths of his cold eyes something stirred and she felt a strong desire to ride away. There was an air of menace about him that entered her heart like a sliver of ice.

'Do you now? And you newly come to Devon. How much do you know, Miss Anderson? I should hate you to be under a misconception and will put you right if you are.'

'I know that you are a smuggler, that even the cleverest smuggler will make a mistake eventually and then he will be arrested or dead.'

His brows rose imperturbably. 'Is that so? I—and more than half the population in Devon and Cornwall—do not see free trading as a crime. Those involved in various ways either buy, sell, or drink—respectable ministers of the church, doctors, lawyers and, yes, even magistrates and Excise men. They all look the other way for a drop of French brandy or a bolt of silk or lace for their ladies.'

He moved closer to her horse, holding its bridle and touching her leg in a familiar way. 'What of you, Miss Anderson? Tell me what would please you—silk? Satin? The softest velvet, perhaps, to wear next to your soft skin?'

He was taunting her and she stiffened with anger. She met his eyes, so bold, gazing at her, taking in every detail of her face. 'I want nothing from you, Mr Price.'

'No? Not even in return for the loan of your horses? They're fine horses, by the way—worth much more than a keg of brandy.'

'I don't drink brandy—and I would prefer it if you didn't make use of the horses.'

'Too late, Miss Anderson. There are nights when they are needed and brave is the man—or woman—who refuses to help the traders.'

'You are quite mad.'

'No, not mad. It takes a very sane person to plan the things I do.'

'As you say. Now please let go of my horse and I will be on my way.'

'Your horse?' He stroked its mane, leaving his hand

to rest there. 'You must have become friendly with Kingsley for him to let you ride his sister's horse.'

'What he chooses to do is nothing to do with you.'

'No, it isn't, but to see you riding Lady Cassandra's horse is bound to raise a few eyebrows.'

'Lord Clifton's sister is dead, Mr Price, as you well know. The horse needs to be ridden.'

'There are grooms aplenty at Clifton House to take care of that. Although—when I saw the two of you walk off together in Biddycombe—to the beach… Very cosy the two of you looked.'

'It is none of your business.'

He laughed, a deep, low sound. 'Maybe not, although, with an infant to take care of, His Lordship must have his hands full.'

Tilly felt her heart flip over. 'Infant?'

His lips stretched in an odious smile. 'Oh, yes, an infant. With a house full of servants, more than one is willing to inform Jack Price what goes on in that fine house.'

Tilly looked at him with intense dislike burning in the depths of her eyes. 'You have a black heart, Jack Price. It will be your own wickedness and greed that will bring about your destruction.'

'You could be right.'

Immediately, she pulled her horse away from him. 'Good day, Mr Price.'

'Good day, Miss Anderson.' He half turned and then looked back at her, capturing her gaze. 'The infant? Who is he? Who does he belong to?'

Tilly stared at him. He had spoken softly, slowly, a hidden purpose in the depths of his evil eyes. She tossed her head. 'How on earth would I know that? Lord Clifton's affairs are his own.' On that note, she rode away from him.

'Are you all right, Miss Anderson?' Graham asked, looking at her with concern. 'I saw the man step out in front of you and recognised him as the man who sometimes takes the horses in the night.'

'I'm all right, Graham. Let's go home. I don't like this place.'

'Nor me, Miss,' Graham mumbled. 'I don't like him either.'

The night Tilly went to Clifton House would always stand out in her memory. It was early evening, the heat of the day having left the land, but it was pleasant and warm, the air heavily perfumed with wild honeysuckle. Aunt Charlotte was excited to be visiting and was looking forward to being introduced to the Earl of Clifton at last.

Tilly was strangely excited, more about seeing Lord Clifton than anything else. Wanting to look her best, she had taken care over her toilette and had chosen to wear a high-waisted, square-necked gown with puffed sleeves in powder blue. It was a lovely contrast to her ebony hair, which she wore loose, held back with a broad ribbon to match her dress.

Driving the carriage drawn by four of the bay carriage horses, Dunstan negotiated the narrow lanes with care. It rocked gently from side to side, the harness jangling. The sunlight was warm and a faint breeze blew in from the sea towards the high moor. They passed through parkland with enormous oaks, beneath which a small herd of deer grazed serenely, looking up with a singular lack of interest as the carriage passed by.

They entered through the high gilded gates of Clifton House, which was magnificent, with its tall chimneys and mullioned windows. Two cylindrical towers flanked either side. There was something medieval about it. Tilly felt that she was passing into another age, a time long past. The stately gardens and carefully maintained parkland were surrounded by woodlands of ancient trees and in the distance the English Channel.

A butler admitted them to the house, where two liveried, bewigged footmen waited to take any outer garments. Handing one of them her bonnet and the light shawl she wore round her shoulders, Tilly looked about her. She recalled the time William had taken her to Cranford and how awestruck she had been as she had tried to take in all the grandeur and that was how she felt at that moment, for Clifton House was just as grand but in a different way.

'So, you have arrived.'

The voice came from above and Tilly turned and looked up the wide staircase. Lord Clifton was coming down. When she saw him, with a strange sensation of fatality she was aware of the stir the sight of him caused in her heart as he continued to advance. Everything about her disappeared into a haze. Her attention was focused entirely on him. Had she wanted to look away she could not have done. She was not even conscious that her aunt was watching her.

Never had Tilly seen such a fine figure of masculine elegance and as handsome as a god with those perfectly chiselled features. In contrast to the times when she had

seen him, Lord Clifton looked so poised, so proud and
debonair. His movements, his habitual air of languid
indolence, hung about him like a cloak. The perfect fit
of his claret coat and the tapering trousers accentuated
the long lines of his body, his white neckcloth pristine
against his sun-bronzed features.

With his hair brushed back, he looked every inch
the well-heeled titled nobleman—and a great deal more
dangerous than the average country gentleman. It was
impossible not to respond to this man as his masculine
magnetism dominated the scene.

When Tilly met his eyes, at that moment she became convinced that there were no eyes in all the world
that were brighter than those which now smiled at her.
Mentally casting off the spell he unwittingly cast, she
scolded herself for acting as addled as a dazzled school-
girl. Closer now, a half-smile curved his lips. He looked
down at her.

'Welcome to Clifton House.' He shifted his gaze to
her aunt standing beside her. 'And you must be Miss
Charlotte Anderson, Silas's younger sister. Commiserations on your loss. Silas was a fine man—one of
the best. I am delighted to meet you at last. I have encountered your niece on one or two occasions—a most
interesting young lady. I thought it was time you both
visited Clifton House.'

'And what a lovely house it is,' Aunt Charlotte said.

They were unable to say more for at that moment the
butler admitted a gentleman and his wife. Lord Clifton went to greet them, bringing them to where Tilly
stood with her aunt.

'I would like to introduce you to Reverend Leighton and his wife. They are old and valued friends of the Kingsleys. And this is Miss Charlotte Anderson and her niece Miss Tilly Anderson. They are in residence at Drayton Manor at present. Silas was Miss Charlotte Anderson's brother, Miss Anderson Silas's niece.'

'May I say we are truly delighted to meet you both and welcome you to Devon,' Reverend Leighton said as he raised Tilly's hand to his lips. 'I am delighted to see Lord Clifton has lost no time in inviting you to Clifton House.'

'Lord Clifton is a very persuasive man, Reverend,' Tilly replied without looking at their host, but she suspected there was a mocking gleam in his eyes.

'I understand we are to be neighbours, that you have taken up residence in Drayton Manor,' Reverend Leighton said. 'Such a lovely old house. Silas was a good friend of ours and we were sorry when he passed on. He was a great asset to the community and will be sadly missed in these parts.'

'Reverend Leighton spent the early years of his ministry in London and moved to Biddycombe fifteen years ago when the appointment became available,' Lord Clifton explained.

'And I bless the day I did. I enjoy ministering to the parishioners who belong to the fishing community, the farmers and the miners. I look forward to seeing you at church one of these Sundays, Miss Anderson. I think you will enjoy my sermons.'

'You will,' Lord Clifton said, laughing. 'Reverend Leighton delivers them with tremendous enthusiasm in case any of his parishioners are indiscreet enough to be caught nodding off.'

Their conversation was interrupted when Lord Clifton's other guests arrived—Mr and Mrs Ainsley. Mr Ainsley was a stout, jovial man, with a warm smile and the relaxed congeniality and confidence that came with the privileged position he held as the local magistrate. His wife was a handsome woman, with an easy, open manner.

They took a moment for introductions and for them to get to know each other before Lord Clifton led them towards the drawing room where drinks were to be served.

Tilly's attention was caught by a gilt-edged portrait tucked away in the corner of the hall. She stopped to look at it. The subject was a lady of perhaps twenty-five or more, wearing a gown in a style no longer fashionable. Mesmerised, she stared at the fair features. The lady was wearing a wig so she was unable to note the colour of her hair. Her features were delicate, giving her an air of fragility, but the artist had captured a steely determination in her blue eyes. Tilly knew instinctively that this was Elizabeth, Lord Clifton's grandmother, the lady who had preferred death to living with the violation inflicted on her by Jack Price's grandfather.

Lord Clifton turned as he was about to enter the drawing room to see what had captured her attention. He came to stand beside her.

'Is this your grandmother?' Tilly asked, her gaze on the painting.

'Yes. That is Elizabeth.'

'She was beautiful.'

He nodded. 'She was also very brave.'

* * *

When dinner was announced they progressed into the dining room of Jacobean design, with chestnut panelling and a great impressive fireplace showing the arms of the Kingsley family. It was a large and high room, with an elaborate plaster frieze depicting a forest with the court of Diana and attendant assortment of animals along with scenes of country life and hunting. Tilly loved it and began to relax, pleased to see Aunt Charlotte was enjoying herself.

They dined in generous style, the conversation light and lively as they talked of local matters and people known to them all. But Tilly had the disconcerting impression that Lord Clifton's other guests were weighing her up with every move she made and every word she uttered, though she was sure they meant to be kind.

'You must learn to swim, Miss Anderson,' Mrs Ainsley said, wiping her mouth with her napkin, 'living so close to the sea. Silas loved the sea. He was a regular swimmer—every night and morning, I believe. He had some steps hewn out of the cliff to save walking half a mile along the cliff path.'

'Yes, I have found them. It's an advantage being able to get to the beach quickly. Do you swim, Mrs Ainsley?'

'Goodness me, no. I never go near the sea—can't stand the way the sand gets into everything. Most unpleasant it is.'

'Miss Anderson expressed to me only the other day when we...er...met quite by chance on the beach her desire to learn to swim. Is that not so, Miss Anderson?' Lord Clifton said, his penetrating eyes watching her intently, a mischievous twinkle in his eyes. 'I think she would take to it like a duck to water.'

'Yes, Lord Clifton, I do remember,' Tilly said, looking at him directly, remembering all too clearly how he had dragged her on to the sand after the wave swept her off her feet. 'But I have had a change of heart since then. I prefer my feet on dry land and will be in no hurry to take to the water.'

Over the glowing expanse of white tablecloth and gleaming plates and cutlery, Aunt Charlotte was regarding her with suspicion. Tilly had told her she had met Lord Clifton when he had called at the house to see Mrs Carstairs and again in Biddycombe, which was where he had invited them to dine at Clifton House. She had failed to inform her they had met before that on the beach.

The meal was a relaxed affair, the food delicious. Seated at the head of the table, Lucas found his eyes drawn to Tilly Anderson like a magnet, where she sat on his right and next to Reverend Leighton. When she had entered the house, the vision she had presented in her blue gown had snatched his breath.

She was beautiful and bewitching and he was drawn to her in a way he wouldn't have thought possible when he'd arrived from Spain. She lit the room simply by being present. Looking for unease or nervousness on her face, he found nothing but calm and the soft glow of light in her velvet-dark eyes.

She had been fully tutored in the conventions of society and was clearly experienced in social repartee. She was lively, amiable, a laughing, beautiful young woman in possession of a natural wit and intelligence. The more he saw of her, the more his need to know more about her grew—and the more he wanted her to be his wife.

'What has been happening in my absence?' Mr Ainsley asked. 'No doubt the smuggling fraternity are as busy as ever.'

'They are.' Mrs Ainsley leaned towards Miss Anderson and her aunt. 'Have you seen anything untoward at Drayton Manor? You know—smugglers, that sort of thing?'

'Aunt Charlotte was not well when we arrived and has been confined to her room,' Miss Tilly Anderson said. 'But there was one occasion when I was awakened in the early hours by strange sounds and, peering from behind my bedroom curtains, I have seen horses being moved.'

A twinkle entered her eyes when she flashed a look at Lucas, reminding him of that night when the smugglers had come to Drayton Manor to return the horses, and he smiled in collaboration.

'And what did you do?' Mrs Leighton asked eagerly.

'What could I do? Not that I would wish to do anything. One thing I have learned since coming to Devon is that the gentlemen are not openly discussed. The men involved in the illicit trade have a reputation for brutality and it would be most unwise to apprehend them.'

'Not without foundation,' Mr Ainsley said. 'They have no respect for anyone—be it man or woman—who gets in their way. They are quite unscrupulous.'

'Then I will take the greatest of care not to get in their way,' Tilly replied.

'Very sensible, my dear,' Mrs Ainsley said. 'The matter of smuggling must be treated with levity. Half a dozen free traders were captured along with their cargo a sennight past off Liskeard and imprisoned. They are awaiting trial. The new Revenue Officer, Lieutenant Foster, is like a man possessed in his desire to eradicate smuggling in this area. He has achieved more than his predecessors—although Jack Price is still at large. He's grown rich on the trade.'

'Then why don't you arrest him?' Miss Charlotte Anderson asked, having finished eating the fish course and sipping her wine.

'Because there has to be tangible proof and because he's clever, Miss Anderson. He's also feared among the smuggling fraternity. No one dares to speak against him. Too many men are in his debt. He manages to escape the Revenue men every time and the Dragoons. The Revenue men are vigilant in these waters, but it grieves me to say they are not all honest. Some of them are in Price's pay.

'Price is greedy, but as careful and as slippery as an eel. He has the distribution routes well planned and has markets for the smuggled goods. He knows all the inlets and coves where a vessel might hide. He also acts as agent and banker with the merchants across the Channel, where the goods to be smuggled to England are purchased.'

'Price is the uncontested victor over his counterparts, but the lucrative trade will turn against him,' Lucas said. 'His days are numbered.'

'Maybe so. I hear old Ned Price is thinking of selling the boatyard. Now Edmund has gone he's reluctant to hang on to it. Jack hasn't raised any objections about selling it.'

'He never did show an interest in ship building,' Lucas said quietly, 'unless the yard was building boats to service his own smuggling needs. I'm not surprised he's thinking of selling. The Price family own enough property up and down the coast to live in comfort. The boatyard will be a prosperous business for somebody— and Edmund kept the workers' cottages in good repair. He would have been saddened to see it sold off.'

With the signal that dinner was at an end, they convened to the drawing room, where coffee was served and something stronger for the gentlemen.

While Reverend Leighton and Mr Ainsley indulged in a game of cards with brandy on the side, the ladies were content to sit and gossip and drink their coffee. Tilly, who was feeling restless, was happy to oblige when Mrs Leighton asked if she played the pianoforte. She was reasonably proficient and played a few easy pieces she had learned by heart. When she had finished, she was applauded and complimented.

'You play well, Miss Anderson,' Lord Clifton said. 'You are a young lady of many talents.'

'My mother made me practise religiously every day. She was of the opinion that every young lady should be able to play the pianoforte—and to sing—but I have not been blessed with a voice I would inflict on others.'

Feeling the need of some fresh air, Tilly slipped out through the French doors on to the terrace, walking down a flight of shallow steps. The terraced gardens were filled with flowers and sweet-smelling shrubs and an enormous fountain shot plumes of water into the air. The sun was sinking, casting long shadows on the smooth lawn.

On a sigh, she breathed in the sweet fragrance of the garden. The night was so quiet. She had come to Devon to escape a scandal, hoping for a few weeks' respite before returning in the hope it would have died a death and she could resume her life as it had been before she had encountered Richard Coulson. Instead, she had inadvertently become embroiled in something quite new to her.

She was tempted to return to London and leave it all behind, but a pair of warm blue eyes held her. She felt bemused. She sensed there were many different facets to Lord Clifton. He was dangerous to her sensibilities and yet she still found him attractive. She was never a rational person—her misdemeanour with Richard Coulson gave evidence to that—but this time she should have the good sense to heed the warning and walk away.

What she could not understand, and what worried her, was this strange, magnetic pull she felt towards her illustrious neighbour emotionally. There were times when he spoke to her in that deep, compelling voice of his, or looked at her with those penetrating eyes, that she almost felt as if he were quietly reaching out to her and inexorably drawing her closer and closer to him. Her mind was telling her to dismiss his sensuality and the attraction she felt for him, but her heart was saying something else entirely.

A footfall sounded behind her. A pulse fluttered in her throat when she turned her head and saw Lord Clifton.

'Oh,' she said softly. 'I thought I was alone.'

'I beg your pardon, Miss Anderson. I didn't mean to startle you. I saw you leave and thought you might like some company. Reverend Leighton is happily drinking his brandy and his wife and your aunt are deep in conversation.'

'So you thought you would come and find me.'

'Something like that. To talk with a lovely young woman on a moonlit night in a beautiful garden is a pleasure beyond compare. I hope you don't mind.'

Feeling her heartbeat quicken alarmingly, Tilly was amazed by the effect his sudden presence was having on her, but she was resolved not to let it show. 'Not at all. It's your house, Lord Clifton, your garden. You are allowed to go where you please.'

'I am—but I will return to the house if you would prefer to be alone.'

'No—please stay. There is something I would like to talk to you about—two things, actually.'

'Oh? I am all ears.'

'It's about the smugglers.' Immediately his expression became serious.

'Have they visited Drayton Manor again?'

'Yes—once. I did as you told me to do, but I couldn't resist having just a peek. They were leaving the manor and I'm certain one of them was Jack Price.'

'I expect you're right, but as long as he doesn't approach the house you shouldn't be in any danger. They have drop-off points inland to use when necessary.'

'Where?'

'Anywhere that is suitable.'

'Is it likely they would use the stables at the manor?'

'I think it's highly likely. Since Silas died the out-buildings will provide the perfect hiding place.'

'But…what if they were using it before Uncle Silas died? Would he have known?'

'I imagine he did, but as I told you before, it's a fool-ish man who doesn't turn a blind eye to the workings of the smugglers. They often pay people to keep quiet—especially if there's a big run. Usually it's small fishing boats, their owners out to make a little money, but for those who have got rich out of the business—Jack Price coming to mind—they have bigger, faster craft that will outrun the Revenue men. When they come ashore with the cargo, that's where the horses come in, a great number of horses, to carry a large cargo away from the coast before dawn.'

Having come to a wall separating one part of the garden from another at a lower level, he paused, leaning against it and holding her gaze with his own. 'There is something else. You said there were two things you wanted to talk to me about.'

'Yes. When I was out riding the other day, I rode further than I intended. I ended up at Trevean—which I now know is where Jack Price lives.'

Immediately, his expression hardened. 'It is. Did he see you?'

'I'm afraid so.'

'Please don't tell me you were alone.'

'No. Graham was with me. We exchanged few words, but what he did divulge was that he knows about Tobias—that you have a child here at Clifton House. He asked me what I knew about it. I told him I knew nothing about a child.'

'Someone must have talked. I expected it to happen at some time.'

'What will you do?'

He shrugged. 'What can I do? I will have to be extra-vigilant.' He moved closer to where she stood so still. 'Now, if I am to stay, what would you like to talk about? Excluding smugglers and children.'

Standing beside him and looking at the garden below, she said, 'About anything. What do you suggest?'

The answer was slow in coming. 'Anything? Then why don't you begin by telling me something about yourself?'

Tilly laughed softly. 'About me? But I'm not in the least interesting.'

'I disagree. Everyone has something interesting to tell about themselves, Miss Anderson—even you. All my sins have been revealed to you.'

'What? All of them?' she teased.

'Maybe not all.' Reaching out, he gently fingered one of her glossy curls admiringly. 'You have beautiful hair, Miss Anderson—the most beautiful hair I have seen on a woman.'

'And you have known many to measure me by,' she remarked.

'Some,' he said, not bothering to deny it. 'I freely admit that I didn't live the life of a saint before I went to Spain.'

'And now you have returned? Will you revert to your old ways?'

He smiled and shook his head. 'I don't think so. A lot has happened to me in the past year.' His eyes captured Tilly's, a lazy, seductive smile passing across his handsome face, curling his lips, and against her will she felt herself being drawn towards him, knowing the sensible thing to do would be to step back, but she was too inexperienced and affected by him to do that. Belated warning bells screamed through her head and her eyes became fixed on his finely sculptured mouth as he came closer still and she knew he was going to kiss her.

Chapter Seven

Tilly was trapped and she knew it. She was mesmerised by him, like a moth to a flame, and she felt her heart suddenly start pounding in a quite unpredictable manner. He was looking into her eyes, holding her spellbound, weaving some magic web around her from which there was no escape.

She favoured him with a melting smile, which made Lord Clifton's blood run warm in his veins and the heat of it move to his belly. 'I want to kiss you, Miss Anderson—if you don't mind, that is.'

'Yes—I mean, no...'

Taking her hand, he drew her close, his mouth almost brushing her lips. 'It doesn't matter,' he said huskily.

The darkening of his eyes, the naked passion she saw in their depths, seemed to work a strange spell on Tilly, but it was his tone and not his words that conquered her, and, without knowing what she was doing, she found herself moving closer still.

His arms came around her and her entire body began to tremble with desire and fear. There was nothing she could do to still the quiver of anticipation as he lowered his head and covered her mouth with his own. The contact was like an exquisite explosion inside her.

The shock of his lips on hers was one of wild, indescribable sweetness and sensuality as he claimed a kiss of violent tenderness, evoking feelings she had never felt before. Richard Coulson had kissed her once, but it had been nothing like this. This was a man several years older, experienced, worldly, who could have any woman he wanted at his feet.

Imprisoned by his protective embrace and seduced by his mouth and strong, caressing hands, which slid down the curve of her spine to the swell of her buttocks and back to her arms, her neck, burning wherever they touched, Tilly clung to him. Her body responded eagerly, melting with the primitive sensations that went soaring through her, her lips beginning to move against his with increasing abandon as she felt his hunger, unwittingly increasing it.

The sweetness of the kiss, of yielding to it, made her confused with longing. When he finally withdrew his mouth from hers an eternity later, Tilly reluctantly surfaced from the glorious Eden where he had sent her, her face suffused with languor and passion, her eyes luminous. His powerful masculinity had been an assault on her senses. She had been unable to resist him. She swallowed a smile. Aunt Charlotte would have an apoplectic fit if she should see her kissing their host.

Lord Clifton touched her cheek with his finger, looking down at her upturned face, and in that instant they both acknowledged that a flame had ignited between them. 'I do believe you have cast a spell on me, for I do not seem to have the strength or the inclination to resist you. I have been too long alone, too long on the move, too long looking for Cassie, my life often fraught with danger. Little did I know that as soon as I reached Devon, I would encounter someone like you.'

Tilly laughed softly. 'I think we will both remember our first encounter. I had only been in Devon twenty-four hours myself when you landed on the beach and played havoc with my temper.'

'So,' he said, leaning against the wall and folding his arms across his chest. He was a tactician by nature and a frontal assault wasn't always to be relied upon. There were often more effective ways, but he wanted to know all there was to know about her. 'What of you? I am curious as to the real reason that brought you to Devon. You are a beautiful young woman. I would have thought you would have the whole of London at your feet.'

'Not quite,' she said carefully as she gathered her thoughts, deciding to stick as close to the truth as possible while disclosing nothing about her unpleasant affair with Richard Coulson. Having grown closer to Lord Clifton over the past weeks, she sensed that their relationship might progress. And now that he had kissed her once more, she was beginning to think he was of a mind to take things further—perhaps even to offer marriage.

If she told him about Richard, there was a danger that it would fundamentally change the newly developed accord between them. Perhaps it was selfish of her, but she hoped he would never find out.

'My coming out is next Season—if I agree to fall in with everyone's wishes, that is. When Charles got the letter informing him that Uncle Silas had left him his property in Devon, but was unable to come himself, Aunt Charlotte and I couldn't resist coming to take a look.'

'And now you have seen it, do you think you could you live here—in Devon?'

He seemed to be watching her carefully, waiting for her response to his question. Half turning, she let her gaze drift towards the sea in the distance. 'Yes, I think I could,' she said softly. Turning her head, she looked at him. He, too, had turned and was looking at the sea.

She looked at his proud profile etched against the sky, strands of his dark hair stirring slightly in the breeze. His strong hands were by his side, his feet planted firmly on familiar ground. Here was a man in his own element—a man she believed she could love. Suddenly, she could not bear the thought of taking up her life in London—or the thought that she might lose him.

'I think we should return to the house,' she said. 'We will have been missed and Aunt Charlotte will more than likely scold me for being out here alone with you.'

'In which case I agree. We should return—but I will invite you back to Clifton House very soon.'

'You are a very gracious host.'

'I can be charming when I am doing what I like to do.'

'I suppose we all can.'

'I want to know all about you, Miss Anderson. Are you happy in London—with your family and the hustle and bustle of town?'

'I'm as happy as most people,' she replied as they made their way slowly back to the house. 'Although happiness is rarely a permanent state. One would be fortunate to achieve that.'

'And are you happy now—at this moment?' he asked, glancing sideways at her.

She hesitated before answering. 'Yes—I am. I am interested in this change to my environment—being close to the sea and the solitude. It is all so new to me.'

He walked on, seeming to contemplate her reply in thoughtful silence. Tilly found a certain pleasure in watching him. She felt very strongly about him. He was the sort of person she disliked most. It was more amusing and interesting to have deep feelings about people and she was one to have such feelings. She disliked or she loved—and she did both most intensely, which often made life most exhausting. One thing she was certain about was that she was looking forward to the days ahead spent in this man's company and getting to know him better.

The evening over, Lord Clifton handed them up into the carriage and closed the door. They drove past the oaks and deer that had so delighted Tilly earlier. In the gathering dusk a lowering copper-and-gold-toned sun cast elongated shadows across the land.

Settling against the upholstery, she let her eyes drift to the sea in the distance. It was still light enough for her to see where it met the sky on the horizon. She was unable to still the confusion of thoughts in her head. Her mind was preoccupied with that moment of intimacy in the garden, when Lord Clifton had kissed her.

Closing her eyes, she allowed the memory of the kiss to invade her mind—the kiss, vibrant and alive, soft, insistent and sensual. When he'd bent his head and placed his lips on hers, she'd wanted it to go on and on and to kiss him back with soul-destroying passion, to feel his hands on her bare flesh—and more.

Dear, sweet Lord! How could she have felt like that? That one kiss and the strange feelings and emotions it had brought had changed her. A peculiar inner excitement touched her cheeks with a flush of soft pink, and a special sparkle was in her eyes at the memory. Aunt Charlotte was seated across from her and her sharp eyes picked up on it.

'You are enjoying your time in Devon, Tilly?' she asked. 'You look pensive—has something happened? I noted you were gone a while—as was Lord Clifton.'

'We took a walk in the garden. Where Devon is concerned, I could live all my life here. I love everything about it—the scent of the woods and the sea. It's so clean and fresh—so very different from London.'

'And much kinder to one's health than the dirt and grime and the smog of the city, although Cranford is a lovely place to live. You could spend more time there if you wished. I am sure Anna would love to have you stay for longer periods.'

'Yes—I know she would. But I do so love it here— so much so that I would not mind if we were never to return to London.'

'Which we will have to do when Charles leaves for India.'

'I expect we will, but I don't see why I should live there. I'm going to ask Charles to let me come back— to live in the house indefinitely. Let's face it, Aunt Charlotte, when he goes to India he could be away for years—and he has no desire to live in Devon anyway. I don't see why he would object.'

'Are you serious about this, Tilly?'

'Very. It's what I want. All I have to do is persuade Charles. And if I do, Aunt Charlotte, if you have a mind to, you can come and live with me. I know you like it down here.'

'I do—very much. I believe you could find real happiness here—and then, of course,' she said, with a knowing smile, 'there is Lord Clifton. Such a charming man.'

'Yes—he is,' Tilly replied, averting her eyes.

'I have noted your sudden interest in His Lordship. You told me you met on two occasions and yet he mentioned meeting you on the beach.'

'Yes, briefly—and again when he came to the house to visit Mrs Carstairs. I did tell you.' Tilly hadn't told her about the night when the smugglers had come for the horses. She couldn't see the point in worrying her aunt unnecessarily. But when it had entered the conversation at the dinner table, her aunt had picked up on it.

'Did you really see the smugglers come during the night?'

'Yes, Aunt Charlotte—briefly. Apparently, when they have a lot of contraband to move, they borrow people's horses, returning them before sunrise.'

'Goodness me! That is shocking.'

'I agree, but there is nothing one can do about it.'

'You will have to be careful, Tilly.'

'Don't worry about me, Aunt Charlotte. I can take care of myself.'

'And if Lord Clifton decides to pursue you? He is a handsome man—and you are an attractive young woman.'

'I'm sure Lord Clifton has enough to deal with just

now. He is grieving for his sister, don't forget, and he lost both his parents just before that. I doubt he has a mind to pursue anyone at present.'

Tilly did not see Lord Clifton for several days. Aunt Charlotte was keen to see something of the surrounding countryside and they spent their days exploring and walking on the beach. They even managed a trip into Plymouth to do some shopping and went in to Biddycombe often. Mr and Mrs Ainsley came to tea, as did Reverend Leighton and his wife. The Reverend was pleased to see them among the congregation on a Sunday.

Two weeks passed in this manner and then one day a letter came from Charles informing them that he was to leave for India with the Company sooner than he had expected and he would like them to return to London before he went. A cloud descended on Tilly, less over the mention of Charles leaving than because she would miss seeing Lord Clifton. She would live in hope that Charles would agree to allow her to return to Drayton Manor indefinitely.

The sharpness of her disappointment that he might not took her by surprise. God alone knew what she had been hoping for. Perhaps that the close relationship that had developed between her and Lord Clifton would oblige him to ask her to stay. He could not know how much he had come to matter to her and his absence from her life would be a source of grief.

There was no use denying it or fighting her attraction for him. Nor could she regret it. How could she regret knowing this man, even if it was for such a short time?

Until then her heart and body had been dormant, waiting for the spark that would make it explode into life.

If Lord Clifton had not ignited it, she would have spent her whole existence not knowing what it felt like to have a fire inside her soul, would never have known that such a wild, sweet passion could exist. Better by far to experience that passion for such a short time than never to have known it at all, even if it brought such pain and heartache, or to die not knowing such joy was possible.

It was unfortunate that now she had had a taste of the intoxicating sweetness of Lord Clifton's kiss, she realised it was completely separate from what she really yearned for—an intimacy of the heart.

Although Tilly didn't know it, Lucas was missing her and, try as he might, being kept busy with important estate matters, he couldn't get to see her. Having been told by Reverend Leighton that having received a letter from her brother, she was to return to London shortly, he was determined to see her.

He had hoped they would have had more time together, to get to know each other better, to eventually ask her to be his wife. She was young and had yet to make her debut and for some reason she was opposed to marriage, which did puzzle him somewhat, but if her willing response to his kiss was an indication of her feelings for him, then he felt she could be persuaded. He could not bear to lose her.

He found it impossible to banish her from his mind. She had a way of getting under his skin and insinuating herself into his mind. No other woman could outshine her. She was physically appealing, with a face and body that drugged his mind, but she was also appealing in other ways, with an intelligent sharpness of mind and a clever wit that he admired, making her pleasant company and interesting to be with.

He was woken when Florence screamed—indeed, it was so loud that it woke the whole house. Immediately, he was out of bed, thrusting his arms into his robe and dashing along the landing to the nursery. Florence, in her night attire, was utterly distraught.

'Oh, My Lord,' she wailed when he appeared. 'Such a terrible thing has happened. Tobias has gone—disappeared. He wasn't there when I went to feed him. Where can he be?' she said, looking wildly around her as though the child might, at the age of five months, have climbed out of his cot and be somewhere in the room. 'I fed him and put him down. He was asleep in no time like the good baby he is.'

Her voice rose to fever pitch, for Florence had experienced the horrors of the battlefields in Spain and witnessed the full horror of nightmares of losing her own child at birth, but surely this was the worst.

Immediately, Lucas took charge of the hysterical Florence, sitting her in a chair.

'Calm down, Florence, and tell me what has happened. Did you hear anything, see anything?'

She shook her head, her eyes filled with fear. By now, servants had gathered on the landing and were peering inside the nursery, curious as to what all the fuss was about. Lucas went out to them.

'The child has gone. I want every one of you to search the house—inside and out. He must be found.'

Florence came forcefully towards him, a fierce look in her eyes. 'She's got him. She's taken him, I just know it.'

Lucas stared at her. 'Who, Florence? Who has got him?'

'That Lizzy who works in the kitchen. Lizzy Tomlinson. She's a sly one, that girl, always creeping about up here on one pretext or another, asking questions— questions about Tobias.' Suddenly, she seemed to crumple and tears flowed from her eyes. 'Oh, where is he—my lamb? Why would she do such a cruel thing as to snatch a baby from his cot—and who will feed him?'

Lucas indicated to one of the maids to come inside and console Florence. Fury burned inside him. He knew exactly who was capable of kidnapping Tobias. Jack Price. It had to be him. Had not Miss Anderson told him that Price knew there was a child at Clifton House? He was surprised he had not taken him before. Returning to his room, he dressed quickly and was soon striding to the stables.

He didn't have to ride far. Lizzy Tomlinson was found outside the gates with the baby in her arms. She was about to pass him to two of Jack Price's men waiting there with a wagon. The child had started to cry, alerting those who were looking for him. The two miscreants absconded without the child and, after being questioned and confirming it was Jack Price who had ordered the child's kidnapping, Lizzy Tomlinson was dismissed from her position at Clifton House.

Chapter Eight

Jack Price's attempted abduction of Tobias had given Lucas much to think about. He could no longer keep Tobias's existence secret and while ever Jack Price lived, he would pose a constant danger to the child. Something had to be done. After decades of feuding with the Price family, Lucas decided it was time to face up to the old man, Ned Price.

On the day he rode to Trevean, Lucas had no doubt in his mind about Ned Price's feelings toward him or his unexpected visit. He hadn't seen the old man for a good many years. Ned might refuse to see him in retaliation for past grievances, but Lucas refused to dwell on that possibility. Prior to this, he had made quite sure Jack was out of the area.

Fortunately, Ned Price agreed to see him. He was admitted into the large, sprawling building perched on the cliffs above the sea. Without the touch of a woman—Ned Price's wife had died many years ago and he had never remarried—the house was badly in need of renovation and modernisation.

Ned Price was a man of around seventy years and not in the best of health. He used to be a big, upright man, but now he was gaunt and stooped with a sparse covering of white hair.

He greeted Lucas warily in his study, studying him closely with penetrating grey eyes.

'Lord Clifton! Forgive me if I appear surprised,' he said, his voice deep and rasping. 'A lot of tides have rolled on to Devon's shores since any Kingsley graced the halls of Trevean.'

'Yes—and many more will roll in before there is another.'

'It must be an important matter to bring you here.'

'It is—and I am not here to heal the breach. Had I the choice I would not be here at all. I will be brief and to the point and as civil as I can be.'

'I would appreciate that. As you see, my health is not what it was.'

Ned Price lounged back in a high-backed chair, motioning for Lucas to be seated in the one opposite. He did so, eyeing the man across from him.

'I intend to get this ordeal over with as quickly as possible.'

'You know Edmund is dead?' Ned said quietly.

'Yes—I was in Spain at the time.'

The old man nodded. 'He should not have gone. He took after me—not wild and headstrong like Jack. They were always at odds with each other. I taught Edmund all I know about building boats. Jack was a disappointment. The days are gone when I begged him to find an honourable profession.'

'You have no one to blame but Jack and yourself for

what happened. Jack resented the fact that Edmund was the eldest, the heir, that he would inherit your estate and boatyard on your death. Edmund was content to work the boatyard—it was what he was good at.'

Ned glanced resentfully at him. 'I don't need you to tell me that.'

'No. Rumour has it that you are to sell it.'

'So, that's why you've come. And if I am, what's that to do with you? Don't tell me you want to buy it.'

'Yes. And when I tell you what I know you will agree.'

He laughed, a harsh, humourless sound. 'You fool, Kingsley. Jack would never agree. A Kingsley owning the Price boatyard? Never.' He shook his head, looking away. 'I have to sell. Jack is only interested in one thing—you don't need me to spell it out. When he's not up to his illegal activities, he's wenching and gaming over in Plymouth. He profits from the smuggling he's invested in.'

He grimaced. 'It won't last. Jack has a streak which will get him into trouble with the law, which he cannot evade for ever, which is why I've decided to sell the boatyard. Trevean and the yard have always been locked together. It's a hard thing for a man to acknowledge his son has no interest in what keeps the family afloat. But Jack would rather see it go to rack and ruin before letting a Kingsley set foot in it.'

'Jack doesn't have to know.'

Ned Price looked at him closely, eyes narrowed. 'What are you saying?' he demanded. 'That I deceive my son?'

'That is precisely what I'm saying. What I am about to disclose is for your ears alone. Do you understand?'

'I am intrigued. You'd better tell me?'

'Two nights ago, a child was kidnapped from Clifton House, a child who is just five months old. Fortunately, we managed to apprehend the servant who was working for your son. It was Jack who arranged to have the child abducted.'

Ned Price stared at him in confusion. 'Jack? What in God's name are you talking about? What would Jack want with a child?'

'The child is called Tobias. He is Edmund's son. His mother was my sister, Cassie.' His words rendered Ned speechless. 'They wanted to be together. I refused to sanction the match—which I am sure is what you would have done. My sister was determined they would be together, that not even Bonaparte's army would come between them. She followed Edmund to Spain.

'When I discovered what she had done, I went after her. It was no easy matter tracking her down. I saw Edmund before he went into battle. I also saw that Cassie was with child, his child. I arranged for them to be married—shortly before Edmund was killed.'

'And your sister?'

'She died in childbirth. Edmund and Cassie are buried together in Spain.'

'And the boy?'

'He is at Clifton House. I promised Cassie before she died that I would take care of him. Somehow, Jack got wind of it and tried to abduct him. I have no doubt he sees Tobias as a threat to his inheritance. With Edmund's death your estate would have passed to Jack. I will leave you to imagine what Jack would do with a five-month-old child who stands in the way of what he now considers to be his inheritance.'

'So, I have a grandson—Edmund's son.'

'He's a fine boy.'

'But…what has all this to do with you buying the boatyard? If the boy is indeed Edmund's son, then it will pass to him in time. Knowing this, I will not sell.'

'No? Think about it. Yes, it is what Edmund would have wanted, but will Jack allow it? I cannot trust him and you will not be around for ever. Can you imagine that Jack will let such an injustice go unavenged? Jack rules by brutality. He served a year in prison for assaulting a man—in fact, he will probably end his days in gaol. Is that anything to be proud of?

'Leave Jack Trevean if you must. That is your affair. The only way to safeguard the boatyard for Tobias's future is to sell it to me on the understanding that when he comes of age it will be his to do with as he sees fit. If you allow me to buy the yard, it will be Tobias's when he is of an age to work it himself. That I promise you.'

'And Jack?'

'Would not know that I am the buyer—not for a long time.'

'You are asking me to deceive my son?'

'I am asking you to do this for Edmund.'

'And in the meantime? Who will work the yard?'

'There will be no change. You have some skilled workers. It will continue to be worked as you yourself have done.'

Ned Price nodded slowly, thinking it over. 'It is profitable now, but I'll not pretend. The shipbuilding business needs careful scheduling to run efficiently and profitably. You also have competition. The Price boat-yard is not the only boatyard on the coast. There are times when customers cannot meet their investments. Terms have to be renegotiated, but often you are left with a half-built vessel. Overheads of a shipyard are immense.'

'I have the income of the Clifton Estate to help support it in times of crisis. I am willing to take the risk for Tobias's sake.

'There will be legalities involved. The investors will have to be told that the yard has changed hands.'

'I deal with legalities on a daily basis. I will ensure that everything is done legally and above board and with your approval. I have a lawyer who will act as my representative and therefore my name will not appear. It will secure Tobias's future.'

'You have it all worked out.'

'I am up against Jack. It has to be done this way. If you agree, I will have my lawyer draw up the documents. It's a complicated business, but it will work providing Jack doesn't find out I am the owner.'

'How do I know I can trust you?'

Lucas produced a letter from the inside pocket of his coat. 'This should convince you. It is from Edmund. Fearing he would not come through, hoping Cassie would bear a son, he wrote it before he went into battle.'

With trembling fingers, Ned Price opened the letter and read it. At length he raised his head. 'He says he wants your sister to raise the child at Clifton House.'

'Since Cassie is no longer able to do that, the onus is on me to do it for her.'

'May I keep this?'

Lucas ignored the mistiness he saw in those grey eyes. 'Yes, of course.'

'And my grandson? Can I see him?'

'It will be arranged at a time when Jack is not around.'

The old man lowered his head, deep in thought. When he again looked at Lucas, there was a determined look in his eyes, as if he had come to a decision. 'I'm not ignorant of Jack's way of doing things. I have no sway over what he does any more. You are right. Jack is a danger to the child. How will you keep him safe?'

'That is something I have already decided. I intend to send him away for the time being—somewhere Jack will not think of looking.' When Lucas made to walk away, Ned Price's next words halted him.

'One more thing. Your parents—I heard what happened to them. For what it's worth I was sorry to hear of it. A storm, they said.'

Lucas paused in his stride and then he turned and fixed him with a hard gaze. 'There was no storm that day.'

'Then...what happened?'

'I think you should ask your son about that. I have proof his vessel was in the vicinity that day, but no one will talk. If I find he was responsible for the death of my parents... That he should still be walking about is unthinkable.'

A darkness entered Ned Price's eyes. 'If it is true, then I will finish him myself—even though he is my son.'

Lucas nodded and said nothing more.

Lucas arrived at Drayton Manor with the intention of seeing Miss Anderson's Aunt Charlotte, only to be told by the maid that Miss Charlotte Anderson was resting and her niece was in the garden.

'I shall go and fetch her this instant if you will be so good as to wait in the library.'

'No,' he said, as she was about to disappear. 'Thank you, but do not trouble yourself. I shall find her myself.'

He stepped briskly outside and was walking along the paths, drawn towards the sound of something creaking among a group of trees way beyond the house. He moved through the shrubbery, following the winding narrow path until he eventually came to a clearing.

There seemed to be a golden mist about him, heightening the hues of a beautiful copper beech, resplendent in all its summer glory, its branches spread out like a gigantic parasol. Hanging from one of them was a swing and sitting on its board was Miss Anderson, gently swooping to and fro, careful not to let her feet touch the ground, her wonderful mane of raven-black hair flowing behind her.

Momentarily taken aback by the sight of her, Lucas paused, transfixed on seeing her like this. He had forgotten what a wonderful rich colour her hair was and seeing her again made every one of his senses clamour for her. There was that same fierce tug to his senses on being near her as there had been that time he had seen her on the beach when she had fallen into the sea.

She really was a beautiful young woman, with her softly rounded limbs, the way her head moved with a swaying grace and a soft, inviting, lilting expression to her lips. He watched as her skirts and petticoats lifted when she stretched out her legs to gather momentum on the swing, revealing her shapely stockinged calves and fancy blue garters.

With her translucent skin and her violet eyes, which were as wide and solemn as a baby owl's, she had an ethereal quality. His heart took a savage, painful leap at the sight of her. She seemed like someone looking more at home here than she would in the salons of London.

He wanted to go to her, take her in his arms, kiss her and tell her how he felt. Ever since they had met, he had been plagued with so many conflicting emotions where she was concerned, becoming lost in a turmoil of contradiction and insoluble dilemma.

Yet until he had settled the business of buying the Price boatyard and making sure that Tobias was safe—and waiting to see what Miss Anderson's brothers had in store for her in London—he was resolute in his decision not to further their relationship until it was over.

Absorbed in her thoughts, Tilly did not realise Lord Clifton was there until he stepped in front of the swing a short distance away. Shocked out of her reverie, immediately she scraped her feet on the ground and stopped, the intimacy of their time spent in the garden at Clifton House springing instantly to the fore.

Lightning seemed to scorch across the space between them, burning, eliminating everything in its path. Everything was obliterated but that invisible physical force searing through her body, so that she felt her flesh throb in agony as every nerve sprang to a trembling awareness of him—and instinctively, she knew it was the same for him.

An unbidden flare of excitement rose up in the pit of her stomach. She watched him, wishing she could cool the waves of heat that mounted her cheeks. She left the swing and stood utterly still. Like a free spirit she faced him, her head poised at a questioning angle, her hair spread over her shoulders like a shining black cape. Until that moment she had thought she remembered exactly what he looked like, his well-chiselled features stamped indelibly on her mind.

'Lord Clifton—you take me by surprise,' she said, forcing herself to ignore the fluttering in her stomach.

'I didn't mean to do that. So,' he said, stopping in front of her, 'no sooner do you arrive in Devon than you are to return to London.'

'Yes. How do you know that?'

'Reverend Leighton told me. Were you going to leave without telling me?'

She shook her head, brushing back a stray lock of dark hair from her eyes, eyes that were bright and inquiring. 'I would have written. It's come as something of a surprise. I was hoping Charles would not be leaving for India until next year.'

'I came to see your aunt, but I was told she is resting. The maid said this was where I would find you.'

'As you see.'

Lord Clifton's eyes softened and a slow smile curved his lips as his eyes swept slowly over her. 'You looked charming on the swing,' he murmured. 'There was a moment when the tantalising young lady eluded me and I saw how you must have looked as a girl.'

A rush of warmth pervaded Tilly's whole being, reawakening the nerve centre which had been numbed since she had last seen him. Hearing the warm words, being here with him now, she felt a sudden, keener awareness of her feelings for him.

The feeling was so strong that for an instant she had a wild impulse to tell him how she felt, but she recollected herself just in time. The man in front of her had merely complimented her on how she looked on the swing and might not wish to listen to a declaration of her feelings.

'It isn't so long ago that I was just a girl. But something tells me you have not come to talk about the garden—or the swing, which Graham very kindly made for me. You have something on your mind—I can tell.'

He smiled. 'How perceptive you are. You are right. The reason I am here is because I wish to enlist your aid in a matter that is of extreme importance, which you will no doubt consider a gross imposition. It concerns Tobias—and Jack Price.'

Lord Clifton's handsome, aggressive face became hard in that particular way Tilly had seen before when he had mentioned Jack Price. His eyes were filled with a mixture of rage, apprehension and dread—dread that Price would succeed in harming Tobias.

'Price has shown his hand. I thought he would,' he said bitterly. 'How dare he make a child the instrument of his vengeance?'

'I am sorry to hear that. But I cannot see what that has to do with me or my aunt. Why are you here, Lord Clifton? Although if you would prefer to wait and speak to Aunt Charlotte then you may do so.'

'No, you would have to know anyway. You are to leave for London. Would you take Tobias and Florence with you? While ever he is here, he is in danger.'

Tilly stared at him. He was watching her uncertainly.

She could feel the tension in him. This really was important to him. 'You…want us to take Tobias with us?'

'Believe me, Miss Anderson, I do not ask this lightly. I did not want to come here…to burden you with this. I have no right, but I am desperate.'

'Why? Has something happened?'

'You might say that. Two nights ago, Florence woke to find Tobias had been taken from his crib. One of the servants whose family is answerable to Jack Price took him. Fortunately, she had only taken him minutes before and we managed to apprehend her as she was leaving the grounds.'

'But that is terrible. Was he harmed in any way?'

'No—just hungry. Apparently, the maid was to have passed him on to one of Price's cohorts waiting in the lane outside the gates.'

'I see. Then if you have him back and he is unharmed, I fail to see how we can be of help. London is a long way to travel with a small child.'

'So was Spain, Miss Anderson,' he said pointedly.

'Yes,' she said quietly. She didn't have to be told what an arduous journey, fraught with many dangers, that must have been for both him and Florence with a young baby. 'I—I am sure it was.'

Noting her hesitation, his lips set in a grim line. 'If you have an aversion to my request, then I will bother you no longer.'

Tilly stared at him as if he had struck her. Lord Clifton saw the pupils of her eyes dilate until the violet had almost disappeared, and all the blood drained from her face until even her lips were pale.

'If you think that, then you do not know me. You

have never been more wrong. No matter what my circumstances are, if I were the meanest, poorest creature on God's earth, I would put the welfare, the safety, of any child before myself.'

His jaw tightened, his eyes burning furiously down into hers, while feeling a surge of relief and thankfulness that she had spoken as she had. 'In all conscience it would appear I have no alternative but to ask your help if I am to keep Tobias safe. His very life is at stake if he remains in Devon. Price will not give up. While ever Tobias is alive, he is a threat to Price.'

'Are the servants aware that Tobias is your sister's son?'

'It's difficult to keep something like that secret. Florence keeps very much to herself in the nursery, but servants talk—so, yes, I believe they will know by now.'

'What will you tell them when Florence and Tobias leave Clifton House?'

'Florence will let it be known she is visiting her sick sister in Dawlish. Since Tobias is dependent on her then it is only natural that he goes with her.'

'And the girl who tried to abduct him?'

'Has been dismissed.'

Tilly hesitated. How could she possibly travel all the way to London with a baby—and how on earth would she explain that to Charles and William? Then came the realisation that there was no guarantee that Charles would allow her to return to Devon.

Even though Lord Clifton had made her no promises, agreeing to take Tobias and Florence to London had given her a link to him. Everything paled beside this. She did not want the strands which tied them together to unravel just yet—if at all.

'Very well,' she conceded. 'You are right. Tobias must be kept safe at all costs. I would never forgive myself if anything were to happen to him because we refused to take him to London. I will help you—*we* will help you—I am sure Aunt Charlotte will agree with me. Tobias has to come first.'

Lord Clifton's expression softened. 'Thank you. I can't tell you how grateful I am. When do you expect to leave for London?'

'Two days. Naturally we are going to have to speak to Aunt Charlotte before anything can be arranged for definite about Tobias, but I cannot see a problem, although I imagine she will have a few choice words to say to me when she finds out I have known about your nephew all along. We will go inside and see if she is available. So you see, Lord Clifton, I may have been painted many things, but I am not uncaring.'

His gaze lingered on her face. 'I do not recall saying you were,' he murmured.

Hearing the tenderness in his tone, Tilly felt her stomach lurch and she turned her head to hide her confusion. 'No, perhaps not.'

On a more tender note that made Tilly's heart flutter and brought her head up, he said, 'There is nothing ordinary about you, is there, Miss Anderson?'

'I hope not. I should hate to be predictable. No doubt you disapprove.'

'Most certainly not. I applaud the wildness and individuality I first saw in you.'

'As I recall it was my bad temper that you noticed the day when we met on the beach.'

Lord Clifton laughed quietly as he fell in to step beside her as they walked back to the house. 'That is something I will always remember about you.'

'Will you take Gracie back with you? Thank you for letting me ride her.'

'She will be at Clifton House, if you manage to persuade your brother to let you return.'

'Yes, thank you. I hope he will.'

'The smugglers are going to miss the use of your horses.'

'That's too bad. I was never comfortable with that. I can only hope that when the time comes for us to leave, they have not made use of them during the night, otherwise we will not get very far before they have to rest.'

'We must work out what is to be done. I intend leaving for London myself shortly. I have some business to take care of, but I have yet to finalise my plans. By that time, I hope to have bought the boatyard, or at least set proceedings into motion. Will you be making for London or Berkshire? I must give you the address of my cousin and his wife. They won't mind taking care of Tobias and Florence until I can get there.'

'If Aunt Charlotte agrees to Tobias coming with us, then we will be going to her house in Chelsea village before I go on to Cranford. If, for some reason, your cousin is not at home or there is a problem, then we will take him to Cranford. William and Anna have a son who is of a similar age to Tobias. Anna is involved in many charitable works, including opening a school for less advantaged children, so I'm sure they wouldn't mind us staying there.'

Having reached the house, they went inside to find Aunt Charlotte had come down from her rest and was in the parlour.

'Ah, Lord Clifton,' she said, smiling broadly at the sight of their visitor. 'How nice to see you again. I'm sorry I was not able to receive you—I do like my little nap in the afternoons, more so since coming to Devon, which I put down to the sea air—but I see my niece has been taking care of you.'

'Aunt Charlotte, Lord Clifton has something to ask of you—something you need to consider very carefully. He is faced with a problem and he believes we can help.'

'Oh?' she said, looking from one to the other. 'I am intrigued. Please, Lord Clifton, take a seat and tell me how I can help you.'

Lord Clifton did as she bade, seating himself opposite and crossing his long legs as he proceeded to tell her his reason for coming to Drayton Manor. He went on to tell her a good deal of what had transpired since he had arrived back in England—all about Jack Price and his illicit activities, the attempted abduction and the threat he posed to Tobias. She listened avidly, her eyes fixed on him in fascination, sometimes with shock, but mainly with great concern.

'Dear me,' she said when he fell silent. 'What a tragedy. That poor motherless child. I can't believe anyone would want to hurt him.'

'What do you think, Aunt Charlotte? Will you agree to take the child with us? If Lord Clifton truly believes that he is in danger at this present time, then we cannot refuse to help in any way we can if he is to be kept safe. He has asked that we take him to his cousin in London. Lord Clifton is to travel to London himself shortly. Maybe by then it will be safe for Tobias to return to Devon with him.'

Aunt Charlotte nodded. 'I see. If it will help you, then we will take him with us. There is room enough in the coach for all of us.'

'Thank you. I am most grateful.'

'I will leave you to make the arrangements, Lord Clifton.'

'Should Lord Clifton's relatives not be at home, I thought Tobias and Florence could go to Cranford, Aunt Charlotte. I'm sure William and Anna won't mind—Tobias will be company for their Thomas.'

'You seem to have it all thought out.'

'Not really. It just seems to be the most sensible thing to do.'

'Very well,' her aunt said. 'I can only hope the journey will not be too taxing with a baby in the coach.'

'I don't think there will be a problem about my cousin not being at home. It is normal practice for them to go to their estate in Oxford closer to Christmas. I will write telling them to expect you. In the meantime, I would appreciate it if you did not mention this to anyone—especially Mrs Carstairs. No one must know Tobias is to go with you to London. I will arrange the time and place where we can meet. It must be kept from Dunstan and Graham until you are away from here.'

'Do not worry, Lord Clifton,' Charlotte said when Lord Clifton got up to leave. 'You can rest assured that our lips are sealed.'

Tilly walked with Lord Clifton to the door, when she paused and looked at him. 'We will take Tobias to London and keep him there until the time when it is safe for him to return to Devon.'

'I know you will.'

He wanted to say more, Tilly could tell, but he remained silent. She wanted to say more, too, words that would make it easier for them both, but the words remained clogged in her throat.

'I will let you know the details,' he said. 'Until then we will go about our daily lives with no hint of what we intend.'

'Very well. If we don't hear from you, we will know you have changed your mind about the whole thing and we will leave for London.'

'I won't change my mind. This is the only thing I can think of to keep Tobias safe for the present.'

Chapter Nine

When Ned Price arrived at Clifton House and was introduced to his grandson, Lucas saw the raw emotion in the man's face. Losing Edmund had affected him deeply, but knowing he had left him his son went a long way to lessening the pain.

Afterwards the two men sat over a brandy to discuss Tobias's future and the sale of the boatyard.

''Tis ironic, wouldn't you say, Lord Clifton, the two of us discussing a business proposition? After all, I and many of my forebears were enemies of your family.'

'The irony of it has crossed my mind,' Lucas said smoothly.

'Aye, well, it's done with. I've paid many times for past mistakes and it's a wonder I'm not long since dead. The young lad is what matters now—and he's a fine lad. I trust you to do what is right by him.'

Lucas was silent for a long moment. 'You have my word.'

Ned nodded slowly; his eyes narrowed on the man opposite him. 'I will come and see him again. It's an odd thing, but you are the only person I feel that I can trust.

I knew your grandmother and father and you, Lord Clifton, all as opponents. Sometimes a man comes to respect an enemy more than a friend. There have been few men I would turn my back on, but you I would do so without a qualm.'

Draining his glass, he stood up and without another word left the house to where his carriage waited in the drive. Lucas watched him go. Ned Price's admission had surprised and touched him as few other things had done.

Everything was arranged, the luggage strapped to the coach and Mrs Carstairs was waving them off. She would carry on running the house in her usual efficient way until further notice.

An anxious Tilly sat back with a deep sigh, knowing she would not be at ease until they had left Devon behind.

The coach had passed Biddycombe when they met up with Lord Clifton. He was in a closed carriage with Florence and Tobias. Immediately, he got out and held the door open for Florence. Taking Tobias in his arms, he waited until Florence was seated beside Daphne before passing the child to her. Dunstan and Graham secured their baggage behind the coach.

Tilly climbed out, sensing Lord Clifton's pain on this parting from his nephew. The remorse that gripped her was powerful and sudden.

'I can understand how difficult this is for you,' she said quietly.

'Yes, it is. The last thing I wanted was to send him away.'

He spoke softly and she looked at him. The sheer male beauty of him took her breath. Morning sunlight speared his hair to shining jet. She wondered what he would say if she were to reveal what was in her heart. He didn't know the extent of her feelings, feelings she had for him, deep and abiding feelings, feelings that would last a lifetime. She didn't really know him, either. Beneath the surface he was deep and complex, a man of moods, a man of principle, who cared deeply about his commitments and about those he had lost.

'You have Aunt Charlotte's address in London and Cranford in Berkshire. Should your cousin not be at home, that is where we will take him. You have written to your cousin telling him to expect us?'

'I have.'

'Have you encountered any further trouble from Jack Price?'

'No, none. I pray it remains that way until you are well on your way to London.'

'Yes, we won't delay lest we are seen. Tobias will be well looked after; you can depend on that.'

'I know. It saddens my heart to part with him, but it is for the best.'

'Yes.' She turned from him and as she was about to get into the coach she turned back. She saw his eyes fixed upon her with an expression of such sadness in them that it wrenched her heart.

'Farewell, Lord Clifton.'

And so they began their return journey to London.

Florence was a friendly young woman who was excited to be going to London. Tobias was a lovely baby.

His hair was dark brown with tawny lights in it. When he was awake, he gazed at them wonderingly, his little hands curling round anything within his reach.

He was clearly a contented baby and that was something to be relieved about. It would make the journey so much easier. Florence was clearly fond of him. When she dozed Daphne was more than happy to take the child on her knee and entertain him.

'I've never been to London,' Florence said on leaving Devon. 'In fact, until I followed Edgar, my husband, to Spain, I'd never been further than Dawlish, which is where my sister lives. I've all sorts of ideas about it. I've read about it and heard people talk of it and it sounds daunting and exciting at the same time.'

'So it is,' Tilly told her. 'It's a big city, with lots to see and everybody bustling about. It has its lovely, fashionable parts with big houses and parks to see and enjoy, but there is also the other side where poverty abounds. Should Lord Clifton's cousin be out of town we will go on to my brother's house in Berkshire. It's called Cranford and is not unlike Clifton House.'

'I was so grateful to Lord Clifton when he asked me to take care of Tobias. When I lost my husband and then when my baby died, I didn't know what to do. Nothing seemed to matter any more. The conditions were so awful out there.'

'I am so sorry for your loss, Florence. What an awful time you've had. What happened to you happened to Lord Clifton's sister also.'

'I know. We knew each other—being in the same boat, so to speak, with both of us losing our husbands. Except that poor lady lost her life, leaving her baby without a mother—poor little mite. Lord Clifton's arrival was a godsend, I can tell you—although, at the time, his sister gave him what for for following her. I'm right glad he did, otherwise there's no telling where her bairn would have ended up—or me, for that matter.

'He applied himself to the matter at hand and did what had to be done about getting back to England. With so many people displaced because of the war, some dangerous individuals who would think nothing of shooting you for a coin or a horse, we could not allow fear to take hold. Meeting him made me realise that even though I had lost so much, I still had a lot to live for.'

Only then did Tilly begin to realise what a terrible experience it must have been for Florence. Her heart went out to her. She was also aware of a new side to Lord Clifton she had not seen before, of the way he had taken care of Tobias and Florence with a doggedness and determination born of pain and hopelessness that had pushed him to get back home. An immense pity welled up from the bottom of her heart towards this man and Florence, whose sufferings she was beginning to understand.

'I'm so very sorry for what happened to you, Florence, and I'm glad things turned out for the best.'

'So am I. At least I have a roof over my head—although what I'll do when His little Lordship has no further need of me, I shudder to think.'

'Plenty of time for that later,' Tilly said. 'Perhaps Lord Clifton will keep you on as Tobias's nanny?'

Florence's face broke into a wide smile. 'I don't mind telling you I would welcome that.'

* * *

After five long, tedious days of travel they finally arrived in London. Heading for Mayfair where Lord Clifton's cousins, Lord and Lady Marchant, lived, they traversed the streets that were congested and noisy with traffic of every description. London was a city made up of theatres, churches, palaces and lovely parks, the skyline dominated by the twin towers of Westminster Abbey.

The river was a busy waterway, with barges and wherries and boats of every description scurrying up and down like busy beetles. The darker side of the city, where squalor abounded, was made up of gin houses and brothels, where thieves and prostitutes, clerks and thieves rubbed shoulders with members of the nobility looking for less refined entertainment. It was a city of the destitute, of piles of rotting rubbish, but it was also a city of vibrancy and splendour that was the unique essence of London.

Not until they reached the more salubrious area of Mayfair did the roadways become quieter. On finding the house of Lord Marchant, they were informed by his butler that Lady Marchant was not in the best of health so Lord Marchant had taken her to their estate in the country. With that, they had no option other than to go to Charlotte's house in Chelsea village. When Charlotte had received Charles's letter in Devon, asking them to return to London forthwith, she had written to her housekeeper instructing her to have rooms prepared for their arrival.

The house was a large three-storey red brick Queen Anne house with Dutch gables. It was a large comfortable residence close to the river. To the rear was a coach house and stables and a well-planted substantial garden. Once inside, with Tobias nestled against her shoulder wrapped in a shawl and sound asleep, Florence followed the housekeeper and Daphne up the stairs where a room was prepared.

As soon as Charles arrived and called her name, Tilly flew into his arms. After giving her a welcoming hug, then holding her at arm's length, he laughed on seeing her sunburnt face.

'Well, just look at you. Devon clearly suited you.'

'It did, Charles, and I simply love Drayton Manor, as did Aunt Charlotte. It's a lovely old house. You should see it. It's perfect.'

'I don't doubt that. But it's a long way from London.'

'I do so hope you won't sell it. It's close to the sea and the most delightful villages,' she enthused. 'In fact, Charles, I would very much like to live there—if you permit it and keep the house.'

Charles stared at her as if she had taken leave of her senses. 'Live there—permanently? I think you're suffering from too much sun, Tilly. Your place is here—with your family.'

'We'll talk about it later—Aunt Charlotte also loves it down there. We could live there together, but come and see her,' she said, taking his hand and pulling him into the drawing room to greet Aunt Charlotte.

Tilly was proud of her brother. Tall and slim, with deep blue eyes and terribly good-looking, he appeared every inch the successful businessman, which he indubitably was, which the smile he cast on his two favourite people seemed to say.

Aunt Charlotte's face was wreathed in delight as she watched her nephew stride into the room. 'Charles! I can't tell you how good it is to see you at last.'

The following ten minutes were taken up with excited chatter—mostly from Tilly as she told her brother all she had learned about Devon. He was quite happy to listen until the distinct cry of a baby was heard coming from the upper regions of the house.

For a moment silence reigned, then, looking up as if he expected the perpetrator of the cry to materialise through the ceiling, he said, 'Would either of you care to explain why there is a screaming baby in the house?'

Aunt Charlotte looked at Tilly perched on the edge of the sofa. The moment when she would have to inform Charles about their tiny guest could not be put off any longer.

'His name is Tobias, Charles. He is five months old and the nephew of Lucas Kingsley, the Earl of Clifton. Lord Clifton was deeply concerned about the child's safety and asked if we could bring him with us to London.'

Charles stared at her in disbelief. 'Are you completely mad?'

'Not at all. We have our reasons for bringing him here. If you will sit down and listen, I will tell you.'

Which she did as well as she could, while her brother stared at her wide-eyed, trying to take in what she was telling him.

'I cannot believe you have done this,' Charles said flatly when she had finished. 'It was a blasted foolish thing to do. I don't know what possessed you to agree to it.'

'The child was in danger, Charles…'

'From his own uncle? What manner of man would threaten his own nephew—a baby, for heaven's sake?'

'A man as wicked as Jack Price.'

Charles drew himself up out of the chair in frustration, combing his fingers through his hair. 'You have gone too far, Tilly. I sent you to Devon in the hope that you would see the error of your ways over that sordid affair with Richard Coulson—the scandal is still raging, by the way—and you come back with fantastical tales of smugglers and kidnappings.'

'Just the one kidnapping,' Tilly interjected.

'Don't be flippant. It doesn't matter how many. Here we are with a baby to take care of—the nephew of a man none of us has ever heard of.'

'He knows William—at least he has heard of him.'

'Of course he has. William is the Marquess of Elvington, for heaven's sake. Everyone in England and beyond has heard of him.'

'Please, Charles, don't be cross. I know when you sent me to Devon you were only trying to protect me, but I can't bear to think of it. I realise now that I was wrong and stupid and I'm sorry for all the trouble I've caused, but please be reasonable about this. Lord Clifton needed our help at a difficult time. We could not refuse to help him.'

'In fairness to Lord Clifton, Charles,' Aunt Charlotte said quietly, 'he belongs to an important and highly revered family in Devon, whose ancestry is as proud and impressive as that of the Lancasters, with a noble pile to equal that of Cranford. Lord Clifton has suffered greatly recently—losing both his parents at sea followed closely by his beloved sister in Spain. Tobias is the only member of his immediate family he has left.

'The man is desperately trying to get some normality back into his life, but he is bedevilled by the child's paternal uncle—a violent individual who threatens the child's existence. Lord Clifton is to come to London himself shortly. Until then I ask you to bear with the situation.'

'How old is Lord Clifton, Aunt Charlotte?'

'Oh, I wouldn't know—perhaps twenty-eight or nine.'

Charles looked at his sister. 'And you have become friendly with Lord Clifton, Tilly? How friendly?'

Tilly flushed a delicate shade of raspberry. 'A...a little. He...invited us to dine one evening, along with other guests.'

Charles scowled. Always protective of his sister, he had a proprietorial air as he regarded her and was not prepared to see another philanderer such as Richard Coulson take advantage of her. 'Aunt Charlotte will know better than I what mischief you have been up to in Devon, Tilly.' When the flush deepened on her cheeks, he added, 'I think you have developed a special interest in this gentleman.'

'We...saw each other on occasion. Lord Clifton and Uncle Silas were good friends.'

'Lord Clifton is also a handsome devil,' Aunt Charlotte said with a low chuckle, 'and has the charm to match. Any young woman would be flattered by his attention—and those not so old,' she muttered to herself.

Charles considered what she had said for a moment, then gave a philosophical sigh. 'Very well. Where the child is concerned, I can hardly turn him out on to the streets, can I? But I will have a few choice words to say to this gentleman when I meet him—if he turns up before I have to leave for India. Lord knows what William is going to say to all this. He will not be best pleased.'

'Thank you, Charles,' Tilly said, throwing her arms about his neck. 'I knew you would understand when I explained it all—and I'm sure William will be just as understanding as you are. We intend having a couple of days here before travelling to Cranford. Will you come with us?'

'Not immediately,' Charles replied, beginning to relax and looking at his sister fondly. 'But I will if I have the time—which shouldn't be a problem since the voyage to India has been delayed. I would like to spend a little time with you before I have to leave.' He caught her in a warm embrace. 'I'm so glad you came back. I'm so used to having you around. I missed your funny face. What am I going to do without you in India?'

In the brilliant sunshine of a lovely July day, Tilly gazed out of the coach window at Cranford's splendid façade. She had only been away a few weeks, but she had missed the warmth of the family to be found within.

They were welcomed warmly by William and Anna. There was a great deal of fuss as they settled in and explanations to be made regarding Tobias. William was concerned while Anna took it all in her stride and Tobias was soon ensconced in the nursery with Thomas.

Tilly soon fell into a daily routine of pleasurable country pursuits and assisting Anna with her many charitable works.

After an invigorating ride out with Anna, the two sat on the terrace overlooking the garden, a tea tray in front of them. Tilly took great pleasure in her friendship with her sister-in-law. Tilly had made many friends when she had been at the academy, but since she had left, Anna was the closest friend she had. She found she could talk to her sister-in-law freely and she was sure she felt the same about her. Although Anna was three years older, they shared the same pleasures in life.

'I'm so glad you're back, Tilly,' Anna said, pouring the tea and handing a cup to Tilly before helping herself to a dainty piece of cake. 'We've missed you—especially William. He does so enjoy your company.'

'William has you, Anna. Never have I seen a married couple who are so absurdly happy. You make a splendid case for the married state.'

Anna laughed, flicking cake crumbs off her lap. 'It is truly a happy state to be in, Tilly, and the fact that we fought so hard to achieve it only makes me appreciate it more. I feel a love so strong for William and Thomas that it scares me. I hope one day you will feel it for yourself.'

'Yes—perhaps one day,' Tilly said, envying Anna her happiness.

'Tobias is a lovely child, Tilly—and Florence is so good with him. It's such a tragedy what happened to his parents—although his uncle obviously cares for him.'

'Yes, he does. Lord Clifton and Lady Cassie were very close.'

'And this Lord Clifton?' Anna said with a curious light in her eyes. 'Do you find him handsome, Tilly?'

'I think some would consider him so,' she answered with an artificially bright smile.

'That wasn't what I asked you. Do *you* find him handsome?'

'Yes—yes, I do.' She sighed, taking a sip of her tea as she watched one of the peacocks strut across the lawn beneath the terrace, trailing its exotic feathers behind him. 'We were getting on so well—and then I had to leave.'

'Did you tell him about what happened—with Richard Coulson?'

'No. I—I didn't want to spoil things.'

'I see. Well, if he cares for you, it shouldn't matter.'

'Perhaps not, but I couldn't tell him.'

Anna studied her calmly. 'I think you care for Lord Clifton more than you are letting on, Tilly. Tell me about him.'

Once Tilly had begun her confidence, she seemed unable to stop. She told Anna about their volatile first encounters and how, as they had got to know each other better, she had begun to see a different side to him and a new accord had grown between them.

'Charles was right when he told me that nothing good comes of a woman who falls short of society's expectations. I broke the rules and I really don't know how I'm going to move on from it, least of all tell Lord Clifton.'

'You didn't break all the rules.'

'No—maybe not all of them. Although everyone believes I did. In a fit of spite, because I refused his proposal of marriage, Richard Coulson let everyone believe the worst of me.'

'When Lord Clifton comes to London for Tobias, if

he has a mind to take things further in your relation-ship, Tilly, will you tell him?'

'I don't know. I honestly don't think I can.'

'Better coming from you than someone else. There is still gossip.'

Tilly looked at her beseechingly. 'I don't think I can manage to do that, Anna,' she said at last.

'He will be arriving shortly to take Tobias away. William received a letter from him explaining the reason why he begged your help in the unfortunate matter. But, what of you, Tilly? What is it *you* want?'

Tilly fixed her gaze on the peacock once more. 'I knew you would ask me that and the answer is, I don't know.'

'Can you not wait and see what happens? See what the day brings when he comes for Tobias? You really like him, don't you, Tilly?'

She nodded. Her parting from Lord Clifton had been like a pain in her heart, a pain mingled with an odd sort of longing. She dared not call it love. In another woman she would think it foolish, yet this feeling had such a hold on her heart.

'I think if I am not careful, he will break my heart. There was a woman in his life some time ago. I don't know what happened, but when it ended, he never got over it, apparently.'

'He has spoken to you about this woman?'

'Not much—and it is not my place to ask him. But… how can I live with a man who mourns the woman he still loves?' A man who, she thought, because of that one tragic experience, now considered marriage to any other woman a convenience—without love.

'When he comes for Tobias he will return to Devon. I've asked Charles to keep Drayton Manor on, to let me live there—me and Aunt Charlotte, who loves Devon. I would still see Lord Clifton.'

'And what did Charles say?'

'He will consider it.' Placing her cup and saucer on the tray in front of them, she looked at Anna and smiled. 'Now enough of Lord Clifton. Tell me what you have planned in the way of entertainment now I'm back.'

Lucas arrived at Cranford Park three weeks after Tilly. He had set off at first light so he could return to London with Tobias and Florence before dark. He was impatient to see Tilly. He had missed her more than he'd thought possible. He couldn't explain it, nor could he understand it, but marriage to Tilly just seemed right, as if it was meant to be. It was not as if he hadn't been looking for a bride anyway, and Tilly was eminently suitable—well-born and well-connected.

Smiling inwardly, he thought he'd hardly behaved like a perfect gentleman, taking advantage of her by kissing her, which would have insinuated in her mind that he wanted to take their relationship further, and, if not, risking her reputation should it become known. Marrying Tilly Anderson was simply the right and honourable thing to do and he had the feeling that she would not need much persuading to accept.

Seeing Cranford in all its splendid magnificence, he could not fail to be impressed. It was fascinating because of its overall effect, not just due to the splendour or beauty of the architecture and the rich golden-yellow stone of which it was built, but because it was enormous, ancient, powerful and beautiful. With dramatic grace, it stood against a backdrop of sweeping lawns and a terraced courtyard.

A smiling Lord Elvington received him as though it were the most natural thing to receive unknown visitors. On arriving in London and going to his club in St James's, he had made discreet inquiries concerning the Marquess of Elvington. His name was not unknown to him, but they had never met.

Everything he was told was favourable. The same was said about his half-brother, Charles Anderson—although it would appear that their sister had got herself into a bit of a tangle some weeks back. Considering it was in her best interests for her to disappear for a while, she had been sent away to spend some time in the country.

Lucas hated gossip and avoided it whenever he could. No doubt it was over something and nothing and Miss Anderson would enlighten him when next they met.

'I have to thank you for the kindness you showed my sister and her aunt in Devon,' Lord Elvington said, handing him a brandy as they sat opposite each other in his study.

'We were neighbours—indeed, Silas and I were friends for a good many years. He was a fine man, a clever man, and he is sadly missed in the community. I am indebted to you for taking care of my nephew. I assumed my cousin Lord Marchant would be at home to care for him. It was indeed kind of Miss Charlotte Anderson to take him in. I explained the unfortunate circumstances of why it was necessary to remove him from Clifton House in my letter—and I am sure your sister and her aunt have filled you in on the matter.'

'Of course. We are happy to help in any way we can. I trust the situation is resolved and it is safe for Tobias to return to Devon?'

'Unfortunately not, but I will take him back with me. I have several matters to take care of in London so I will be there for a while longer.'

'Aunt Charlotte did not accompany Tilly to Cranford. After journeying up from Devon she was tired of travelling and preferred to remain in town. Charles is here…somewhere. You'll meet him later. You are welcome to stay with us overnight and travel back in the morning if you prefer.'

'That's very kind of you. Thank you. That would suit me—although I have to see my lawyers in Oxford. It would help me greatly if Tobias could reside here a few more days until I return. I could travel on to Oxford from here in the morning.'

'That won't be a problem. Make yourself at home. The servants will see to your every need while you are a guest under my roof. I'm afraid my wife has become besotted by Tobias and will be reluctant to see him go. She is in the nursery at present. Come, let us go up. I will introduce you—and I am sure you are impatient to see your nephew.'

'And, Miss Anderson, your sister? Is she at home?' Lucas asked, trying not to sound too eager to speak to her, to feast his eyes on her again, to hear her soft, musical voice and to know the exquisite sensation of being close to her.

Lord Elvington gave him a long, considered look and

then he smiled. 'I believe she is out riding somewhere—spends most of her time on horseback. Perhaps you would like to take a stroll to the stables? She should be back shortly.'

Glad of the opportunity to stretch his legs, Lucas found his way to the two-storeyed stable block and coach houses to the rear of the house, built round a central yard with a huge fountain spouting water up into the sky in the centre. He paused, taking in the activities of the grooms and stable boys, all busy with their tasks.

Turning his attention to the deer park beyond, his eyes lit on the person he was looking for. He had been driven by a ridiculous eagerness to see her. His loins tightened as he recalled the way she had yielded her lips to him in the garden at Clifton House. The sweet desire she had felt for him had been there. She had wanted him, and he had wanted her more than he had ever wanted anything in his life.

Atop a spirited mount, she was cantering across the grass towards the stables, riding expertly in the side-saddle, urging the raw-boned gelding, a glossy chestnut horse, on. She presented a slender figure and it seemed incomprehensible that she could control the great beast, so much stronger and more powerful than Gracie. The groom in the Lancaster livery rode some distance behind, hard pressed to keep up. Her hair beneath her riding hat was loose and rippled gracefully behind her and the long skirts of her riding habit billowed against her horse's flank.

Since parting from her in Devon, it had been a time of great bemusement for Lucas. The longer they were apart and the more she was in his thoughts, the deeper he fell under her spell. Watching her deftly controlling her mount as it frolicked and pranced beneath her, he was reminded of the days they had ridden together, and his heart swelled with tenderness.

He observed her from some distance away, but she was unaware of his presence as she rode into the yard and dismounted, her cheeks as rosy as a delicious apple. Her riding habit was a shade of apple green and simple in its cut, but not even her plain clothing could hide Tilly Anderson's beauty. Her shining hair framed a face of striking, flawless beauty and glowing with health he remembered so well.

His mind drifted back to the times they had been together. How exquisite she had been when she had emerged from the sea that day, with her dress all wet and clinging to her perfect body, her face as pink as a rose in the warm sunlight glinting off the sea, the sight of her making him light-headed, reeling with her sensuality. What a firebrand she was.

Chapter Ten

Tilly had risen early, the sun shining out of a speedwell-blue sky. The torrential rain which had saturated everything the day before had stopped shortly after she had gone to bed. She entered the stable yard—the sight of the horses' heads peering out over the half-stable doors and their soft whickering never failed to excite and cheer her.

She breathed deeply, inhaling the familiar smell of the tack room, of warm leather and saddle soap. She acknowledged the polite, respectful good mornings cast her way by the grooms with a smile and asked for William's horse to be saddled. The groom set about it without question. Miss Anderson was a competent horsewoman and His Lordship allowed her to ride his horse whenever she had a mind.

She had taken her time to enjoy her ride, so it was some time later when she rode into the stable yard. Feeling relaxed and invigorated, she dismounted and handed the horse to a groom. Suddenly, she saw Lord Clifton coming towards her, lean and immaculate. Her heart gave a leap of surprise, consternation and excitement.

He stopped in front of her, wearing a look of uncon-
cealed appreciation on his handsome face, his glorious
blue eyes locked on hers, which, unbeknown to her,
shone with a heart-stopping brilliance. During the time
she had been without him, she had done nothing but
think of him—now they were face to face, all she could
do was stare at him, feeling painfully self-conscious.

There was a silence about them. They stood quite
still in those first few moments, savouring each other,
their eyes seeking the truth, which was what they had
felt for one another when they had kissed was still there.

'Lord Clifton. You take me by surprise.'

'Do you think we could drop the Lord Clifton and you
call me Lucas?'

'If that is what you want.'

'You look well.'

The tone in which it was said brought a warm glow
to her cheeks and her voice trembled a little when she
spoke. 'I am. You have met my brothers?'

'I have met Lord Elvington and his charming wife.
I'm here to take Tobias back to London. I'm staying in
my cousin's house for a couple of weeks or so—I have
several matters of business to take care of. How has
Tobias been? No trouble, I hope?'

'No, he's such a good baby. We…will miss him when
you take him away. How were things in Devon when
you left? Have you managed to do anything about buying the boatyard?'

He nodded. 'Ned Price agreed to the sale. It's going
through.'

'Did he get a chance to see Tobias before we left for
London?'

'He did. He tried hard not to show it, but it was an emotional moment for him. He was closer to Edmund than Jack. His death hit him harder than he cares to admit. The fact that he has a grandson has given him a new lease of life. There will have to be some adjustments made to his will and he doesn't intend losing any time in doing so. How he will deal with Jack is his business. The fact that he said not a word about Tobias has angered him.

'Had I not called on him to offer to buy the boatyard he would have been none the wiser that he had a grandson. What Jack intended to do with Tobias if the kidnap had been successful, I shudder to think. Which brings me to the reason why I had to come to London.'

'Oh? Please,' she said as they left the stables, unsure that she wanted to be privy to his private affairs, 'don't feel that you have to tell me. It is your affair.'

'I would like to tell you. I'm probably jumping the gun, so to speak, but I have to be practical and consider the future logically. It is important that I prepare for every eventuality should anything happen to me.'

Tilly's eyes flew to his in alarm. 'Why? Are you in danger?'

Having no illusions about Jack Price and what he could expect—a bullet or a knife in the back—he nodded. 'I may be—from Jack Price. Until I produce offspring of my own, Tobias is my heir. When Jack Price works it out—which he will—then he will move heaven and earth to get his hands on the Clifton estate through Tobias. He is devious and ruthless and will stop at nothing, even murder.'

'Surely you exaggerate. Jack Price would not go that

far.' As soon as the words had left her mouth, on recalling her own encounters with the smuggler, she acknowledged Lucas had good reason to fear what he would do. She could see and almost feel the tension in his body. He was not a man to lie or exaggerate. It made her suddenly fear for him. 'What precautions will you take to deter him?'

'In case the worst should happen, then I intend to set up a board of trustees to administer the estate until Tobias is of age. I will have to travel to Oxford to see my lawyers.'

'I can understand that. It is a wise move. What about the boatyard? Does Jack Price know you are buying it?'

'He's raised no objections to the sale, although it would be a different matter should he discover I am the one buying it before the sale goes through.'

'Then I hope that everything is finalised before he finds out. Are you travelling back to London today, or has William invited you to spend the night at Cranford?'

'He has, and I was happy to accept. He has been most generous. His wife is more than happy for Tobias to remain here while I travel on to Oxford to meet with my lawyers tomorrow. I shouldn't be gone more than a couple of days. I will be for ever in Lord Elvington's debt for the care he and his family have taken with Tobias.'

'Have you seen him—Tobias?'

'I certainly have. He has grown since I last saw him.' His face became set in serious lines. 'Florence looks better than she has for a while. She has become indispensable to me. Out of our misfortune came the luckiest moment of my life when I met her,' he said quietly, his expression grave, which left Tilly in no doubt as to the strong bond that had developed out of extreme hardship between Lord Clifton and Tobias's nursemaid.

'I imagine it was—and I am sure Florence feels the same. What will you do when Tobias no longer needs her?'

'Keep her on—if that is what she wants. There will always be a place for her at Clifton House—and if I am so blessed, there will be other children to care for in time.' He paused, pronouncing his next words carefully. 'My coming to Cranford to see Tobias is only half the reason.'

'Oh? Then pray tell me what else brings you all this way.'

'To see you—although I thought you might have returned to London to enjoy the short Season and whatever other pleasures are to be had. Are you not sad to have left Devon?'

'Yes, yes, I am, although I am happy now to be at Cranford.'

'I can understand that. When I was in Spain, I, too, knew how it felt to be far away from home.' As he took in a deep, appreciative breath, his gaze did a wide sweep of the house and beautifully landscaped gardens. 'I have to say Cranford Park is quite splendid. I imagine you will be reluctant to leave here for the city—although,' he said, turning to look at her, 'you may be impatient to partake of the frivolities there after your time in Devon.'

She met his gaze, a frown creasing her brow. 'Why on earth would you think that? I thought you understood that I much prefer the country.'

'And it has nothing to do with you getting yourself

into some kind of tangle and your brothers thinking it wise for you to have a spell away from town?'

Alarm shot through Tilly. She stood rigid, fighting against the fear and nausea. He must have heard the gossip. She felt the pain of memory—those awful days following her reckless behaviour with Richard Coulson and the horrible scandal about to burst hanging over her.

'Now you are frowning,' he said. 'You are remembering something unpleasant, I think.'

'Disastrous, more like.'

'As bad as that?'

Taking a deep breath, she stood and faced him. Since he had raised the issue she had hoped to avoid, she realised she could do so no longer. 'Yes, I'm afraid it was. If you know anything at all about London society, you will know there is no surer way for a girl to ruin herself than to take up with a profligate nobleman. No self-respecting gentleman would want to marry her after that.'

He frowned, a growing suspicion in his eyes. 'And that is what happened to you?'

She nodded. 'Yes. Something like that. Charles handled the matter as discreetly as he could—and then decided it would be prudent for me to disappear for a while, which is why I found myself in Devon.' Throwing caution to the winds, she found herself telling him about Richard Coulson, how she had misjudged him and how he had meant to ruin her reputation for rejecting him.

'And he was believed?'

'He's popular, so yes. Everyone believed him because it gave the gossipmongers something to talk about—

and they love to gossip—especially when every word is true.'

Lucas's eyes narrowed below a frown. 'True, you say?'

'Why—yes. I cannot deny my friendship with Richard and every damning word that dripped from his mouth was believed. Besides, he is a man and they'll ignore his part in the nasty affair because he's charming and very rich.'

'Why did you reject him? With your reputation in question, did your brothers not insist that you marry him?'

'No—I had no wish to marry him. I will not be pushed into some misalliance. Marriage was not on my agenda at that time—although,' she said, laughing lightly, 'he did offer me a diamond engagement ring as big as a dinner plate if I accepted him.'

'Was he in love with you?'

'Goodness me, no. He was something of a narcissist—completely in love with himself.'

'And you have returned to London in the hope that your ruination is only temporary?'

'Yes, exactly. London did not smile kindly on me and I left in somewhat of a hurry. Apparently, the scandal hasn't gone away and if I were to appear in society I am sure I would be treated with contempt and condemnation. At all costs I will try very hard to hold on to my dignity. It's true that I am no lady and I hold my place in society through the generosity of my half-brother. At present, my place in society is too insecure for me to risk making any more mistakes.'

Lucas looked down at her. 'Tell me something. Did you enjoy my kiss—when we kissed in the garden at Clifton House?'

She stared at him in bewilderment, thinking it a strange thing for him to ask. He stood there, a perturbed look in his eyes, his mouth in a tight line, and a frown cut a furrow in his brow. What was wrong? Why had he suddenly changed? 'Yes, of course I did. I—I've never felt that way before.'

'Then the young man you say compromised you cannot have been a proficient lover if he neglected to give you pleasure. As for myself, I don't like being played for a fool.'

'I wouldn't do that.'

His frown grew deeper, his mouth grew tighter, and the expression in his eyes was a mixture of reproach and accusation. 'I didn't know you well enough and yet you kissed me—twice, as I recall. Why did you do that?'

'Because I wanted to. In the light of what you've just told me, I'm beginning to think that it was a mistake.'

A deep flush spread over Tilly's cheeks. To her dismay she realised he thought she had done this before, that she and Richard Coulson had been lovers in every sense. But she hadn't. She'd been the recipient of nothing more than a few chaste kisses. She might be prone to scandal, but she wasn't wanton. His expression was unforgiving. There was a silence.

Tilly averted her eyes, never having felt so wretched. She forced herself to look at him, having no trouble reading his expression, and her heart sank. She had been hoping he would look more kindly upon such an admission than its concealment. He was disgusted, yet she could not regret telling him the truth.

Now he knew what she had done, she could not blame him for his reaction, nor had she expected it to hurt quite so much. But she would not be cowed. Stepping away from him, she averted her eyes. If Lord Clifton had decided to judge her and think the worst, then so be it.

'Yes—I agree with you. Goodness me! I didn't expect you to make the ritualistic proposal that follows a kiss.' She glanced at him sharply. 'Please tell me you weren't going to do that.' He remained silent, watching her intently. She laughed mirthlessly. 'You were, weren't you? Well, if it will make you feel any better, I will tell you now that I don't want to marry you—and if you had offered for me I would have respectfully refused.'

His lips twisted in a mirthless smile as he looked down into her deceptively innocent eyes. 'Then it's as well for both our sakes that I didn't make you an offer.'

'Absolutely,' she uttered flippantly, his utter lack of caring causing her heart to squeeze in the most inexplicable way. She longed to say that of course she wanted him to make an offer, but the words wouldn't form. She simply stood looking at him, the familiar ache in her heart. She wanted to reach out to him, but her body stayed still, unbending.

'I am also fresh out of diamonds,' Lucas told her coldly. 'How can I possibly put my life in order and restore some kind of peace to my house if I have to defend my wife's reputation? You have beauty, wit and spirit and you are exciting to be with—I actually *like* being with you, but if your recent scandalous behaviour is anything to go by you will make an abominable wife.'

Her chin lifted in self-defence. 'And you, My Lord, would make an abominable husband. I really don't want to marry you—or anyone else for that matter. I'm not in the market for a husband,' she said, trying to sound as indifferent as he.

'Then you shouldn't have allowed yourself to be compromised. You certainly have a propensity for scandal and a disdain for the rules of society.'

'Oh, dear me,' Tilly uttered mockingly. 'That is bad indeed. I was raised to understand that society makes the rules and if one wants to live among society then life must be lived according to them. I failed at the first hurdle. If you must know, I made an utter fool of myself and I am ashamed because of the hurt it brought to my family. But it's too late now to change that.

'So, you see, you really must look elsewhere for someone to wed. I cannot for the life of me see that you and I have anything in common. You say you like my spirit and find me exciting to be with, but after your severe and unfair condemnation of my character I fail to understand how you can possibly feel that way.'

'Then I ask your pardon. But when you made me aware of your reason for going down to Devon, I had to wonder at your ethics.'

'Then don't,' she cried firmly, uncaring that she was unable to defuse his wrath. 'What I do is none of your business. Yes, I was a silly, naive fool and I make no excuses for becoming involved with Richard Coulson. You have clearly misinterpreted what I said, but that is beside the point now.'

'If I have done so, then perhaps you would care to explain.' He was trying to hold on to his anger.

'No, I do not. You do not have the right to judge or condemn me. Not that it will matter since you will be leaving for Devon shortly so I doubt we will meet again—even if I do decide to return to Drayton Manor in the future. I realise that you must despise me for what I might or might not have done, but that is for you to deal with, not me.'

'I do not despise you, quite the opposite, but what you did no respectable woman would have dreamed of doing—which is a category from which you chose to eliminate yourself when you took up relations with the likes of this…this Richard Coulson,' he said derisively.

Tilly stood before him, straight and erect, as if carved from stone. Her cheeks burned from the casual cruelty of the remark. 'That is condemnation indeed.'

His eyes narrowed, but otherwise he ignored her comment. 'There are times when you remind me of Cassie—when you are angry.'

His tone was sombre while something sad and bleak tugged at her heart, despite his animosity towards her of a moment before. She had forgotten for the moment that his own past was not bereft of tragedy. He was still mourning his sister's death and the woman he had loved in the past still had a hold on him.

Stiffening her spine, she steeled herself and hardened her heart against any sympathetic urges she felt. She didn't want to feel that way lest it weakened her resolve to preserve all her resources for herself. Stepping away from him, she squared her shoulders and lifted her chin.

'And for that very reason I would refuse to be your wife. I am my own person. I think and feel and do what I like. I will not be any man's wife because I bear some resemblance to his sister. You can go to the devil, Lucas Kingsley—and take Richard Coulson with you. When I look in the mirror, I want to see a strong woman, not a victim. My reputation might be in tatters now, but that is my problem. It is certainly not your place to lecture me or to sit in judgement.'

He looked at her, his face sculpted against the brightness of the sun. It was without expression. He seemed remote, untouchable. 'I think you have said quite enough.'

'It is clear to me that because of the scandal I have created, my presence offends you. Since you are to stay the night, to show courtesy to my family we will behave as if nothing untoward has happened between us. You have made it plain that you don't approve of me, but there is no need to turn this into a spectacle.'

As they walked towards the house, the atmosphere between them was charged with a subtle tension. When Tilly had seen him waiting for her at the stables, she had wanted nothing more than for him to take hold of her, to crush her in his arms, to feel his lips on hers once more, but he had done none of that.

A strange, icy calm came over her. Taking a look at the hard planes of his face, the subtle aggression in the line of his jaw, and the clear intent that stared at her from the depths of his deep blue eyes, she felt a slight trembling sensation skitter over her skin. Ignoring it, she looked straight ahead and continued to walk on.

There was a pain in her heart she couldn't identify. All the days leading up to seeing him again she had looked forward to, but now…? Nothing. She had felt excited in a way she had never felt before as something was beginning to grow inside her, something bright and beautiful that filled her heart like a gentle piece of music, soft and sweet that would grow and burst into a crescendo of… What? She tried to identify the elusive feeling inside her, but she couldn't.

She wondered why the thought of losing the man who did not care for her should affect her heart in such a pitiless manner. It was an enigma too complex for her to analyse. And yet it should be simple. She cared deeply for him. He did not care for her. But that was for her head to work out, not her heart, which could only feel the hurt, the pain, the emptiness. And yet the heart still mourned, still grieved.

Reaching the house and seeing Charles in the entrance to the hall, she waved. He came to meet them, shaking Lord Clifton's hand warmly on Tilly's introduction. When they began to indulge in polite conversation, she managed to make her getaway.

For the rest of the day and through dinner Tilly was reeling between confusion and dread—and more than a little anger because Lucas had been so ready to judge her. Where she was concerned, his eyes were always guarded. They were polite with one another, pleasant even, both of them doing their best to begin the process of making something of being together under William's roof.

Whatever illusions Tilly might have had where Lucas was concerned were gone. When she anticipated his visit to Cranford, there had been a soaring of her spirit and excitement had heated her blood. Now she swallowed against an overwhelming sense of loss. The pain of her emotion was sharp. She tamped it down and reminded herself that if his reaction to her fall from grace was what she could expect if she conceded to Aunt

Charlotte's wish and made her debut, then what was the point of it all? She was ruined by her own stupidity.

Maybe she was judging Lucas too harshly. If she told him the whole truth—that her virtue had not been violated—maybe he would no longer feel the disgust she had seen in his eyes when he looked at her. At least then, with time to mull things over, there was the possibility that his attitude would become soft with understanding.

Lucas had much to think about when he left Cranford for Oxford. Tilly's confession, followed by the sense of betrayal he felt, was as powerful as anything he'd ever experienced before. When she had told him about the scandal she had created in London, it had taken a moment for the full significance of her words to sink in. His mind had registered disbelief. It started to shout denial, even while something inside him slowly cracked and began to crumble.

Was she just some shallow little rich girl looking for excitement? No well-bred young lady, who would normally have been seen exclusively among the company of the social elite, would have risked her reputation by indulging in such wanton behaviour that would damage any chance she might have of making a decent marriage. He had to admire her courage, he thought with much bitterness, if not her standards. At least she had been honest.

He'd believed Tilly was different to other women. Discovering that she was not so pure was like being kicked in the gut. It puzzled him that it should make him angry that she could give herself so easily and his anger was exacerbated both by a kind of rage that she should demean herself and by an inexplicable disappointment. He'd been so enamoured by the wonder of her, by her wilfulness and the spirit of her, by her freshness, that he'd been blind to her real nature.

What she had told him touched the part of a man's life that was sacrosanct—his woman—even though she'd never declared herself as such. There could be no kind of relationship, no future for them together with the scandal she had created lying between them like some eternal obstacle. Her weak moral standards left her wanting in his eyes. Everything he'd felt for her, all his expectations of forming some kind of future for them together, left him abruptly. All that remained was a cold, sick rage.

And yet nothing could be softer than those eyes, or softer than that skin, those lips, nothing purer than that face or more exquisite than that form, but that was just a small part of her. He had been hurt by a previous lover, beautiful, treacherous Miranda, who had shown the kind of betrayal her kind were capable of once their love had paled and someone else came along. The experience had left him wary of all women. He had vowed never to fall into the same trap twice.

Lucas's meeting with his lawyers to set up a board of trustees for Tobias should something untoward happen to him was dealt with to his satisfaction. He spent an extra night in Oxford to put other matters affecting his life into perspective. Gradually, his anger towards Tilly diminished and there followed a time of soul searching. There had been so many adversities in his life. Fate had been cruel to him, it had mocked him, but it would not triumph. Fate could be overcome.

He could not escape the fact that Tilly was branded deep inside him and he could not hold out against his need. She had a way of getting under his skin and insinuating herself into his mind and his heart that troubled him. Where she was concerned, he felt the same aching loss he had felt when Miranda left him, followed by the loss of his parents and then again when Cassie had died.

He had reacted to what she had told him very badly and assumed the worst. Now, as though to punish him for his condemnation of her, it was all turned about. Something about what she had said nagged at his mind—that he had misinterpreted what she had told him. How? What had she meant by that? It puzzled him. Had he indeed misconstrued her words?

Guilty or innocent, it no longer mattered. He would not abandon her. If she would have him, he would marry her in spite of everything. After the upheaval of his feelings and emotions he realised at last that he wanted her in his life, that he did not want to lose her.

Would she forgive him? he wondered—that defiant, wilful woman with a spirit and a will to match his own. She was clever, she was lovely and as slick as oil, and yet, for all that, she was as vulnerable as a child. She could not have known what she was doing when she had taken up with Coulson.

Memories of his sister came to mind, of how she had fled to Spain to be with her lover and how he had gone after her to bring her back before she came to harm in a war-torn land. He had failed to do that and the memory of his failure haunted him still.

High-spirited Tilly reminded him of Cassie. With this scandal hanging over her, her future looked bleak. He could not let that happen to her. He would not abandon her. He would go to her and fall to his knees if need be and beg her forgiveness.

The hour was late when Lucas arrived at Cranford. The ladies had retired, but William and Charles were seated before the fire in the library enjoying a late-night glass of William's excellent brandy. They insisted Lucas join them. He had never known the companionship of brothers and he envied them their closeness.

The three of them talked companionably about their various business interests and Charles's imminent departure for India, and they showed a particular interest in the smuggling operations in Devon and Tobias's future. Having discussed these topics at length, they turned their attention to what was uppermost in all their minds—Tilly. Charles was hoping she'd return to London with him.

William propped his feet on the low table between them, loosening his cravat. 'She's reluctant, Charles. Accept it. She really doesn't want to go and I'm quite happy for her to remain here. Your aunt will be disappointed, I expect, but there's no point in forcing her into the maelstrom of society until she's ready.'

'Perhaps she's afraid of meeting the young man who damaged her reputation,' Lucas remarked casually, swirling his brandy round the bowl of his glass.

Surprised, Charles stiffened as if he were trying to withstand a physical blow. 'She told you about Coulson—the scandal that ensued?'

'Yes, she did.'

'Then…you must have become…close, for her to do that. It's not something she likes to hear mentioned, let alone discussed. Coulson is a rake of the first order, for God's sake. Tilly did not lose her virtue—if that's what she told you—but when she rejected him, he spread malicious gossip about her wantonness and laughed about it with his friends. He was believed.

'When I found out I wanted to strike out at him for what he had done to my lovely, vulnerable sister. From the moment she was born I have never stopped thanking God for the gift of her, for the beauty of her, the joy of her. And now Richard Coulson has brought her to this. I am not a violent man by nature, Lord Clifton, but when it comes to something as serious as this—when a damned reprobate has intentionally damaged Tilly's reputation, then I can be as outraged as the next man. I could kill him for this.'

William looked at his brother with concern. 'Don't upset yourself, Charles—and for God's sake don't suggest she goes with you to India. I've worked for the Company in India, don't forget. You'll have enough to take care of without a wilful sister hanging on to your coat tails.'

'Where is this Coulson to be found?' Lucas asked.

Charles shook his head. 'As to that I can't say. He disappeared weeks ago. I heard he'd gone for an extended tour of the Continent.'

'He proposed marriage to her?' Lucas asked.

'Yes—although we never knew how serious he was. We couldn't consider it, of course. Coulson is a philanderer—a reprobate. He would have made her life a misery. We couldn't allow that, not for Tilly. She was not yet nineteen and she was to make her debut—have a Season. The whole of London would have been at her feet.

'Coulson—with an inflated opinion of himself—took that from her, making her the victim of malicious tongues. She was young, vulnerable, wilful and when he gave her his attention she was flattered and besotted as any innocent young woman would be by the attentions of such a handsome, well-favoured young man.

'I've always looked out for her, and when it wasn't me, then Aunt Charlotte or William when he came back from India. Collectively, we failed. She fell prey for the first dissolute character that came along. That beautiful girl was put in such an impossible situation by him that we felt compelled to send her away—hence her departure for Devon.'

'Where she met me,' Lucas remarked quietly. 'Why on earth did she lead me to believe her virtue had been taken from her?'

'Lord knows! I've ceased wondering how my sister's mind works. If you offended her when you believed the worst and you want to make amends, you must apologise to her—and hope she'll accept it. But then again, she might very well tell you to go to the devil.'

Lucas grimaced. 'She already has.'

'The gossip is proving hard to get rid of,' William said. 'It's been blown out of all proportion. We hoped that by the time she came back from Devon it would have died and some other unfortunate would have become the topic of malicious tongues. I hate to think of the damage and the heartache this has caused her. Before she met Coulson, she was like any other young lady looking forward to her debut.'

'I will not stand idly by while our sister's name is sneered at and pulled apart,' Charles declared, his lips tight with anger. 'I hate to be going off to India and leaving her like this.'

'Then allow me to offer a solution before you go that far,' Lucas said.

The two brothers looked at him. 'How?' they asked in unison.

'Since my arrival at Cranford I have been a detached observer, but I am not inexperienced in dealing with the female mind—my sister was very much like Tilly. However, your sister has right on her side. The way I see it is simple. Her name has been unfairly besmirched. She no longer has the desire to make her debut into society, yet she cannot hide herself away—that would be a scandal in itself.'

'Then what is it you suggest?' Charles asked.

'That she gives the gossips something to gossip about. Instead of retreating from the battlefield, she takes the initiative…and marries me.' The brothers stared at him in astonishment.

As Lucas watched their reaction to his suggestion, now that he had admitted to himself his desire to marry Tilly, he wanted her with an urgency that was almost irrational. The desire she ignited in him every time they met was eating at him like a fire licking at his insides. He wanted her so badly that he ached with it.

His growing need for her made him feel vulnerable and uneasy, for he knew from past experience how vicious, how treacherous, the female sex could be. Despite this, he could not stop himself from wanting her and his firm hope was that she would want him, too.

'You would do that?' Charles said, looking at him, his piercing eyes alive with anticipation.

'I would. Marrying Tilly was very much on my mind before she left Devon, but there was so much going on in my life—having just returned from Spain, having lost my sister, Tobias to take care of and a damned smuggler out for my blood. I was shaken when she implied she and Coulson had been lovers.'

'And now you know the truth.'

'I do—although I had become so enamoured of your sister that I had decided to set her lapse from grace aside. As her guardians it is the correct thing for me to ask your permission to marry her.'

William nodded slowly, thinking it over. 'At present it would stop the gossip that will surely ruin Tilly if it carries on much longer. There are many kinds of persecution that are not readily apparent, such as the whispered conjectures, the gossip and subtle innuendoes that can destroy a reputation and inflict a lifetime of damage.'

'Which marriage to me will put an end to. I have much to offer her. My name, my title and an estate that has belonged to the Cliftons for generations. I would have it remain so for many more generations.'

'Do you have feelings for Tilly?' Charles asked.

Lucas nodded. 'I have come to have a high regard for her—and, yes, I adore her.'

William gave him a considering look. 'So—you have come to realise what a dear, sweet girl she is.'

Lucas laughed softly. 'I would not describe Tilly as

sweet. It didn't take me long to appreciate that that high-minded woman is the most exasperating female I have known in my entire life—although she only comes a close second to my dear, departed sister. Tilly is also the woman I want for my wife.'

Charles, having taken special note of the way Lord Clifton's gaze had lingered tenderly on his sister momentarily before he had left for Oxford, was not surprised by this. 'And Tilly? How do you think she will react when she knows you want to marry her? Has it not occurred to you that she might very well turn you down?'

'It has, but I am confident she can be persuaded. I care for her—more than I have ever cared for any other woman, which is why I want her to be my wife. I want to marry her as soon as it can be arranged.'

William nodded and looked at his brother. 'What are your thoughts, Charles? Do we give this gentleman permission to wed our wilful, spirited, troublesome yet adorable sister?'

'Gladly—although I must insist you woo her first, to observe all proprieties. We don't want to intimidate her, nor do we want to do anything that might exacerbate the situation with society. Let people see you together before you announce your betrothal. When it's announced, I have no doubt it will be received with tremendous shock.'

'Four weeks,' Lucas stated.

'Four weeks?' Charles gasped. 'But surely that's too soon.'

'Three weeks is the time it will take for the banns to be called.' Lucas smiled, catching Charles's eye. 'You are due to leave for India shortly. Do you think Tilly would not want her brother to be present on her wedding day?'

'Yes, I suppose there is that. I shall have to extend my leaving if it can be arranged.'

'I also have to return to Devon. There are important matters that need my personal attention.'

'It will certainly give society something else to talk about,' William remarked, draining his glass.

'This is quite splendid,' Charles enthused, crossing to the sideboard. 'Now that's out of the way, I think a toast is in order—and we will sit and discuss the kind of wedding we want for Tilly—along with the terms of the betrothal and the dowry.'

Picking up the decanter of brandy, he filled their glasses, already thinking how much easier it would be for him to go to India without the worry of Tilly's predicament hanging over him. 'I pray she looks on you with favour, Lucas, and agrees to be your wife without argument—otherwise we are all going to have dreadful headaches in the morning without anything to show for it.'

The following morning found Tilly up with the lark and riding over Cranford's luscious acres. She loved to ride through the park when the dew was heavy on the grass and the deer were grazing nearby.

As he had done on his arrival at Cranford, Lucas walked to the stables, hoping to meet her on her return. He was not disappointed. Her ride concluded, she was on her way back to the house.

He'd paused, as if distracted, and turned his gaze

to the beautiful panorama that stretched out as far as the eye could see. He was already lost in his thoughts.

As she slowly approached him, Tilly studied him. For a man of such herculean stature, he had an elegant way of moving. Wearing a dark green coat, his long legs were once again encased in biscuit-coloured trousers and highly polished dark brown riding boots.

His hair was dishevelled from the breeze, the black curls brushing the edge of his collar. The sun illuminated his bold, lean profile and that aquiline nose that gave him a look of such stark, brooding intensity. His mouth seemed hard and grim. She watched him raise his hand and, as he absently rubbed the muscles at the back of his neck, her treacherous mind suddenly thought of the exquisite pleasure he would make her feel were his hand to caress her in that way.

On the times they had been together she had made no effort to know the man who lived beneath the surface of the man who dwelt there, who had seen her as a future bride, a woman he could wed before, like a silly girl, she had told him of her association with Richard Coulson, leaving him to believe her virtue was no longer intact. How could she have done that? It had mattered to him. She should have seen that, instead of seeing only how it affected her and had taken offence.

Her heart suddenly swelled—with what? Admiration? Affection? Love? No, not that. She could never love a man who was in love with another woman. Could she? However hard she tried, she couldn't help but want him. But then, hadn't Aunt Charlotte once told her that the heart wasn't always wise when one's body was driven by base desires.

Recollecting herself, she shook away such thoughts. She was being an utter fool romanticising Lucas Kingsley, simply because he was a handsome man, sleek and fierce as a bird of prey and incredibly skilled in arousing her desire—and because she was a spineless idiot who was disgustingly and helplessly attracted to him.

Becoming aware of her approach, he turned and looked at her. Her cheeks were flushed and her eyes glowed from her ride. 'At last,' he said. 'I was beginning to think I would never get you alone. I thought I would have seen you at breakfast.'

'I like to ride early. I heard you were back. You are leaving for London shortly, taking Florence and Tobias with you. It is doubtful we will see each other again.' She was doing her best to hold in the resentment she felt, to be dignified, as a lady of her class would be, but it was very hard and her expression was softening.

'And that pleases you—that you and I will part without resolving our differences?'

'Really, Lucas,' she said, walking round him and proceeding to walk on, 'I cannot for the life of me think what else you and I have to say to one another.'

'I disagree. I merely want to talk with you privately for a few moments. After all that has happened, I thought it especially needful before I leave Cranford.'

'Why on earth would you think that? What is the point?'

Deeply moved by her outburst, Lucas took hold of her arm and turned her to face him. 'Tilly, please stop this. I am sorry if I upset you when you told me about Coulson. I should have been more understanding—but I am not your enemy.'

'No? Then what are you?'

'The man who wants to marry you.'

A silence fell between them that could be sliced with a knife. Tilly stared at him through eyes huge with shock and disbelief. 'Marry me? You *want* to marry me?'

'That is what I said. Is it so strange that I want you to be my wife?'

'Yes, yes, it is when I think of the harsh words we exchanged before you left for Oxford. I told you that I didn't want to marry you or anyone else come to that."

'It was a misunderstanding, Tilly.'

'But—but why do you want to marry me? Isn't that a bit extreme? It's quite ridiculous.'

'I see nothing ridiculous about a man asking a woman to be his wife. I have approached your brothers on the matter and they think it's a splendid idea— providing I court you in the proper manner of course.'

'I would have to go to London?' He nodded. 'I'm trying to avoid being seen, remember,' Tilly retorted cuttingly. 'What will everyone say when we suddenly appear together?'

He grinned. 'They'll see how weak you are, that you find it impossible to resist my manly charms.'

She looked at him coolly. 'Don't flatter yourself— and don't you think you should seek Aunt Charlotte's favour first?'

'I don't think your aunt will raise any objections and will be happy to combine forces if it stills the gossip.'

'You mean I'm not completely ruined?'

'Not if you marry me.'

'I recall you telling me in no uncertain terms that

you didn't want to marry me,' she said with cool dignity, lifting her chin and stiffening her spine.

'That was then. This is now. The way I see it, you have been unfairly maligned.'

'Thank you for your concern,' she remarked with heavily laden sarcasm, 'if it is genuine. You didn't think so before.'

'That was partly down to you leading me to believe the worst. I realise that I have done you a terrible injustice—but I still cannot understand why you did that.'

'No, neither can I,' she said, her mood beginning to soften. 'It was very stupid of me; I know that now. At the time I think I wanted you to think I was sophisticated and more experienced than my nineteen years. It was wrong of me. I suppose my brothers told you the truth.'

'They did, but it didn't make any difference. I had time to think in Oxford and I realised that I want you in my life. I'd already decided that I wanted to marry you before I reached Cranford.'

Gazing at the cool, dispassionate man standing before her, looking so powerful, aloof and completely self-assured, Tilly managed a nervous little laugh. 'It would seem that you and my brothers have it all arranged. Pity you didn't think to ask me first. Is it pity or guilt that has prompted you to ask me?'

He shook his head, knowing she would suspect that—and as proud as she was, her pride would make her oppose him. 'Neither. I care enough about you to be hurt by the dreadful way you have been treated by society. You do not deserve that.'

'No, I don't—but please do not feel under any obligation to marry me.'

'I don't. It just so happens that I want to marry you. That aside, I am offering you a lifeline, to enable you to hold up your head in society and not have to listen to the slights and slurs, the whispers and jeers. I ask you to put aside any objections you might have of marrying me and see marriage to me as a way forward, otherwise...'

'Otherwise?'

'You will be terribly unhappy—as I will be.'

'And you expect me to be grateful for your generosity? You speak of marrying me as if you're discussing a business arrangement—without any feeling or emotion, without even the pretence of...'

'Of what, Tilly? Of love?' His eyes suddenly became warm as his hands went to her shoulders and he drew her near, his voice low and seductive. 'I find myself attracted to you. When we are apart I think of you all the time. It just so happens that I want you, Tilly—you cannot condemn me for that—and I know you want me. We have wanted each other every time we have been together. You are beautiful, innocent and courageous, passionate and stubborn—and I hope you will forgive my wrongdoings and get to like me.'

Feeling perilously close to tears, Tilly dropped her gaze, unable to absorb the amazing revelation that he was actually attracted to her. 'I can understand your reaction when I told you about Richard Coulson, but I acted in all innocence, unmindful of propriety and plain good sense.

'I liked Coulson when we first met,' she whispered. 'After a while I couldn't stand the sight of him and couldn't wait to be rid of him. It would seem that I have poor judgement in the matter of men. Maybe I should change my mind about considering marriage to you or anyone other man for that matter.'

'Tilly,' he said softly, 'you have no choice if you want to come out of this with your reputation intact. Come, let me look at you,' he cajoled gently. When she complied by raising her head, his brows gathered in perplexity. The tears glistening in the long, silken lashes were hard to ignore. Laying a hand alongside her cheek, he gently wiped away a droplet with his thumb. 'What has happened is not so bad that you should feel a need to cry.'

Embarrassed because she couldn't contain her emotions, Tilly responded with a shake of her head, wiping away the remainder of her tears with the back of her hand in frustration. 'I never cry. It's a silly weakness I could do without.'

'Why? If you are unhappy, it's the most natural thing in the world to cry.'

'I'm not unhappy,' she argued. 'Quite the opposite.'

'That's a relief to hear. Marry me and we'll be ecstatically happy together. I would like us to reach an understanding before I leave Cranford today. As the Earl of Clifton, I have much to offer you, Tilly. I want to give you my name and everything a woman could want. Our wedding will be the likes of which London has not seen in an age and afterwards a grand ball to which everyone who is anybody will want an invite. Before you know it, you will have every distinguished family in London leaving cards and you can thumb your nose at the lot of them and come to Devon with me.'

Chapter Eleven

'You make it sound so easy,' Tilly murmured. He had told her he wanted to give her everything, everything a woman could want—everything but love. She was unable to fathom that cynical remark, because he took her hand and drew her into the shrubbery, away from the sight of prying eyes, his firmly chiselled lips beginning a slow, deliberate descent towards her.

'I'll give you riches beyond anything you've ever dreamed of,' he murmured, his free hand cupping the back of her head and tilting her face up to his for his kiss. 'In return, all you have to give me is yourself.'

Strangely, Tilly thought he was selling himself too cheaply, asking so little of her when he was prepared to give her so much. His eyes peering down at her were like flames of fire, scorching her. She was astounded at her body's reaction on being held so close to him and she tilted her head to make her lips more accommodating to kiss.

Then he was kissing her face, her cheeks, caressing her lips with his own. His lips moved on hers, the fierceness changing to softness, to the velvet touch of intoxication. An eternity later he pulled his mouth from hers and looked down into her eyes, which were warm and velvety soft.

'Oh, dear,' Tilly murmured, her senses all over the place. 'That was a mistake.'

His lips quirked in a faint smile. 'Then let's make another one.'

As he spoke, he drew her further into the gloom of the shrubbery. His tall figure dark against the shadows, he pulled her to him once more.

Tilly was astounded at her body's reaction to this man. A touch, a kiss, a look and he could rouse her and something rose and shouted for the joy of it. Her heart was pounding in her breast and she could feel his beating against hers to the same rapid rhythm.

She pressed herself close to him, not with fury but with delight, with something she had felt before when he had kissed her, which she knew was the female in her responding to the male in him. It was madness. She made a sound in her throat and she threw back her head in the exultation of the moment.

'You *do* want me, don't you, Tilly?' Lucas said triumphantly, softly, her breath sweet and warm against his mouth as she still clung to him. 'Say it. Your heart beats far too quickly for you to claim uninterest, my love.'

'Yes,' she whispered, 'I do want you, Lucas.' She was dazed, her eyes unfocused with that soft loveliness that comes when a woman is deep in the pleasures of love, her senses completely overruled by this magic that had sprung up between them. Cupping her chin, he began to kiss her face, her eyelids, her cheeks. Her lips trembled as she claimed them fiercely with his own.

'My God,' he whispered hoarsely, his blue eyes even deeper in the gloom as he looked at her upturned face. 'You are the most beautiful, wilful woman I have ever met, traits I admire in any woman. But you are also so lovely and desirable. Do you enjoy being kissed?'

Regardless of all the raw emotions quivering through her, Tilly gave him a wobbly smile. 'Yes, but I'm not used to being kissed twice in one day.'

'You must expect to be kissed more than that if you consent to being my wife. For the present, I will try to control my urges.' He gave her the ghost of a smile. 'But it will be no easy matter.' For a moment neither of them spoke, then he said, 'I promise you I will not take advantage of you. For now, you are quite safe from me.'

May God help her, she did not wish to be safe from him. As he turned his head away, she wanted to beg him to kiss her like he had a moment before, to ignore all his good intentions, but he was already drawing her out of the gloom.

Emerging into the open once more, they continued to walk on in silence.

Tilly went through a great deal of deliberation and heart searching, deciding that, with cool calculation, marriage to Lucas might not be so terrible after all. She could hardly believe how deep her feelings were running and the joy coursing through her body melted the core of her heart. The feeling was so strong there was no room for anything ese. Ever since their first meeting they had moved towards this end and now there was no doubt in her heart.

Lucas represented security and a release from the gnawing fear and uncertainty of being shoved into an alliance with a stranger. But it was all so sudden. Was she about to give in too quickly? Could it be? Could it work? It was, as yet, only a whisper inside her, but it was growing, becoming more insistent. She allowed the whisper to extend to the hope that Lucas might one day feel for her what he had felt—might still feel—for that other woman he had once fallen in love with.

On reaching the house, Tilly stopped walking and turned to him. 'You said you wanted the matter settled before you have to go to London.'

'That is what I want. May I have your answer? Will you marry me, Tilly?'

She kissed him then. That was her answer. 'I hope I can make you happy, Lucas. I think I can.'

Lucas raised her hand to his lips and kissed the soft white skin of her wrist. 'I have no doubts about that. What do you think? Are we compatible?'

'Yes. Yes, I believe we are. You have twisted my emotions from the very first.'

An incredibly tender smile flitted across his lips. 'I adore you, Tilly. It's as simple as that.'

'I see,' Tilly exclaimed, unable to believe the evidence of her eyes. But there it was for her to see, the powerful emotions that moved him. She could hear it in the vibrant tones of his voice. Hardly daring to believe what her heart told her, a frisson of delight shot through her, her own feelings revealed by the bright flush on her cheeks. His arms closed around her; his lips brushed hers.

When they parted, he glanced towards the double doors of the great house and, seeing the three figures standing there, he laughed. 'I see we have a reception committee. Are you ready to face your family and tell them what we have decided?'

'Yes. Let's do it.'

'I am surprised,' William remarked as he watched Lord Clifton walk towards them with Tilly on his arm. 'Who would have thought our sister would make such a grand match? Even if it did come about in an unorthodox fashion. What do you think of the Earl of Clifton, Charles?'

'I am impressed by him. He is well-born, titled—an old and venerated title. He is rich and honourable, and if what we have just witnessed is to be believed, Tilly is enamoured of him. I believe he will treat her well.'

William nodded. 'Then with all that to recommend him, I have no objections to a marriage between them. With the scandal still running, it would solve the problem of what to do about a Season for Tilly.'

'That's all very well,' Anna said, having listened with interest to the conversation between the brothers, 'but does Tilly love him?'

Charles looked at her. 'Yes, Anna, I believe she does.'

'Then she must marry him.'

William cast his wife a loving look. 'To my darling wife, Charles, love is the mainspring of any marriage. Without love she is convinced a marriage cannot survive.'

Charles smiled. 'Then it would be prudent to take note of those pearls of wisdom, dear Brother. As for myself, I will never know—not for the foreseeable future anyway. When I finally set sail for India, I would like nothing better than to see my dear sister happily married and tucked away—out of mischief—in Devon, before I go.'

'And Drayton Manor?' William asked. 'Have you decided what you are going to do with it?'

'Not yet. At some point I will go and take a look at it myself. I know Aunt Charlotte grew rather fond of the house when she was there and has fallen completely in love with Devon. I believe she will be quite happy to return and to continue living there for the present.'

'And with Tilly living nearby,' Anna said, 'she will have her darling niece for her neighbour.'

Everyone was delighted at the way things had turned out. It was suggested that since Cranford had its own chapel the ceremony could be performed there. But Lucas intended for it to be a large affair and, since the guests were mainly centred in London, it was decided that they would be married at St George's Church in Hanover Square with the wedding breakfast and ball to follow at the Lancaster town house. No expense was to be spared.

With business matters to attend to in town, Lucas had left Cranford, accompanied by Florence and Tobias. Tilly and Charles had followed a day later to inform Aunt Charlotte of the latest developments.

Tilly found that she had very little time in which to think during those heady days in London. Every minute seemed crammed with activities. It was a happy time. Tilly's feelings were too newly acknowledged to be the firm bond that would develop over time. She and Lucas trod an uncertain path, learning about each other, and there were still some dark areas that lurked in the shadows—Tobias's future being one of them and how to keep him and Lucas safe from Jack Price. The other dark cloud that bedevilled Tilly was Lucas's past love. Did he still harbour feelings for her? It was something that must be confronted eventually, but for the time being, she was too happy not to let that or anything else spoil her world.

Aunt Charlotte had been surprised and highly delighted when she was told that Lucas and Tilly were to be married and in no time at all, although she would have liked a little longer to prepare for it.

'There really is so much to do,' she said when they all sat around drinking tea on the terrace of her lovely house in Chelsea village. 'If it is to be the grand affair you intend, then a guest list has to be drawn up before the wedding invitations can be sent out and there are the menu and the flowers to be taken care of—not to mention Tilly's bridal gown. Really, Lord Clifton, it is obvious you have never been married, otherwise you would know it is virtually impossible to arrange a wedding on a scale that befits the sister of the Marquess of Elvington in four weeks. And do not forget that we have bridesmaids to find and dresses to be made.'

'I don't see why that should be a problem,' Tilly said. 'There are children in abundance among your close friends to choose from who might like a trip up the aisle.'

'Yes, of course, although I still think more time is needed,' her aunt argued.

'Really, Aunt Charlotte,' Tilly said, laughing softly. 'You are one of the most competent and capable women I know. I have every confidence that you will cope splendidly. I will help, too, don't forget—and William's secretary. He will assist us in the preparations and knows how to go about getting things done.'

'Very well,' Aunt Charlotte conceded, knowing everyone's mind was made up about an early wedding and there was no point arguing, but she insisted on the requisite rituals of courtship with equanimity until the wedding and chaperoned Tilly wherever she went.

'There is bound to be a great deal of speculation as to why Tilly has skipped her coming out,' she remarked, 'but you, Lord Clifton, are exactly the kind of bridegroom that all young ladies enter the marriage market for—which is precisely what it is—to catch a titled and wealthy husband. When they see that Tilly has managed to achieve what many young ladies have failed to do, they and their ambitious parents will turn green with envy.'

'But I have no desire to go anywhere before the wedding, Aunt Charlotte. I'm simply not ready to face everyone just yet.'

'Yes, you are,' Lucas countered. 'You have to do it some time. I have every faith in you.'

'I can't do it,' she said, throwing up her arms in despair. 'I simply cannot.'

'Yes, you can.' He spoke in a tone that brooked no argument.

'And it doesn't concern you that I shall be flayed alive by malicious tongues?'

Unbelievably, he laughed outright at that. 'Not a bit. From the conversation I've had with your brothers concerning your behaviour before you ran away and sought sanctuary in Devon, then you deserve it,' he joked, knowing as he said it that she would rear up in indignation. He wasn't disappointed.

His remark made her cheeks flame. 'I did not run away,' she retorted adamantly.

'No?' he said, chuckling softly. 'It sounded very much like it to me.'

It was the sort of thing she would have expected him to say as an act of revenge. 'And I have no doubt that you will enjoy every minute of my suffering.'

Crossing his long legs in front of him, he captured her gaze. 'I may be many things, Tilly, but I am neither cruel nor sadistic. If we are to be married, you have to face society at some point. Since you have a scandal hanging over your head, I suggest the sooner we are seen together the better.

'For your first public appearance since returning to London I've reserved a box at the theatre. We can all go so you will be well chaperoned. There is every chance the scandal will be forgotten when the performance is over.'

Tilly paled at the mention of the scandal. 'I can't. I have no desire whatever to enter society. I can't face anyone just yet.'

'You can and you will,' he said in his determination to convince her of the feasibility and the necessity of the plan. To soften his words, he took her hand and raised it to his lips. 'Take my word for it, you will be a sensation.'

'How can you possibly know that? You are being very stubborn, Lucas, expecting me to do this with no consideration for my feelings.'

Her words were unjust, but Lucas cast them aside

and, when he spoke, the tenderness in his voice was teasing and persuasive. 'I have every consideration for both you and your feelings. It is you who are being stubborn, my love, and if I knew you couldn't do this, I wouldn't put you through it. But you are more than capable of looking every one of your adversaries in the eye and telling them to go to the devil—as you did me on one occasion.'

'Yes, I did—and you deserved it.' Having no wish to argue further, for deep down she knew he was right, and unable to endure his close scrutiny any longer, she shot out of the chair and, ramrod straight, stood apart from him. With a superhuman effort, she took control of her rampaging ire. She looked straight into his enigmatic eyes. 'Going to the theatre to be gawped at in a box by all and sundry is not the solution. It's a nightmare.'

Without another word, she stalked into the house.

Suppressing a smile, Anna placed her cup and saucer on the table and rose. 'Oh, dear. She's still highly sensitive about the whole thing. I'll go and try to calm her down.'

Anna managed to work her magic on Tilly, but not entirely. In the warmth of her bedchamber as she prepared for the theatre, the face that looked back at Tilly in the pier-glass was glowing. Colour flushed her cheeks and her deep violet eyes seemed to have become almost luminous. It was not the heat, but rather the suppressed uneasiness and tension within herself that was responsible.

Standing with William and Charles in the hall, in a moment of stunned silence Lucas saw a vision in a drift of lavender lace coming down the stairs. The neckline of her gown was scooped low, offering a tantalising view of smooth creamy flesh above a minuscule waist.

Her glossy black hair was swept back off her forehead and held in place with a diamond clip, then left to fall artlessly about her shoulders and down her back. Beneath arched brows and long curling lashes, her glowing violet eyes were watching him carefully.

Moving forward, he waited for her to descend, holding his hand out for her to take. Her unparalleled beauty proved a strong lodestone from which he could not drag his gaze. 'I am almost speechless,' he murmured, taking her hand and kissing it lightly. 'You are exquisite.'

Trying to fight down her growing trepidation, she gave him a wobbly smile. 'Thank you, Lucas,' she said, staring up at the handsome, dynamic man standing before her. He looked powerful, aloof and self-assured. 'You look quite handsome yourself.'

'We should be going,' Anna said, looking incredibly beautiful in a creation of pale green silk and lace as she stood beside William and Charles. 'We are late.'

'Don't worry. We can be there in no time,' William replied. 'Besides, Lucas wants everyone there when Tilly arrives.'

The theatre was athrong with theatregoers and every pair of eyes seemed to shift to Tilly as she alighted from the coach. No one looking at her would guess how nervous she was. For a moment as Lucas paused to assist Anna out of the carriage, she stood beside Charles outside the theatre, looking at a sea of nameless faces. Then Lucas suddenly appeared by her side and held out his hand. Tilly placed her hand in his and he tucked it possessively in the crook of his arm.

Lucas felt it tremble and, bending over her, murmured, 'You are nervous, aren't you? I can tell.'

'Terrified,' she amended, pinning a smile to her lips. 'Everyone is looking at us.'

'Tilly,' he said severely, but with a dazzling smile for the benefit of onlookers, 'you are the young woman who brazenly confronted an arrogant stranger on the beach and several times thereafter. Compared to that this is child's play.'

Tilly stared at him askance. 'Did I really do that?'

He grinned down at her. 'Yes, you did. So do not dare turn cowardly now.'

Tilly glanced round at the curious faces, some craning their necks better to see her. 'I'll try not to,' she replied, 'but it won't be easy. Don't they know that it's impolite to stare?'

'Probably not. Ignore them,' Lucas quipped, seeming completely impervious to the stir they were creating. But when he looked at the fashionable throng, how these same people had shunned her and whispered about her, he was angry, but managed to appear superbly relaxed.

The attention that Lucas attracted did not go unnoticed either, as, during the interval when one group after another entered their box, in a flurry of curtsies and flirtatious smiles, inviting glances and a fluttering of fans, the ladies almost fell over each other in their foolish desperation to be introduced.

William and Charles watched it all with amused understanding. 'How does it feel, Lucas,' William enquired as the curtain went up for the second act and the last group departed their box, 'to have become, overnight, London's most sought-after bachelor?'

Relieved that Tilly had been left unscathed, Lucas laughed. 'Bachelor maybe, but no longer eligible—and they will all see that when our betrothal is announced tomorrow.'

All those people who had maliciously maligned Tilly, looking at her as she sat serene and secure in her box, had to admit that Tilly Anderson was beautiful. She had no lack of admiring smiles from the gentlemen who watched from the auditorium and other boxes to where she sat with her siblings. Some of the more adult theatregoers knew Lord Clifton from the days when he had come up to London and had been no stranger on the social scene, but the younger generation were curious to know who that rakishly handsome man who remained attentively by Miss Anderson's side through the evening could be.

They found out the following morning, when their betrothal was announced in the *Post*, giving rise to further gossip, no longer malicious but full of complimentary speculation and excitement as to who would be on the guest list for the wedding.

Nothing seemed real for Tilly during the days leading up to the wedding. She moved into the Lancaster town house in Mayfair where she went through several fittings for her wedding gown. Aunt Charlotte was in her element as she busied herself with arranging the flowers and bridesmaids—six in total with a variety of ages. She was determined that everything would go well on the day. The guest list for the ceremony was for a select assortment of close friends and family, the ball to follow a truly grand affair with guests that would fill the Lancaster town house to overflowing.

It was a happy group that rode into Hyde Park late one afternoon to partake of exercise and fresh air. It was where the *beau monde* congregated, to see and to be seen. Ladies attired in the height of fashion, gentlemen on high-stepping horses and carriages bearing the gilded family crests of the *ton*, liveried servants and matched teams of horses glided along in majestic splendour.

William, Charles, Tilly and Anna were to meet Lucas in the park. They had done a circuit of Rotten Row, jostling along with other riders, when Tilly saw her betrothed astride his horse. He was accosted by a group of other riders and fell into conversation with them. She slanted a long, considering look at him as he sat astride his strong, well-muscled mount. Attired in a dark green coat, gleaming brown leather boots and a pair of buckskin riding breeches that fit to perfection, in her opinion he was by far the most attractive man present.

She watched him as he talked and joked with lazy good humour with those around him, looking completely relaxed. On seeing her he excused himself, but unfortunately he was too far away to reach her before Sir John Paterson, one of the sporting gentlemen in their group who had latched on to them, challenged her to a ride. With an angry scowl on his face Lucas watched her gallop off in light-hearted abandon across the green grass, scattering other riders in their path, leaping over a ditch and clearing a low hedge effortlessly.

Her mare held her own until they turned and headed back to the others, slowing their mounts to a sedate walk. Tilly was happy to converse with the young man about the pleasant afternoon, when a sudden awareness swept over her. One moment she was thoroughly occupied learning the identity of others in the park and the next she was oblivious to everything but the inexplicable realisation that Lucas was close at hand.

The perception was quickly confirmed when his cool voice said, 'If you don't mind, Paterson, I would like a word with my betrothed.' His eyes passed over them both, considering each of them, instilling some discomfort in Sir John.

Even though there had not been the slightest hint of impropriety, Sir John stiffened apprehensively. 'I beg your pardon, Clifton, but Miss Anderson expressed an interest in some of the people present.'

'Then I shall be happy to familiarise her with them myself.'

Sir John fell back and, after excusing himself, rode away.

One quick look at Lucas's face convinced Tilly that he was furious with her. Not only were his eyes glinting like shards of ice, but the muscles in his cheeks were tensing to a degree that she had never seen before.

'It's a pity your riding skill is not exceeded by your common sense, Tilly,' he reproached her severely. 'Did you have to ride off alone with Sir John? And did you have to take those jumps? You could have broken your neck.'

'Really, Lucas, there's no need to get all hot and bothered about a few measly ditches and hedges. You've seen me ride harder terrain than this and jump obstacles far worse in Devon. And you should not have spoken to Sir John like that—making him think you are jealous…'

Lucas squinted in the sun's bright glare. 'Damn it, Tilly. I *am* jealous.'

His simple acknowledgement confused Tilly so completely that for a moment she could think of nothing to say. To feel jealousy, one had to care. As usual, his tall, hard body radiated strength and vitality, but his eyes held a dangerous glitter. A winsome smile touched her lips. 'Why, Lucas, you really are quite terrifying when you're angry—and jealous.'

'I'm jealous of any man who claims even a moment of your time when that moment could be spent with me. Was it too much for you to wait and ride with me?'

Tilly gasped, astounded that he should argue about something so trivial. 'Really, Lucas, I was just enjoying myself—and I could see you were engaged in conversation with others. But there is no need to be jealous of Sir John.'

'He's a handsome fellow with many conquests. The very idea of you being pursued by another rankles sorely.'

'It wasn't like that,' she answered softly, truthfully, in an attempt to placate his ire. What he said confused her, for it was in complete variance to his behaviour of late. Unhooking her leg from the pommel, she slipped off her mount with an easy grace. 'Of late we've spent little time together, Lucas, and our wedding is only days away. The others are riding along the Row so let's walk together. There is something I would like to talk to you about.'

Dismounting and leading their horses to where the park was less busy, Lucas took her arm and drew her into the shade of a large beech tree, out of sight of prying eyes.

'I'm sorry if I've made you angry,' she said. 'I didn't mean to.'

'You are right,' he said. 'We've had precious little time to ourselves of late. I'll be relieved when the wedding is over and we can leave for Devon.' Placing a finger lightly under her chin, he tipped her face up to his, his anger of a moment earlier dissolving. 'I'm sorry, too. I didn't mean to speak so harshly. What is it you want to talk to me about?'

Biting her lip, Tilly hesitated. Would what she was about to ask him make him angry? But she had to know about Miranda. How much had he loved her? Had he grieved for her so much that he wanted to die? Would he ever come to terms with their parting? Would he ever be free of her? Until she had the answers to these questions, how could their marriage succeed?

'I—I would like you to tell me about Miranda, Lucas. Before you marry me, I need to know if you are still mourning her loss?'

Pain clouded his eyes. 'Miranda? How do you know about her?'

When Tilly saw the taut line of his jaw and how his expression had hardened slightly, her mouth went dry and her heart began to beat in heavy, terrifying dread as she sensed that he had withdrawn from her. 'Mrs Carstairs told me. I know you are a private person, but if I am to be your wife, if you cannot be open with me, then it bodes ill for the future.'

'You are right. You should know about Miranda—and why I am marrying you. When you told me about Coulson I was repulsed by the very idea of marrying a woman without any regard to the morality of the situation you were in. But I was so consumed with anger that another man had taken what I cherished that I was blind to anything else. Yet much as I wanted to rebel against it, I found myself wanting you.'

Tilly's heart soared and his confession brought a smile to her lips, but the grim expression that suddenly appeared on his face gave her a sense of unease and made her wary. 'I was a fool to let you think Richard Coulson and I had been lovers and I am sorry. I didn't mean for you to suffer. I thank God all was not lost.'

'No, it is not and I will show you,' he murmured, taking her face between his hands.

The sound of his deep, reassuring voice, combined with the feeling of his strong gentle fingers closing around her face and his lips placed tenderly on hers, did much to dissolve Tilly's misgivings. When his lips left hers, her gaze searching his face, she said, 'It would mean a great deal to me, and to our future together, if we could put this behind us, so will you not tell me about Miranda? I don't want to pry into your relationship with her, but it is perfectly natural for a wife to want to know if her husband's old love is still a threat.'

'You do me a grave injustice, Tilly, to imply I would love another woman when you are to be my wife.'

'I'm sorry. I didn't mean to. I know you loved her and that she hurt you when you parted.'

For a long moment his gaze met hers with penetrating intensity. 'Yes, I loved her. I thought she felt the same. I was young and dazzled by her. We were to be married—the wedding was arranged until she went to London and met someone else. She was beautiful—she was also deceitful and treacherous as sin. There had been other men before me—men known to me, who mocked my youth, my ignorance and my innocence.'

Tilly stared at him. 'You are saying that you do not still love her?'

He nodded. 'I came to realise that when I met you. What I felt for her was something more primitive than love. Whatever it was that bound me to her was so powerful that I was in danger of losing my immortal soul. She lived in Truro with her parents, who also had a house in London. It was where Miranda met a rich American gentleman, married him and went to live in America.'

Tilly bowed her head. At last she understood why he had behaved the way he had when she had told him about Richard Coulson, why he would not let his feelings and emotions get the better of him. She could not blame him for not wanting to love any woman. Her heart ached with remorse. For a man as proud as Lucas to have his proposal of marriage flung back in his face, which was what Miranda had done, must have made him furious.

'She hurt you very badly, I can tell.'

'I chided myself relentlessly for having been tempted by her, for having believed she felt as I felt. Remembering, I hated myself with a hatred and contempt that were absolutely bottomless and I swore that the woman I took for my wife would not be like she was. I vowed that my emotions would never again be engaged by a woman. I wanted none of their treachery and deceit.'

'And you thought I was like that. I am not Miranda, Lucas—although I am sorry I gave you reason to believe I was like her.'

'And yet, my love,' he said, 'before I knew the truth, I came to realise that I wanted you so much that it no longer mattered. What I feel for you transcends anything I have felt before. It seems impossible and yet I know it is true, for here I am, totally enamoured with you.'

Tilly looked up at him, his achingly handsome face languid and his blue eyes dark with passion as his fingers gently traced the line of her throat. 'Thank you for telling me about Miranda. We'll be man and wife in just a few days and I can't tell you how relieved I am knowing there will be just me and you, with no other woman in the shadows.'

Walking towards where their horses were grazing on the soft turf, Lucas slipped his arm about her waist and paused, looking down at her. 'There is no one else, Tilly. There never will be. It is important to me that you believe that.'

The intensity of his gaze ploughed through Tilly's composure. The yearning in his eyes smote her. 'I do—now.' Kissing him lightly on the lips, she smiled, looking towards where the riders were parading ahead of them. 'I think I see Anna waving to us. We should go. Just a few more days, Lucas, and we will be man and wife.'.

And then suddenly it was the wedding day and as servants and footmen scurried about in a frenzy of preparations and bridesmaids ran excitedly about the house, Tilly was in her room being dressed in a creation of champagne silk gauze. Anna and her maid had spent all morning getting her ready. Her hair was brushed until it shone and then drawn back from her face into a heavy chignon. Round her throat she wore a necklace made of amethyst gemstones with matching earrings to match the colour of her eyes. They were a wedding gift from Lucas. He would have given her diamonds, but ever since she had told him how Richard Coulson had promised her diamonds if she married him, he had developed a strong aversion for that particular gemstone.

When she was ready and it was almost time to leave for the church, Charles, who was to walk her down the aisle, came to see her.

'Well,' he said, his voice hoarse with emotion and pride as his eyes passed over her appraisingly. 'You look...you look beautiful, Tilly—like a princess,' he said reverently. 'How I wish our parents were here to see you today. They would be so proud of you. Are you nervous?'

'Terribly—but I'm also happy.'

'We should be leaving. William said there are crowds of spectators around the church, with congestion on the roads. It's as if the whole of London has turned out to see you wed.'

'Oh, dear, I never imagined I would be so popular—unless it's the handsome man I am to marry who has drawn the crowd, or even my terribly attractive brothers. I never can decide which of you is the most handsome.'

Charles grinned, adjusting his cravat. 'As far as I'm concerned there's no contest. It's me, of course. Besides, everyone turns out to see the bride on her wedding day and to look at what she's wearing. They won't be disappointed.'

Chapter Twelve

Charles was right. The crowds and vehicles blocked the streets around the church in Hanover Square. The bridesmaids being kept in check by Anna were waiting. The church was bedecked with urns of sweet-scented flowers. The organ music swelled. Drawing a deep breath and taking Charles's arm, Tilly walked slowly down the aisle, bearing a spray of white lilies.

All the radiance in the world was shining from her eyes which were drawn irresistibly to the man who was waiting for her at the front of the church, overwhelming in stature, his ebony hair smoothly brushed and gleaming. His claret-coloured coat, dove-grey trousers hugging his long legs, matching waistcoat and crisp white cravat were simple but impeccably cut. Anna had taken her seat beside Aunt Charlotte, who looked proudly on, dabbing a tear from her eye.

The blue eyes of her husband-to-be held hers, narrowing, assessing, the woman walking towards him snatching his breath away and pride exploding throughout his entire body until he ached with it, for no bride had ever looked so lovely. He stretched out his strong hand and offered it to her. She lifted her own and placed it in his much larger, much warmer one. Lucas felt the trembling of her fingers and saw the anxiety in her large eyes. He gave her hand a little squeeze in an attempt to reassure her.

The music drew to a close. As Tilly spoke her vows, firm and sure, she was aware of little more than his close proximity and his firm hands when they slipped the ring on her finger. At that moment she felt herself possessed and at the same time a rush of happiness that he was the possessor. To this man she had committed her life and at that moment she recognised the emotion that had struck her when he had kissed her at Clifton House. She no longer had any doubts that she was deeply and irresistibly in love and this revelation sealed the bond between them.

They were pronounced man and wife and the next thing Tilly knew was her husband's lips on hers, sealing their union, and they were walking back down the aisle with a drift of bridesmaids behind, smiling broadly to all those who had come to witness their union.

With the aid of grooms outside the church, they were ensconced in the shiny black carriage and managed to get through the snarl up. Along with the rest of the wedding cortège, they were soon at William's house for the wedding breakfast.

Already anticipating the night to come, food was served and wine and liquor flowed. Gifts were received and congratulations given, wedding cake cut. The whole day had an air of unreality about it.

The wedding breakfast over, Tilly went to her room to prepare for the ball.

* * *

When she was ready, with a smile pinned to her face and with Anna by her side, she passed through some of the anterooms to the ballroom. It was exquisitely decorated and festooned with flowers on pedestals.

Some of the fashionable, overdressed gentlemen lounged against pillars, drinking wine and talking and laughing much too loudly as the liquor loosened their inhibitions. Tilly was confidently aware of the gleam of her beautiful wedding dress hinting at the contours of her long shapely legs as she walked. Long gloves encased her arms and her shining dark hair was caught up at the crown in a mass of thick, glossy curls.

She was surrounded by other ladies, beautiful, bejewelled ladies, but when Tilly put her mind to it only she had that perfect self-conscious way of walking. She moved as if every man present was watching her. She walked as if she were irresistible, such was the power of her conviction that she would achieve her goal in what she had set out to do—to retrieve her good name. Even the jewels adorning the throats of the ladies winked at her like bright-eyed conspirators as they caught the prisms of the chandeliers.

Looking ahead, she saw Lucas waiting for her. His midnight-blue evening clothes accentuated his long lean body to perfection, his hair as dark as her own brushed to perfection. The pleasure of seeing him again eclipsed her earlier panic about attending the ball. Lucas Kingsley was as handsome of physique as he was of face. His chiselled features were touched by the light and a gentle ache in her bosom that grew and grew attested to the degree of his attractiveness. His masculine perfection dominated the scene.

A half-smile curved his lips as he watched her come closer. He raised his fine, dark eyebrows. She completely ignored the young women eyeing him with encouraging, flirtatious glances over their fans, tittering and giggling. Where other women might have succumbed to the irresistible pull to see behind the cool façade and start uncovering the man beneath, Tilly merely returned his smile, knowing perfectly well what lay beneath.

Taking her hand, he smiled down at her. 'You look exquisite, my love. Are you ready to take to the floor with me for the first dance? Everyone is impatient to join us on the dance floor, but it would be bad etiquette for them to do so before the bride and groom.'

'Then we'd best not keep them waiting any longer.'

It was quite magical when Lucas led her on to the dance floor and gathered her into his arms for the first waltz. Feeling terribly conspicuous, with all eyes upon them, she hoped she wouldn't trip up and make a fool of herself.

Aware of her nervousness, Lucas murmured, 'Relax.' She almost missed her step, but his arm tightened, holding her steady. 'Focus your eyes on me and you'll be fine.' He steered her into the first graceful steps as the music washed over them.

Gradually, other couples began to step on to the floor. Of their own volition Tilly's feet followed where Lucas led and her mind opened to the sensations of the dance. She was aware of the subtle play of her skirts about her legs and the hardness of her husband's thighs against hers. The closeness of his body lent to her nostrils a scent of his cologne, fleeting, inoffensive, a clean masculine smell. The seductive notes of the music were mirrored in their movements and the sway was a sensual delight. Lucas's hand at her waist was firm, his touch confident as he whisked her smoothly around the ballroom.

The ball became lively as everyone threw themselves into enjoying themselves. Tilly danced with Charles and William and other gentlemen she could not put a name to, for all her thoughts were focused on just the one. Her husband.

They were to spend the first night of their marriage at William's town house. It was almost midnight when they managed to slip away while everyone was still enjoying the festivities. Tilly said goodnight to Aunt Charlotte, who was having a rare old time, the madeira she had consumed having flushed her cheeks a bright pink. Kissing her soundly and wishing her all the luck in the world, Charles and William ushered her on up the stairs, and when she looked back at them, they were still watching her, grinning like a pair of hyenas.

Having removed her wedding finery and the pins from her hair, and wearing a cream silk dressing gown, she dismissed her maid. The room was sumptuously furnished, tastefully decorated in pastel cream and green, with a huge, canopied bed fit for a king.

Tilly sat before the mirrored vanity, brushing her hair until it shone. She tried to ignore her nervousness, not knowing what to expect beyond the basic facts as told her by Aunt Charlotte. Knowing Lucas would be joining her from the connecting room at any minute, her anxiety increased.

When he stepped into the room, dressed in a dark blue silk robe, through the mirror she watched him come close and paused her brushing. Standing behind her, he placed his hands on her shoulders and, lowering his head, pushed aside her hair and placed his lips on her neck before meeting her eyes in the mirror.

'So, here we are at last,' he murmured. 'Happy?'

His warm breath caressed the back of her neck, and then his lips trailed over her sensitive flesh to her ear, while she turned liquid inside. 'Yes—you know I am,' she said, closing her eyes as she enjoyed the feel of his closeness. 'Are you happy, Lucas?'

'Absolutely. I am the luckiest man alive to have you for my wife—and my lady. Countess of Clifton. How does that feel?'

Tilly's heart swelled to hear him say that and her mouth curved in a smile. 'Strange, but I suppose I'll get used to it. It's been a lovely day—although I swear, I only remember the half of it. Did we really get married?'

Laughing softly, he again bent his head to nuzzle her neck with his lips. 'Believe it, my love. It happened—and you looked like an angel in your wedding gown. But I prefer you like this—with your hair loose and wearing nothing but a robe.' Meeting her gaze once more in the mirror, her eyes warm with passion, he gave her a lazy grin and said, 'Shall we go to bed?'

Standing up, she walked into his arms, wrapping her arms around his neck and tilting her head back to look at his handsome face. 'I would like that. But…you… you realise that this is all new to me, don't you, Lucas?'

'Why, what's this? A fit of nerves?'

'A bit.'

'Then don't be. I will be consideration and gentleness personified,' he murmured, slipping the knot on the belt of her robe and sliding it off her shoulders where it settled in a pool at her feet. 'You have the loveliest eyes I have ever seen and I like the way they sparkle when you laugh, and darken when we kiss. I remember an unbelievable softness when I kissed your lips, and a warmth the likes of which set my heart afire.'

A wicked grin highlighted his lips as he glanced at her. 'I also like the way you look in your nightdress— but I would like you better without it.'

Tilly felt the soft caress of his gaze which caused a familiar twist of her heart, an addictive mix of pleasure and discomfort. His warm eyes looked at her in undisguised admiration as his gaze took in her silk nightdress to match her robe. 'You are very eloquent, Lucas, but please don't go on. I would prefer you to show me with your lips.'

'My thoughts exactly.'

Again, his arms went round her and he found her lips, drawing her senses into the heated depths of a kiss, as his hands deftly slipped the straps of her nightdress off her shoulders, revealing the cleft between the round fullness of her breasts. Her cheeks flushed scarlet at his boldness.

Bending his head to pay homage to the soft flesh glowing like creamy pearls in the soft light, he placed his lips in the hollow of her throat where a pulse throbbed. Heat blossomed and spread inside her. But the heat building inside Lucas, fed and steadily stoked, was escalating into urgency. He needed to touch more, to explore without the encumbrance of fabric.

Standing her away from him, he slipped the offending nightdress down over the curves of her hips and thighs, where it joined her robe on the carpet. Her glorious body was a shade of pale gold in the wavering blur of the candles.

Chest tight, eager to seize, to devour, to slake the lust that drove him, every nerve Lucas possessed stilled as slowly, his gaze traced up the curves of her long legs, the gentle swell of her thighs, over her taut stomach and minuscule waist to her breasts, full tipped with rosy peaks.

Tilly's throat dried. His eyes focused upon her figure and the ardour in his dark gaze was like a flame to her senses. Fuelled by a whirlpool of emotions she didn't recognise, much less understand, she fled to the bed, climbed in and pulled the covers over her nakedness.

'When you've finished ogling me, Lucas, kindly remember you're supposed to be a gentleman and take off your clothes, too—unless you intend to make love to me with them on.'

Desire having become a physical torment, he disposed of his robe and joined her in the bed.

'That's better,' she said. 'Now we're the same—and I have to say, Lucas Kingsley, that you're a fine-looking man without your shirt on—although,' she said, remembering another time she had seen him minus his shirt, 'I have a confession to make.'

'You have? Then you had better tell me—although I feel I must tell you that I have an aversion to a divorce,' he teased.

'It's nothing like that…only… Do you promise you won't be cross?'

'Absolutely. It is our wedding night. I'll forgive you anything. I'm curious. What is it?'

'One day—I didn't know you very well, I saw you on the beach. You stripped off to your trousers and went for a swim. You swim very well, by the way. Despite my previous dunking, I would like you to teach me some time.'

'It will be my pleasure. But why on earth didn't you make your presence known? Where were you hiding, ogling me?'

'I wasn't hiding—nor was I ogling. I was sitting among the rocks when you appeared. I liked watching you, which is why I stayed where I was.'

'I see. Well, what can I say, only that I hope you weren't disappointed.'

'No, I wasn't. Quite the opposite, in fact,' she said, snuggling close to him. 'Now, will you please kiss me.'

'It will be my pleasure.'

Gathering her into his arms, as he held her tight against him, his kisses consumed her in the violent storm of his passion. Lowering his head, his mouth moved to circle her breasts, kissing each in turn, before travelling down to her stomach. Operating wholly on instinct since her wits had flown, Tilly craned her neck back and her fingers laced through his thick hair as she abandoned herself to his lips, his hands—intimate and evocative, exploring the secrets of her body like a knowledgeable lover, savouring what he found—and the pleasure that burned through her, expanding, mounting, until her body shuddered with the force of her passion.

When he shifted position to take control, the warmth of his body pressing close against her own, wrapping her arms about him, Tilly opened up to him, her kisses driving him on, inciting his passion until he could no longer control the force that had claimed him. Her hands tensed on his shoulders, but she did not cry out when he entered her. He paused and looked down at her.

'Are you all right, Tilly? Did I hurt you?'

She shook her head slightly, hardly daring to breathe.

'That's good, my love,' he said, his voice low with passion, soothing her so seductively as he began to move.

The discomfort she had felt passed and her body came alive with pleasure, unfolding like the petals of an exotic flower. Never in her imagination had she experienced anything so erotic as this. All her senses became heightened and focused on him and what he was doing until nothing else mattered.

This was how she wanted him, all his iron will stripped from him, his passion for her driving him on. There was no hiding for either of them when they were in the throes of passion, of pleasure, consuming them in undulating waves.

They reached their climax in unison. A blissful aura broke over them. Spent and exhausted, slowly they drifted back to earth, drained and incapable of any movement other than holding each other close. Tilly sighed, the physicality of their lovemaking, her vulnerability and her implicit surrender sweeping over her as her hand caressed Lucas's furred chest.

He eased away from her, and, drifting on a tide of glory, in the aftermath of their passion she curled against him, her body aglow, her limbs weighted with contentment, firm in the belief that her husband was a man of extraordinary prowess. Finding his lips, she kissed him softly, then, lost in the wonder of completeness, naked limbs entwined, with a soft sigh she let exhaustion claim her.

Lucas leaned on his elbow and gazed down at the young woman with a mass of silky hair who was now his wife in every sense of the word. He thought of all the nights to come and his blood stirred hotly at the mere thought. He was engulfed in a swirling mass of emotions, emotions that were new to him, emotions he could not recognise and could not put a name to.

His every instinct reacted to the fact that he had this woman in thrall, that he'd finally breached the walls and captured the elusive creature at its core. He gloried in the fact that she was his, here, without reserve. Gently, he touched her hair, brushing her flesh with his arm, feeling the warm reality of her.

Conscious of the languor that weighted his limbs, of the satiation that was bone deep, he realised that this state had been reached not by mere self-gratification, but by a deep contentment more profound than at any other time in his life. Tilly had succeeded in tapping the source of his well-being where every other woman he had known had failed.

They were soon to leave for Devon. He looked forward to showing her her new home and all the things he had come to cherish as a boy and throughout his life into manhood. Nostalgia swamped him, for it was at a time such as this that he missed his parents and Cassie.

They would have taken to Tilly and welcomed her into the family with open arms.

Tilly sensed the presence of a warm, naked masculine form pressed against her as she floated in a comforting grey mist.

'Good morning,' Lucas murmured huskily. 'I trust you slept well.'

Opening her eyes, she gazed up at him and her lips curved in a smile as she stretched her lithe body. 'I slept very well. In fact, I cannot believe I slept at all after what we did.'

Kissing the tip of her nose, he nuzzled his lips against her cheek. 'Are you ready for breakfast?'

'Absolutely not,' she uttered with mock indignation. 'I have a different kind of appetite now and I am not ready to face the world for, well, another two hours at least. Besides, I must look a complete mess.'

'You, Countess, look quite delectable, but you are also wanton. Despite that, I am willing to oblige you in any way you choose.'

He laughed. She liked it when he laughed. His tousled hair, with an errant wave falling over his brow, was dark against the snowy whiteness of the pillows, and sleep had softened the rugged contours of his handsome face. He was utterly irresistible in his naked state.

Remembering their loving, of how he had lingered over her, guiding her to peak after peak of quivering ecstasy, caressing and kissing her with the skill and expertise of a virtuoso playing a violin, a warm glow engulfed her and she found herself reaching for him again.

Later, she was to look back on this night when Lucas

had lit the spark within her that was like having a fire in her soul. She would never have known such wild, sweeping passion existed were it not for Lucas. Better by far to experience that passion for such a short time, than never to have known it at all, even if it brought such pain and heartache, or to die not knowing such joy, such intoxicating sweetness was possible.

It was a lovely early autumn day when Charles embarked on the East Indiaman, which was to take him to India. They all went to East India dock to wave him off. He had delayed his sailing due to Tilly's wedding. He was excited by the prospect of India and impatient to be on the high seas. Tilly was sad to see him go and cried a little, but her joy in her marriage and the excitement of returning to Devon overshadowed everything else.

They were to travel with Florence and Tobias the day after Charles's departure. William and Anna were to return to Cranford, promising to visit them at Clifton House in the spring. Quite worn out with all the wedding arrangements and looking forward to a quiet time, Aunt Charlotte would travel down to Drayton Manor at a later date.

Their journey to Devon was uneventful. The weather held and, changing horses frequently at the coaching inns, they made good time. Florence had enjoyed her time in London, but was glad to be returning south. Tobias was restless and often fretful at being confined to the coach for long periods. Keeping him entertained was often difficult and, his patience running thin, Lucas would climb up front with the driver and leave them to it.

Both Lucas and Tilly looked forward to the nights they spent at the inns along the way when they could be together. Tilly fell more in love with her husband with each passing day. She would anticipate the nights of love and she would tremble, in part from an inexplicable excitement that his mere touch never failed to evoke in her.

She was delighted to see the sea again and the thought of it being available to her for the rest of her life gave her a warm glow. And then suddenly they were at Clifton House, gracious and almost shining in the clean air. One of the peacocks appropriately appeared on the lawn, strutting along with its head high in his desire for admiration, a peahen following sedately behind.

Lucas had notified the butler when to expect them. Everything had been prepared for their arrival. It was cool inside the lofty hall. Tilly had insisted she didn't want any fuss, but the housekeeper had other ideas on the proper way to welcome the new Countess of Clifton. The servants were lined up in the hall to be introduced to the new mistress, although many of them were already acquainted with her from her previous visit.

Tilly had ridden to pay a visit to Mrs Carstairs and returned, only to find Florence and Tobias were nowhere to be found. Thinking Florence might have taken Tobias into the garden, she scoured the secluded places she might have gone. She was not to be found anywhere. Deeply worried and with a feeling that something was very wrong after speaking to one of the maids who helped Florence in the nursery, she went to find Lucas in his study to alert him to her disappearance.

He looked up when she entered, frowning when he saw the anxiety on her face. 'Tilly? What is it? Is something wrong?'

'It's Florence. She's nowhere to be found. She's taken Tobias.'

Lucas's face hardened and his eyes darkened. Anger flared in them, as sudden and as bright as quicksilver. 'When was she last seen?'

'Mid-morning. One of the maids who helps her in the nursery told me her sister's husband arrived from Dawlish with a message that her sister is very poorly and wanted to see her.'

'And has she gone?'

'Yes—at least she's gone somewhere. I don't like it, Lucas. Something is not right. Wherever she's gone, she's taken Tobias with her.'

'I'll arrange for a search party,' he said, getting up and striding to the door. 'If she was last seen midmorning—two hours ago—she could be anywhere. Did anyone see her speak to this individual?'

'Apparently not,' Tilly said, following in his wake as she went out into the hall. 'She returned to the nursery for Tobias and no one has seen her since. Where can he have taken her?'

'But why did she not speak to you…or me?' Lucas said, raking his fingers through his hair. 'And why take Tobias? Why do I sense Jack Price is behind this? If he is, I shudder to think what he will do to them.'

At that moment the butler was opening the door to a caller. Two mounted Dragoons waited in the drive. The visitor, a tall man with a gaunt face and piercing grey eyes, introduced himself as the Revenue Officer, Lieutenant Owen Foster. Lucas remembered his name being mentioned when the Reverend Leighton and the magistrate had been for dinner before his trip to London.

'Pardon me for coming unannounced, Lord Clifton, but it is necessary that I speak with you.'

'Why are you here, Lieutenant?'

'You are aware that the smugglers use this part of the coast for their runs, Lord Clifton?'

'Very much so. What of it?'

'I have it on good authority that there is to be a large delivery of contraband tonight. We've been waiting for this for a long time and hope to arrest some key figures. The Coastguard and Excise men and the Dragoons will all be ready.

'The sea is choppy, the winds fair, but not a problem at present—no moon, so the conditions are favourable for the free traders. I thought you should know since it may turn violent when the smugglers realise their plans have been blown wide open. If some of them manage to get away, then they will try to make it north over your land.'

Lucas nodded. 'I don't think I need ask the name of the man you seek.'

'Jack Price.'

'I have a problem of my own at present, Lieutenant. I believe my nephew has been abducted—roughly two hours ago. For reasons I do not wish to go into, I believe it is Jack Price who has taken him. The child is seven months old. His nurse is with him. I have to find Price myself before the child comes to harm.'

'And you think your prediction is correct?'

'Yes, I do.'

'I understand your concern, Lord Clifton, but I am compelled to ask you not to try to find him for the present—in fact, I will go so far as to forbid it. If he has taken your nephew we will find him, but Jack Price is a man who must be apprehended. I have been after him for too long to have my plans jeopardised.'

Lucas stiffened. He didn't like being denied by anyone, but he had to admit that the Lieutenant might have a legitimate point.

For the rest of the day both Lucas and Tilly waited in a state of suspended anguish for darkness to come. Despite Lieutenant Foster's orders to leave what was to happen later to him, Lucas was determined to be there to see Jack Price brought down and to retrieve Tobias and Florence. Tilly insisted on going with him. When Lucas objected, she set her jaw mutinously, her eyes shining with determination.

'I will do nothing of the sort. I'm going with you.'

'No, Tilly. You'll be safer here.' His mouth was set in a grim line. 'For once in your life you will do exactly as you're told. You are far too stubborn for your own good.'

Tilly, not to be deterred, squared her chin and met his gaze head on. 'You say what you like, but I will not stay here. Besides, Florence or Tobias might have need of me.'

Reluctantly Lucas relented. 'Very well. But when I tell you to keep out of sight you do as I say. Is that clear?' Tilly nodded. 'You are being extremely difficult,' Lucas remarked, raising a disgruntled brow at her.

'I would have you know I am never difficult,' Tilly

was quick to insist, 'save, of course, for those times when you aggravate me into being so.'

'It will be hazardous on the beach,' he reminded her. 'I'd never forgive myself if some harm came to you. I couldn't bear to lose you.'

The genuine concern in his voice touched Tilly and warmed her heart. She prayed to God that it was so, that he was all hers and would be so for evermore, but until he told her that he loved her a shadow of doubt would always remain. 'Don't look so gloomy. You need have no fears for me. I will behave and not do anything rash. I promise you.'

Lucas drew her close to him. 'If you do, my love, I will tell you now that I will never forgive you.'

'Worry not, Lucas,' she whispered, momentarily managing to overcome her anxiety for Florence and Tobias and force a little smile to her lips. 'I shall still be here to plague you.'

When darkness shrouded the land, Lucas, with Tilly by his side, took to the saddle and vengeance rode with him. His nephew had been taken by a man who he was convinced was responsible for the death of his parents. No man had ever set forth with a blacker rage filling his heart.

The moon was hidden behind a bank of cloud. Her eyes having become accustomed to the dark, Tilly glanced across at her husband. He was bent low over the horse's neck. She caught the gleam of a pistol butt at his waist. Beneath his French cocked hat, his face was set and intense.

This self-contained man with a single-mindedness

had his thoughts on a purpose. He knew they were facing a grave emergency, that from now on the momentum would build until it reached its inevitable climax, and for him there could only be one conclusion.

Tilly found the inky blackness total and terrifying. Gradually their eyes became accustomed to the gloom. Coming to the edge of the cliff, they dismounted and tethered their horses out of the way. Suddenly, she started when half a dozen figures materialised out of the dark. One of them was Lieutenant Foster, two of them Excise men, and the other three Dragoons. All were armed with pistols and swords.

'Everything seems to be going to plan,' Lieutenant Foster told Lucas in a low voice. 'They are not expecting us. Price placed two lookouts on the cliff-top, but they've been taken care of, having given us the signal they were to use with a little coercion. I let it be known I'd be in Plymouth. It's a night of no moon—perfect for a run. I hope to catch Price red-handed. Hopefully they'll run straight into the trap we've set for them. They cannot escape.' His words carried conviction.

'Where are the rest of the troops?'

'They're placed strategically around the cove. They have orders to hold their fire unless any of the smugglers try to escape and not to invade the beach until I give the signal. Price has his men waiting in the gully that opens on to the beach further along with the pack horses. They cannot see the Dragoons waiting on top of the cliffs. The Revenue cutter with the Coastguard on board is round the headland and will appear when the boat is sighted with the contraband.'

Lucas nodded, his face grim. 'Congratulations, Lieutenant. You appear to have thought of everything.'

'I hope to God I have. I've been after Price too long to allow him to slip through my fingers tonight.'

'But what of Florence and Tobias?' Tilly asked, fearful for the nurse and her charge.

'I've received reliable information that Price has them. He's ashore—probably waiting in one of the caves for the vessel to land. When the contraband has been unloaded, he plans to have the lad and his nurse put on the boat and taken to France. What fate he has worked out for them I shudder to think.

'We must apprehend them before the boat sails off—although there's no chance of it getting away if the Revenue Cutter appears on time. Don't worry, Lady Clifton, we'll get to them in time, but we won't make a move until the contraband has been brought ashore.'

For the next hour they played a waiting game. The wind rose and then the vessel they waited for was sighted, its ghostly shape riding the waves towards the shore. The one-masted cutter which brought the contraband from France carried no light. It bobbed about like a cockleshell on the heaving water, perilously close to the cliffs. On shore and on the surrounding cliffs the Dragoons waited.

There was a flash of light from the shore followed by two more signalling it was safe for the vessel to land. When the contraband had been taken off, the smugglers would load their haul on to the backs of horses and make the long climb up the high moor.

Lucas saw men at the oars struggling in well-drilled

unison against the swell of the sea, using brute strength to keep it from smashing into the rocks. A man stepped over the side and climbed into a rowing boat. They watched him row towards the shore, where he climbed out and dragged the boat over the shingle and some way up the sands.

He rapped out orders to some of the men waiting in the shadows, the wind whipping the words from his lips as the sloop delivered her cargo into small waiting boats. At that moment men and horses pulling carts appeared from the gully, scattering like ants over the sand to load the contraband on to the backs of the horses, and from one of the caves further along the beach a man appeared, shoving a woman in front of him, a woman holding a child in her arms.

'Florence,' Tilly said. 'Lucas, that's Florence—and she has Tobias.'

When she made a move to run down to the cove, Lucas took hold of her arm and drew her back. Knowing how headstrong and wilful she could be, he placed his hands on her shoulders and gripped them hard, forcing her to meet the intensity of his gaze. 'What I said to you earlier applies now more than ever, Tilly. Listen to me and listen well. No matter what happens from now on, you will remain out of sight at all times. Is that understood?'

He saw the spark of defiance gleam from the velvety depths of her eyes and the stubborn tilt to her chin. His mouth tightened, his dark brows coming together, and he spoke with grinding resolution. 'I mean it, Tilly. I want you to find it in your defiant heart to obey me on this, otherwise I shall have one of these soldiers escort you back to the house, where you will remain until I return.'

Tilly opened her mouth to argue with him, but his gaze was so hard and unyielding that she bit back any words she was about to utter. 'But what about Florence and Tobias?'

'When I manage to get down there, I will bring them to you, but until then you keep out of sight.'

She nodded dully. 'I will do as you say. But please take care, Lucas.'

He nodded, thrusting her further back. His pistol at the ready, gripped firmly in his hand, he moved to the edge of the cliff and disappeared down the path.

The contraband was unloaded with well-practised precision. From his stance behind some rocks, Lucas had his eyes firmly fixed on Jack Price standing close to the sea edge. He was holding on to Florence while issuing orders to the men. Suddenly, pandemonium broke out as the Dragoons poured on to the beach, firing warning shots into the air.

Lieutenant Foster shouted to the smugglers to stop or they would be fired upon. They ignored the command and began scattering in every direction, half-crazed with fear. They didn't know in which direction to run. Ahead of them were the soldiers, behind them the sea. Soon swords were brandished and torchlight glinted on the cold steel.

Seeing what was happening, Jack Price shoved Florence, holding on to Tobias, towards an empty rowing boat, ordering her to get in. Florence stumbled, almost dropping a mewling Tobias into the water. When he would have hauled her on to her feet and tossed her into the boat, Lucas came up behind Price, his pistol in his back.

'Let her go, Price,' he ordered. 'Move and you're a dead man.'

Slowly, Price turned and faced his enemy, his eyes gleaming like bright slits. 'By whose hand, Kingsley?' he challenged boldly. 'Yours?'

'Why not? I hold the weapon.'

Price had seen the red-coated Dragoons and splashing through the surf towards him was Lieutenant Foster. 'Foster! I might have known,' Price sneered.

Lieutenant Foster nodded, moving closer. 'Surprised, Price? Did you expect to find me absent from Biddycombe?' He laughed derisively. 'How unfortunate for you that I'm not. You've led us a merry dance up to now. But you're finished, Price.'

Price was visibly furious at this unexpected turn of events, and he felt at a disadvantage—a unique experience for him. His presence was noted and from that moment he knew there was no escape. He might be Devon's most successful smuggler, prepared to use any misbegotten, contemptible method to achieve his aims, but nothing had been more important to him than to rid himself of his brother's child, whose very existence threatened everything he considered was his from the moment he had learned of Edmund's death.

'You are guilty of many things, Price,' Lucas said contemptuously as the Lieutenant helped Florence out of the water, 'but the one that concerns me is the crime of kidnap—and you can only think yourself lucky that your crime has not extended to the murder of an innocent babe,' Lucas said with icy calm, 'otherwise I would kill you myself.'

Seeing what was going on around him, that his men were fleeing the scene and the cutter about to set sail, Price saw the imminent threat of defeat, but he was not prepared to give in now. His hard mouth curled in a savage sneer. 'So, Kingsley, you thought to deceive me when you brought my brother's brat from Spain to steal my inheritance.'

'The child is Edmund's son, the inheritance of Trevean his by right.'

'A child with the blood of our enemy—your sister. Do you think I would let a Kingsley take what is mine?'

'Not for one minute—which is why I bought the boatyard. Yes,' Lucas informed him when fury propelled Price towards him. He stepped back. 'I bought the boatyard for Tobias to make sure when you played your dastardly game, he had something that had belonged to his father. Even your own father wanted it kept out of your hands.'

'Damn him.' Price spat. 'I damn him to hell.'

'As you did my parents when you tried sending them to the bottom of the sea? The truth, Price,' Lucas said, ramming the barrel of his pistol against his chest, his free hand clenched into a fist and his eyes as cold and hard as obsidian blackness. 'I've waited a long time to hear it—and since this is your day of reckoning, you might as well tell me the truth before I decide to put a hole through your black heart.'

'The truth is it you want? Then look no further and I will tell you,' Price hissed, a wild hatred filling his eyes as he thrust his face contorted with rage at his most hated enemy. 'I was on a run—me and my fellow trad-ers. The skipper of the sloop your parents were on saw me and tried to stop me. By the time their vessel caught up with me they'd seen our faces. They knew too much.'

Lucas was deadly quiet. 'So, you and your gang of murderers sent the boat and all those on board to the bottom of the sea. There were no survivors—but bod-ies were retrieved.'

'Aye, so I heard and a grand send-off you gave those who sired you—better than was deserved for the das-tardly Kingsleys.'

Lucas would have gone for him then if Lieutenant Foster and one of the Dragoons hadn't pulled him back.

'Enough,' the Lieutenant ordered. 'The man isn't worth hanging for. He'll get his just deserts in the end.'

From her vantage point on the cliff, Tilly watched everything that was happening. She saw Lucas confront Jack Price and the Lieutenant take charge of Florence and Tobias. Suddenly, there was pandemonium as the escaping smugglers made a dash for the sea, milling around Lucas and the Lieutenant. She watched as Jack Price made a lunge for the rowing boat he had tried to shove Florence into. He threw himself into the boat and began to row out to the cutter for all he was worth, try-ing to widen the distance between him and the shore. But the men on the cutter had seen what was happen-ing on the beach and were equally desperate to escape.

It began to move away, faster now she was lighter, having shed her cargo. But not far away were the lights and outline of another vessel bearing down on them. Tilly realised this must be the Revenue cutter. The smugglers were caught like rats in a trap, and as a fusillade of shots broke out from all around the cove, the desperate scramble for life went on.

From the shore Lieutenant Foster shouted to Jack Price to stop or he would be fired upon. He ignored the command, rowing faster against the incoming tide. Suddenly, there was a loud report and a sudden flash or orange flame shot across the night sky as the soldiers opened fire on the boat. The cutter began its own desperate battle to escape the Revenue cutter, only a few lengths away.

The soldiers hauled the boat back to the shore and hauled Jack Price out on to the sand. At first, they thought he was dead but, as if sensing their presence, he opened his eyes, sunk deep in their sockets, forcing them to focus on Lucas. They were filled with so much hatred and contempt that Lucas was seared by it. He tried to speak, but before any word could pass his lips his whole body convulsed. When his head rolled to one side and his lids sagged over his eyes, devoid of life, Lucas knew he was dead.

Tilly, who had ventured on to the beach when she saw the soldiers had everything in control, stood beside Florence, who was clutching Tobias to her. She was numb with shock and cold from her stumble into the sea. Lucas came and placed an arm comfortingly around Tilly's shoulder and drew her to him. He was accompanied by Lieutenant Foster, who draped a cloak over Florence's trembling shoulders.

'Why would he want to get rid of the boy?' he asked Lucas, staring down at Jack Price.

'His reason is complicated—it is a long story, Lieutenant, one that will keep until later.' He clasped his wife tight and placed a kiss on the top of her head, feeling her tremble. 'Come, Tilly. You shouldn't be here.'

'I'll get someone to accompany you and the nurse back to the house,' Lieutenant Foster offered. 'I'm sure your husband will be along shortly.'

'Yes, you go, Tilly—you, too, Florence. Is Tobias unharmed?'

Florence nodded, gazing down at the child in her arms. 'He is. He's been a brave little chap. So very brave—just like his father.'

Epilogue

Later, with Florence and Tobias safely tucked up in the nursery, hopefully none the worse for their ordeal at the hands of Jack Price, Tilly waited for her husband to return. When he walked in, wet and dishevelled and slipped his arms around her, she sighed with contentment, breathing in the manly scent of him—of soap, leather and the smell of the sea.

'Is it over?' she asked softly.

She felt him smile before he lowered his head and placed his mouth on her neck, gently nuzzling her warm flesh. 'Yes, my love,' he murmured. 'It is over. Jack Price is dead. His body is being taken to Trevean. His fellow smugglers have been rounded up, and the cargo impounded by His Majesty's Customs.'

'I can't believe he's dead,' Tilly whispered.

'I have to say that it is no more than he deserved. He was a rogue and a blackguard to the end, who manipulated and cheated all those involved in his illegal operations. He lived a villain and died a villain and leaves a legacy of torture and plunder—excessive evils indeed in a country where smuggling is almost a way of life.

He also confessed to the murder of my parents and all those on board the vessel they were on.'

Tilly's heart went out to him. 'I'm so very sorry, Lucas, but you always suspected him of having something to do with their deaths. At least now you know the truth.'

'Yes—and he's paid the ultimate price. Did Florence tell you why she went to him?'

'Apparently one of Jack Price's men paid a visit to her sister, forcing her husband to come here. He told her Jack Price had asked for her—and to take Tobias with her, otherwise her sister's family would be harmed.'

Lucas's arms tightened around her. 'What a terrible ordeal it's been for her. But it's over now and we can all move on—no more of Jack Price's threats.'

'And his father? He has lost both his sons. The enmity between you will have to end, Lucas.'

'The enmity between our families goes back decades. It became more virulent as the years passed, and when Jack came along, but Ned was never my enemy. I cannot forgive his son for what he tried to do to Tobias. God knows what he intended doing when they got to France—probably to be sold into slavery or some such thing.

'Despite his son, I think Ned has suffered in his own way when he lost Edmund. It left him with a well of loneliness and bitterness. I'd like to think we could become friends.'

'Reconciliation and redemption can defy anything that's gone before, Lucas—forgiveness, too, if you let it. One thing I learned when I was growing up is that it's easy to condemn, but harder being compassionate.

It seems to me you have shown compassion for Ned Price, even if the reason is hard for you to understand just now.'

With his arms around her, he smiled softly. 'You have a beautiful head on your shoulders, Tilly—and a wise one. Ned Price has a grandson—we will have to decide where and how he is to be raised, which we will do between us. I will be neighbourly towards him and welcome the hand of friendship if he offers it, but at this moment it is you who fills my thoughts, you I care about, you I adore and love.'

Filled with a feeling that was part-joy and part-reverence, with love passing between them in silent communication, Lucas kissed her softly, tenderly. Raising his head, he sighed heavily. 'I am so fortunate to have found such a wonderful Countess. I love, admire and respect you. During the past few years, I have lost my close family and there were times when I thought I would never come through.

'But then I met you. You have reinvented my life for me and I am never more content than when we are together. I bless the day I landed on that beach and met you. You have brought purpose and meaning to my life and you make me feel human again—to forget the heartache the loss of my parents caused me, followed so soon by Cassie.'

Tilly lifted her thickly lashed eyelids, and the dazzling brilliance of her wonderful violet eyes lovingly caressed her husband's handsome face. His eyes burned with all the love and passion she had once despaired of ever seeing there and, for the first time in her life, she was able to savour the joy of loving and being loved.

Through a blur of tears, she smiled tremulously. 'Thank you for saying that, Lucas. You already had my heart—and now I know I have yours.'

* * * * *

If you enjoyed this story, make sure to read the first book in Helen Dickson's Cranford Estate Siblings miniseries

Lord Lancaster Courts a Scandal

And why not pick up one of her other great reads?

The Earl's Wager for a Lady
Conveniently Wed to a Spy
To Catch a Runaway Bride
Enthralled by Her Enemy's Kiss

Get 3 FREE REWARDS!

We'll send you 2 FREE Books plus a FREE Mystery Gift.

FREE
Value Over
$20

Both the **Harlequin®** Historical and **Harlequin®** Romance series feature compelling novels filled with emotion and simmering romance.

Get 3 FREE REWARDS!

We'll send you 2 FREE Books plus a FREE Mystery Gift.

FREE
Value Over
$20

Both the **Romance** and **Suspense** collections feature compelling novels
written by many of today's bestselling authors.

YES! Please send me 2 FREE novels from the Essential Romance or Essential
Suspense Collection and my FREE gift (gift is worth about $10 retail). After receiving
them, if I don't wish to receive any more books, I can return the shipping statement
marked "cancel." If I don't cancel, I will receive 4 brand-new novels every month and
be billed just $7.49 each in the U.S. or $7.74 each in Canada. That's a savings of at
least 17% off the cover price. It's quite a bargain! Shipping and handling is just 50¢
per book in the U.S. and $1.25 per book in Canada.* I understand that accepting the
2 free books and gift places me under no obligation to buy anything. I can always
return a shipment and cancel at any time by calling the number below. The free
books and gift are mine to keep no matter what I decide.

Choose one: ☐ **Essential** ☐ **Essential** ☐ **Or Try Both!**
                  Romance   **Suspense**   (194/394 & 191/391
                  (194/394 BPA GRNM)   (191/391 BPA GRNM)   BPA GRQZ)

Name (please print)

Address   Apt. #

City   State/Province   Zip/Postal Code

Email: Please check this box ☐ if you would like to receive newsletters and promotional emails from Harlequin Enterprises ULC and
its affiliates. You can unsubscribe anytime.

Mail to the **Harlequin Reader Service:**
IN U.S.A.: P.O. Box 1341, Buffalo, NY 14240-8531
IN CANADA: P.O. Box 603, Fort Erie, Ontario L2A 5X3

Want to try 2 free books from another series? Call 1-800-873-8635 or visit www.ReaderService.com.

---

*Terms and prices subject to change without notice. Prices do not include sales taxes, which will be charged (if applicable) based
on your state or country of residence. Canadian residents will be charged applicable taxes. Offer not valid in Quebec. This offer is
limited to one order per household. Books received may not be as shown. Not valid for current subscribers to the Essential Romance
or Essential Suspense Collection. All orders subject to approval. Credit or debit balances in a customer's account(s) may be offset by
any other outstanding balance owed by or to the customer. Please allow 4 to 6 weeks for delivery. Offer available while quantities last.

Your Privacy—Your information is being collected by Harlequin Enterprises ULC, operating as Harlequin Reader Service. For a
complete summary of the information we collect, how we use this information and to whom it is disclosed, please visit our privacy notice
located at corporate.harlequin.com/privacy-notice. From time to time we may also exchange your personal information with reputable
third parties. If you wish to opt out of this sharing of your personal information, please visit readerservice.com/consumerchoice or
call 1-800-873-8635. **Notice to California Residents**—Under California law, you have specific rights to control and access your data.
For more information on these rights and how to exercise them, visit corporate.harlequin.com/california-privacy.

STRS23

HARLEQUIN
PLUS

Try the best multimedia subscription service for romance readers like you!

Read, Watch and Play.

Experience the easiest way to get the romance content you crave.

Start your **FREE TRIAL** at
<u>www.harlequinplus.com/freetrial</u>.